A river has its secrets
Far under folds of water
Deeper than the buried dark
Where all is slick and softer

A fire has its secrets
Dancing bare before your eyes
Trimmed in heat and lost in gold
Something in its brightness lies

A boy has his secrets
His fist clasped tight as stone
Watching water, spying fire
In a crowded room, alone

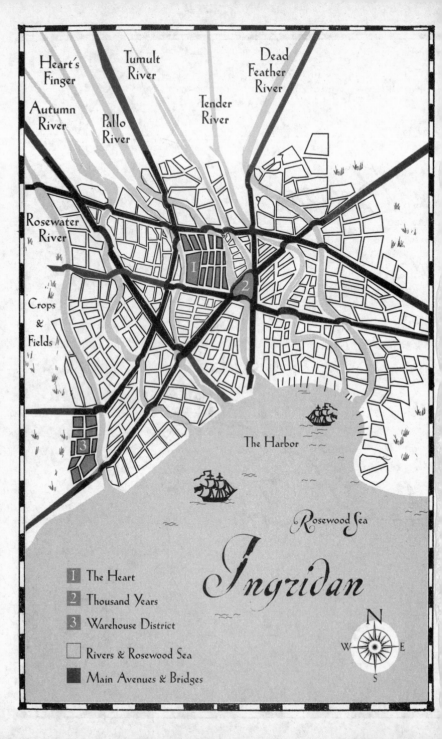

Published by Bloomsbury U.S.A. Children's Books
175 Fifth Avenue, New York, New York 10010

The Library of Congress has cataloged the hardcover edition as follows:
Hale, Shannon.
River secrets / by Shannon Hale. — 1st U.S. ed.
p.   cm.
Summary: Young Razo travels from Bayern to Tira at war's end as part of a diplomatic
corps, but mysterious events in the Tiran capital fuel simmering suspicions and anger,
and Razo must spy out who is responsible before it is too late and he becomes trapped
in an enemy land.
ISBN-13: 978-1-58234-901-5 • ISBN-10: 1-58234-901-0 (hardcover)
[1. Fairy tales. 2. Diplomacy—Fiction. 3. Spies—Fiction. 4. Self Esteem—Fiction.
5. Nature—Effect of human beings on—Fiction.] I. Title.
PZ8.H134Riv 2006   [Fic]—dc22   2005035500

ISBN-13: 978-1-59990-293-7 • ISBN-10: 1-59990-293-1 (paperback)

Typeset by Westchester Book Composition
Printed in the U.S.A. by Quebecor World Fairfield
2 4 6 8 10 9 7 5 3

All papers used by Bloomsbury U.S.A. are natural, recyclable products
made from wood grown in well-managed forests. The manufacturing processes
conform to the environmental regulations of the country of origin.

THE BOOKS OF BAYERN

River Secrets

SHANNON HALE

BLOOMSBURY

For all the boys in my family

But especially, triumphantly, adoringly
for the one and only
Max Stonebreaker Hale

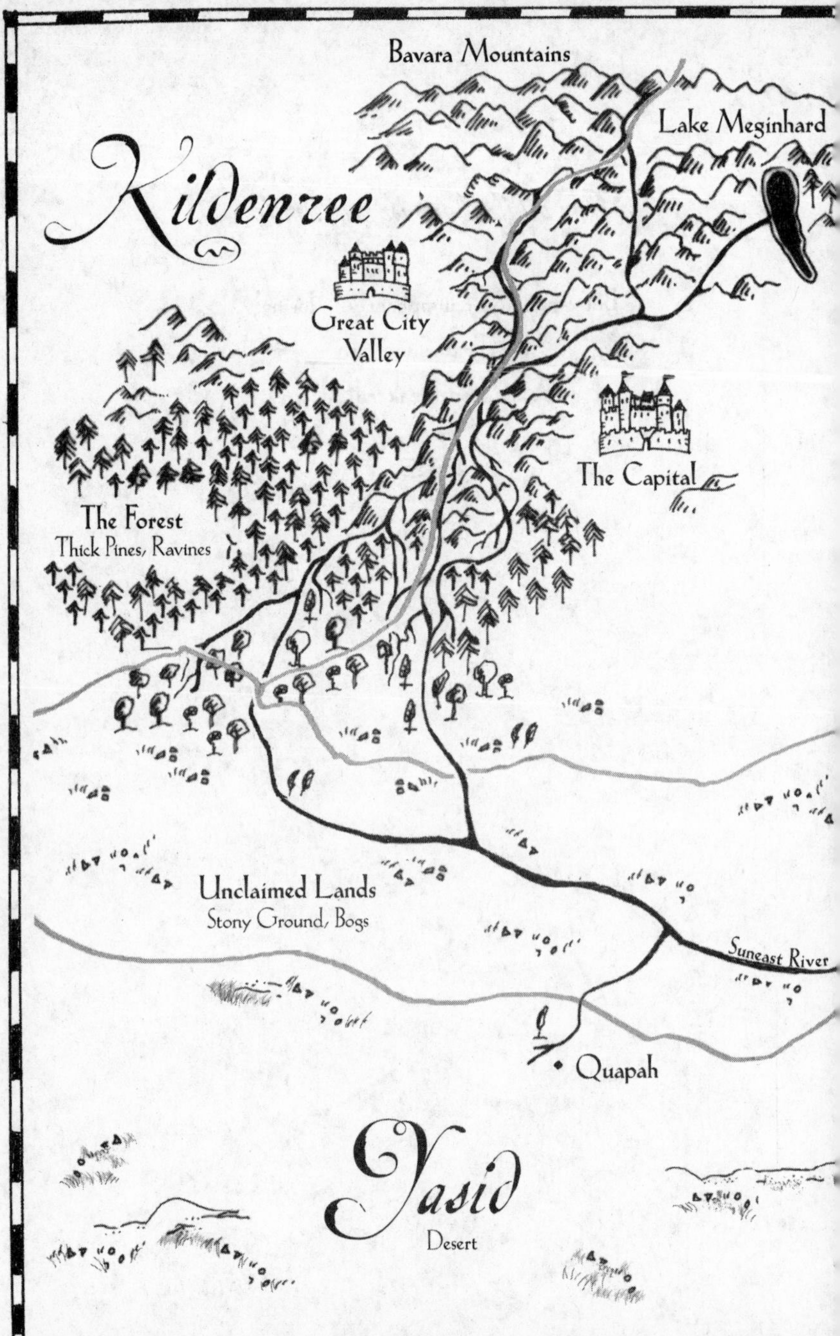
Bavara Mountains
Lake Meginhard
Kildenree
Great City
Valley
The Capital
The Forest
Thick Pines, Ravines
Unclaimed Lands
Stony Ground, Bogs
Suneast River
Quapah
Yasid
Desert

Praise for *River Secrets*

An ALA Teens' Top Ten

★ "This novel will be a special treat for readers of Hale's other two companion books, but it also stands on its own as a unique and tender coming-of-age story." —*Publishers Weekly*, starred review

★ "This high fantasy is rich in detail and lyrical in writing. . . . Fans of the genre will no doubt rejoice in immersing themselves in this magical world." —*SLJ*, starred review

★ "[Hale's] language glimmers like firelight, like sunshine on water as she propels readers along a river of wonderful writing to the tumultuous and heart-tugging climax." —*Kirkus Reviews*, starred review

★ "Suspenseful, magical, and heartfelt, this is a story that will wholly envelop its readers." —*Booklist*, starred review

"The settings, customs, and festivals of both Bayern and Tira are easy to imagine. Fans of Hale's previous books will enjoy this one and will hope that there is more to come." —*VOYA*

"All elements join together to form an adept Tamora Pierce–like fantasy adventure—although when it comes to Hale's subtlety of description and limber turns of phrase, there really is no comparison." —*The Horn Book*

"Hale's imagined world is danger-filled: gruesome deaths are alarmingly frequent, attempts on lives more so, and even talents or gifts are double-edged as potential curses if used incorrectly. It is to the author's credit, therefore, that she has also created a landscape and characters with enough beauty, depth, and complexity to keep readers eagerly anticipating visits." —*BCCB*

ALSO BY SHANNON HALE

THE BOOKS OF BAYERN:

The Goose Girl

Enna Burning

Princess Academy

Book of a Thousand Days

GRAPHIC NOVEL:
with Dean Hale
illustrations by Nathan Hale

Rapunzel's Revenge

FOR ADULTS:

Austenland

Prologue

Ingridan was an ancient city. Memory ached in its stone arches, crept down its narrow alleys, sluiced through its seven rivers. And its newest memory still burned, raw and sore—a failed war, a nation shamed, and an army dishonored.

On the western edge of Ingridan, just across the Rosewater River, someone watched a man die. The man had been poor and desperate for a bit of coin, but now he was just dead, his body black from burning.

When the smoke cleared, the watcher dragged the corpse out of the nearly empty warehouse, rolled it into the river, and kept watch as it floated into the sea.

"They will pay for making me do this," spoke the voice that no one else heard. "I'll see Bayern in flames."

A Journey South

azo hopped up and down, but he could see only backs of heads. Soldiers and courtiers lined the grand hall, craned their necks, stood on toes. And everyone was taller than him.

"That's just perfect," Razo muttered.

Rumors had been buzzing all week that something weighty would be announced today, and now here he was without a hope of a decent view. If only he were in the Forest and could just climb a tree.

He looked up. Then again . . .

Razo squeezed to the outer wall of the chamber and leaped at a tapestry, just catching the lower fringe. A brief sound of tearing, quick as the squeak of a mouse in a trap, and he found himself dangling above a hundred heads, waiting for a terrifying rip to send him down. The tapestry shivered, then held, so Razo crossed his eyes once for luck and climbed up.

He pushed his feet against the wall and sprang onto the decorative shelving. At last he had an agreeable view of his friends Isi and Geric, Bayern's queen and king, seated on a dais three steps below their thrones. Beside them were the white-robed emissaries from Tira and a handful of Tiran soldiers who, Razo imagined, had been handpicked for looking brutish and menacing.

The yellow-haired Tiran woman was speaking. ". . . years of animosity cannot be quickly forgotten, yet we see the benefit of forming an acquaintance with Bayern as we have not for many hundreds of years."

"That is our wish as well," said Geric, "and so we propose an exchange of ambassadors. This spring, we'll send one of our own south to live among the Tiran people in the capital city of Ingridan."

"By the authority of the people of Tira, our assembly, and our prince," said the Tiran woman, "we accept Bayern's invitation and likewise will send our ambassador to live in your capital."

The crowd creaked with astonished silence. One lean Tiran soldier glared at Geric and thumbed the hilt of his sword.

"Great crows," Razo whispered, his belly filling with cold. Just over a year ago, Tira had invaded Bayern with the intention of wiping out the Bayern army, hanging their king and queen, and claiming Bayern land as its own. In a terrible battle last spring, Bayern had finally overcome the invasion and won a rickety peace. Razo had served as a scout and soldier for Bayern and had no desire to roll around again in that whole mess of a war. He staunchly believed that seventeen years was too young to die. Even so, asking Bayern to welcome a Tiran into their midst already was a mighty sticky solution.

The Tiran woman was speaking again. "Know that the wounds of war won't heal easily. Burns can't stop stinging under such a mild salve...."

Burns. The crowd rustled. It was clear she was alluding to the last battle of the war and the mysterious Bayern fire-speaker who had burned one-tenth of the Tiran army.

Razo smirked. It suddenly seemed such a laugh, those angry Tiran completely unaware that the fire-speaker herself was just five paces away.

Enna stood behind Queen Isi's chair, slouching a tad, as though trying to communicate that the gathering was killed and done for already. Her formal tunic was deep red with beads around the neck, and her black hair was loose and growing unchecked to the middle of her back. Occasionally her lips moved and her eyes glanced sideways, as if she were whispering something droll to Finn beside her.

Enna seemed so careless. Yet if those Tiran soldiers discovered she was the secret fire-speaker, Razo realized they would not hesitate to part her head from her shoulders. Suddenly, it did not seem such a laugh. He scratched his neck and clambered back down.

An hour later, Razo was napping on the floor of Geric's antechamber when toes tickled his side. He squirmed and squinted with one eye to see Isi standing above him.

"There you are, Razo! We're meeting in my receiving room. Will you come?"

"Yet another glorious meeting? I'm really tempted, Isi, but you know my schedule right now is—"

"There's food."

Razo leaped up. "I'm right behind you."

A large soldier with dark, shaggy hair walked the corridor ahead of them, peering into open doorways.

"I found him, Finn," said Isi, "asleep on a floor, just like you thought he'd be."

"What do you mean?" Razo rubbed his nose. Sleepiness always made it itch. "I'm not *that* predictable."

"You told him there'd be food, didn't you?" Finn asked.

"The only way he'd come."

"Hmph," said Razo. Finn gave his arm a friendly knock.

Razo was relieved to find the mood in the receiving room had shrugged off the itchy stiffness of that day's formal assembly—at least, Conrad was laughing loudly as he arm-wrestled Geric, even though a couple of ministers frowned in their direction. Conrad was a friend of Razo and Isi from years ago, and since the death of Geric's young brother, the king seemed to have taken to Conrad as more family than friend. Enna was lounging in a chair, and a handful of soldiers chatted at the table. But there was no food.

"That's cruel, that is," said Razo, and Isi patted his shoulder consolingly.

She took her three-month-old baby, Tusken, from a maid's arms and asked her to bring in a plate of something sweet. So Razo stayed, lolling against the wall, half listening to Geric talk about the ambassador exchange, and practicing an expression of supreme indifference so that when he was not asked to go along, his face would not betray disappointment.

Why had Isi bothered to wake him for this meeting, anyway? She was wholly absorbed in Tusken now, cooing and smiling at him, though he was asleep and did nothing but occasionally twitch his lips or rub his nose. The purpose of babies eluded Razo. He supposed it would be different if he were a father, but that would require finding a wife.

And then, unasked for, a memory of Bettin spasmed behind his eyes. She was laughing and wrestling him to the ground to squish an overripe pear into his face. Up close, her eyes were almost green in their blackness.

"Hmph," said Razo. Bettin was married now. To someone else. Remembering that produced an uncomfortable, creeping sensation across his back, like the times he caught himself wanting to chat with an old friend, only to recall that the friend had been killed in the war.

"At spring thaw, we'll send our ambassador south," Geric was saying. "Isi believes trade is one way to pacify animosities, so we'll also convey a load of Bayern dyes, something the Tiran lack. Captain Talone, I'll ask you to lead the ambassador's guard and choose twenty of your own men."

That's hopeful, Razo thought. The gray-templed warrior was the leader of Bayern's Own, the king's personal hundred-band of soldiers, and Razo's own captain. Perhaps he'd have a chance to be a part of the adventure after all.

"Who knows what dangers you'll face?" Geric was saying. "We need boys who can keep a clear head, smart lads . . ."

That's two for me, Razo thought.

". . . strong, too . . ."

Uh . . .

". . . and good fighters."

Counts me out. Razo felt regret creeping into his expression, so he looked for something amusing to distract himself. There appeared to be a small hole in the rug. He stuck in his finger. Now it was a slightly bigger hole.

"Since we can't dispatch an army to protect the ambassador," said Talone, "I recommend Enna take part."

"Enna?" Isi sat up sharp, and the baby grumbled in his sleep. "Enna, you can't go. If the Tiran people realize that you are the fire-speaker . . ."

Enna shrugged. "Most of them never saw me."

"You spent weeks in a Tiran-occupied town—"

"In a tent, with mostly just one other person—"

"Who's dead now, but other people saw you, Enna—"

"Other people I'm not likely to meet in a city of hundreds of thousands of people—"

"There were soldiers in Eylbold who might be stationed in Ingridan's palace barracks."

"They were disgraced, Isi. I seriously doubt they'd be retained in a royal company."

Isi sighed and looked at Geric for support. He smiled sweetly at her, then frowned as he realized that she expected something. "What? You'd ask me to throw myself between you and Enna?"

"Captain," said Isi, turning to Talone, her friend from years past and her only other countryman in Bayern. Often when speaking to him, her voice strayed from her adopted Bayern accent to the stiff, punctuated tones of Kildenree. "You must see the danger—if she is discovered, not only her safety but all of yours will be compromised."

"I see a thousand dangers in this enterprise, my queen," said Talone. "In Enna, we have a secret army. Nevertheless, if you judge best to keep her back . . ."

"No." Enna lurched forward. "Please, Isi, don't say I can't. I need to go."

"But, Enna—"

"Isi, listen, I need to do something with all this." She thumped her chest, the place where she could pull heat inside her, change it somehow, then send it out to become fire.

"I killed so many people in the war, did so much damage, and I swear to you, to all of you"—she turned, her gaze seizing everyone in the room—"that I won't kill again. I'm so sorry about the times when I went too far, when I hurt people I didn't mean to. And now I've got all this power at my fingertips and all this guilt burning a hole through me. If you can give me another chance, I want to prove I'm on Bayern's side. I want to help." She turned her eyes and her voice back to Isi. "Please, you understand, right?"

Isi nodded. "I do. And I'll miss you."

"Thanks, Isi," Enna whispered, looking down. "Thank you."

Isi smiled at her sleeping baby, her forehead pinched.

The conversation tumbled on. Talone named the soldiers he would invite to join the company, including Finn, asking them to go to Tira and remain there for the next year or as long as it took to formalize peace. They all accepted, though many gazed up into the hanging candlelight or down at their boots as if wondering how many of them would return home again.

Razo had beaten down his hope into thin, shaky gloom when he actually heard his own name.

"What?" he said, looking up from the hole in the carpet.

"I believe we will have need of your skills," said Talone.

What skills? Razo almost asked. He knew he should be elated, but he felt knocked flat by surprise and too baffled to speak. After all, Finn as a choice made sense—he had become one of the best swordsmen in Bayern's Own and was as dependable as nuts in autumn. Enna made sense—her talents with fire and wind made her more powerful than a room full of soldiers. Conrad had been named, another Forest-born like Razo who was not too handy with a sword, but he was the best grappler in Forest or city. In fact, all the soldiers Talone had called were the best at something—sword or javelin, grappling or horse mastery. Razo knew he was best at nothing, except maybe cramming two cherries into a single nostril.

He did not have to hear the whispers to know what everyone was thinking—the only reason he had been chosen to join Bayern's Own was because of his part in ending the war. He and Finn had protected Enna while she had chased the Tiran army away during the last battle. That was all right, except Razo had taken a sword in the ribs and barely scraped by with his breath intact.

He did not have to hear the whispers, but he heard them all the same.

"A brave fool," one soldier had murmured to another when they'd thought Razo was asleep in the barracks. And there had been others. *A child that fell into his armor and didn't know how to get back out . . . A puppy dog with noble friends . . . The worst swordsman this company has ever boasted . . .* And Razo thought they must be right. Months he'd been a member of the Own and had never been asked to be a part of any assignment or counsel of importance. So why did Talone suddenly want him for the most important mission of all?

Razo realized everyone was still staring at him. He laughed self-consciously and said, "Of course I'll go, you know that."

"Excellent." Geric reached for the baby. "And now that's settled, so give me my boy."

Isi passed Tusken to his father. "Careful, he's still sleeping."

"He's been asleep long enough, and I haven't seen those huge blue eyes since early this morning, what with everything we've done today." Geric bounced Tusken in his arms until the baby produced a huge, toothless yawn, opened his eyes, and stared unblinking at his father. "Hello, there he is! You see, I knew he wanted to wake up."

Isi kissed Geric's cheek and laughed against his neck, calling him impossible. She picked up her blue skirts and sat on the floor next to Razo. Enna plopped down beside her, leaning against Finn and resting her feet on Isi's lap.

"It hardly seems a fair trade," said Isi, patting Enna's legs. "The company of my three best friends for Tiran dignitaries. If it weren't for Geric and Tusken, I'd trade the crown to go with you."

"I'm not worth a crown," said Enna. "Well, maybe a handful of jewels."

"*My* handful, maybe," said Finn. "Your hands are too tiny."

"Fair enough." Enna took Finn's sword hand and rubbed the calluses on his palm.

Isi began to pull her yellow hair free of its pins. "At least you'll have the winter to spend at home."

"So," said Razo, simmering with excitement and unable to sit on the question a moment longer, "why did Talone choose me, do you think?"

"To give us a good laugh," said Enna.

Razo tilted his head in his *be serious* expression.

"Who knows?" said Enna. "Who can read the mind of Captain Stoneface? But it's bound to be more of an adventure with you along and twice as fun as potato mush fights."

"Sounds like sticky business—"

"Tira or the food fights?"

"And if my luck holds up, I won't be getting out of this without another scar. You either, Finn."

"If you think you've never seen me angry," said Isi, "just watch what happens if any of you goes and gets yourself hurt. If things turn ugly, just get out of there and come home."

Razo sniffed. "What exactly do you think might happen?"

"Death, war, possibly some maiming," said Enna.

Razo did not care. Out of one hundred of Bayern's best soldiers, Talone had chosen him. Whatever the reason, Razo was determined to show his captain he had not made a mistake, no matter the cost.

2

A Rumble of Javelins

Before frost could thicken into snow, Razo hurried home for the winter. His mother's Forest house stood in a clearing of pine trees, encircled by the five cottages his older brothers had built for their own families.

Razo was shocked to find his little sister, Rin, suddenly taller than him—that is, she would have been taller if his hair lay down flat, which he made certain it never did. Sometimes when no one was looking, he ran a little pine sap through his hair, pulling his finger-length locks upright.

He passed the weeks chopping wood, slinging for squirrels and hares so his ma's dinner pot never lacked meat, wrestling his young nephews and nieces to the ground, and in turn being wrestled down by his legion of big brothers.

"But why do you have to go off again, Razo?" His mother ripped the hide off a dead hare, the latest offering from Razo's sling.

"I'm a member of Bayern's Own," said Razo. "It's the king's own hundred-band, the best of the soldiers, and I'm one of them. It's an honor. It's like . . ." He could think of nothing in her own life to compare it with. The thought made him feel already hundreds of leagues away.

When early spring began to shiver the cold from the air, Razo's excitement tickled him awake at first light. *Talone chose me*, he remembered. *I'm going on an urgent, dangerous mission. Me, Razo of the Forest.* He spent two days working till dark to ready his ma for the next marketday, then made his farewells. Rin became quiet and fluttery as if she would miss him, which made his heart pinch. Brun, his oldest brother, grappled him into the hangman's hold.

"Not running after that Bettin again, are you, Razo?" said Brun. The other brothers laughed. At age fifteen, Razo had thought he was too young to propose marriage to the pretty, strong-armed Forest girl. Then, on hearing that she was suddenly engaged to Offo, he had run across three days of Forest in two. He'd arrived before the wedding, red faced, triumphant, gasping for breath, and spewing words that sounded like poetry to his own ears. Bettin had just laughed and rubbed his head.

"But I love Offo," she'd said. "Good old Razo."

His brothers could tease him about his height or the number of scars he was collecting on his body. He could take the joke when they said he would die having never won a fair wrestling match. But the topic of Bettin still smarted too much. He'd imagined being with her always. Now when he closed his eyes, he had trouble imagining anything else.

But it was useless to fight back, so he just went limp in Brun's hold until his brother dumped him on the ground.

With a last kiss for his ma, Razo ambled on his way. He felt a chill skitter across his back and kept looking behind him, fearing that the Forest had folded in half and the homestead ceased to exist. His gut felt hollow, so he tried to fill it with his ma's nutty travel bread. That worked pretty well.

Two days of walking later, he found preparations in the capital well under way, horses exercised, barrels and casks loaded, tents rolled. Razo felt the energy like a muscle twitch. Journeys always took too long, but never as long as the readying.

He was hanging around the stables, chaffing the boys as they shoveled manure, when one of Bayern's Own, a wiry man with a nose that looked sharp enough to have its own sheath, came up close to Razo. He stank of ale and appeared to be proud of it.

"Perfect," Razo said under his breath.

"Ho there, sheep boy! I've been wanting you to explain something to me . . . to you, to me . . . about you going to Tira, huh? Why're you going, huh? And I'm not. That's what I'd like to know."

Razo winced. "You're aware that you smell like a privy?"

Two other soldiers gathered in behind the first, and

emboldened by his friends, the man poked Razo in the shoulder. Several times. Razo gritted his teeth and kept his eyes on the ground. It never did any good to fight back.

"You're no soldier. You're just friends with the high and mighty, eh?"

"What's this, Razo?" Enna stalked away from her horse, brush still in hand. "Your pretty friends here are certainly loud about their opinions."

"This has nothing to do with you," said the man.

She folded her arms. "If you've a problem with *my* friend, then it has everything to do with me, Lord Puke Breath. Why don't you explain the situation, I'm oh so eager to hear."

In short order, there was a very pleasing shouting match going on. Razo settled back into a stack of hay to enjoy Enna at her best.

"Aren't you going to help?" asked one of the stablehands.

Razo laughed. "Enna can handle three brawlers with her eyes closed. If there were twenty, then I might do something. I'd go find Finn."

"I'd dig my own grave," said another stable-hand, his back turned to Razo, "afore I'd sit back and let someone else fight my battle."

Razo opened his mouth but found himself suddenly emptied of jokes. *Why fight my own battles if everyone else does it so much better?* he asked himself, but the thought irritated him, a bug bite he could not scratch.

By the time Talone finally heard the riot and took over, Enna had the soldiers looking like puppies with their tails between their legs.

"What *is* the ruckus?" A stout woman draped in too much yellow fabric came lumbering into the stable. She caught sight of Razo lounging in the hay. "Are you responsible for all this uproar? This is a work area and closed to loafers. Who are you?"

"I'm Razo, a member of Bayern's Own," he said, stopping himself from adding, "Loafing is just a hobby of mine."

"Bayern's Own? But you're a child."

Razo looked up to the sky. "I'm not a child, I'm just *short.*"

"Hm," she said through her nose. "I don't know what kind of man this Talone is to enlist boys. . . ."

"I am Talone," he said, approaching. "And who are you to interfere with one of my men?"

"I'm Lady Megina, cousin to His Highness the king and chosen ambassador to Tira. I may as well tell you right now that I'll expect cooperation from my military escort, not demands."

Talone crossed his arms, appearing twice as wide. "Regardless, my men have one captain, and you are not it."

Her eyes widened briefly, like the upward surge in flames when new fuel is added. "Very well. You'll command your men, Captain Talone, and I'll command you."

They strode away in opposite directions while the stablehands snickered into their shoulders.

Razo had heard of Lady Megina before, a childless widow of twenty years and cousin to the king. Geric had credited her for ending a water dispute in southeast Bayern and managing her brother's estate with precision. Still, she could have been nicer.

The night before departure, Isi and Geric held a feast for the travelers but had not shown up by the time the feasting began. Razo was on his second turkey leg and fifth berry pie when Isi climbed onto the bench next to him, resting her elbows on the table, her brow on her hands.

"What's happened?" asked Enna.

Isi met eyes with Talone, seated across from her. Her voice quavered. "We've had word from Tira. Over the winter, many Tiran citizens started calling for a return to war. It got quite bad, and to appease them, the assembly agreed to vote on the matter in the fall."

Finn shook his head and seemed likely to strike something.

"That won't give us much time," said Talone.

"*If* you go." Isi looked up, as though to keep her eyes dry. "I'm thinking of . . . of canceling the mission. By the time you arrived, Lady Megina would have less than a month to meet with the assembly members before they all leave for their summer estates. Once they return to Ingridan, she'd have two more weeks at most until the vote. It's not enough time to sway their opinion in favor of peace, and I'm afraid your company would have a tricky time just keeping her alive. Keeping all of you alive." She took Enna's hand and began to talk faster. "But I'm also so afraid that if you don't go, there'll be no chance. It's easy to believe complete strangers are your enemies. If they knew us . . . But how can you go, Talone? How can I bear to risk all of you? You'd be traveling into a hornets' nest."

Razo scratched at the flea bites on his arms, then realized they were goose bumps. He was not much fond of hornets' nests.

Talone stood. "Bayern's Own." The rattle of dishes stilled, all faces turned. "Our queen informs me that Tira has used the winter to stir up thoughts of war. If we go, the people just might decide to cut our throats one by one. The queen is giving us a choice. Even if we go, it's likely we will fail. Are you willing to take that chance? Will you march with me to Tira?"

The quiet that followed made the room feel tight and small and airless. Then Finn thumped his javelin against the tiled floor. Razo smiled at him and echoed with his own javelin. Enna banged her fist on the table. The sound of two javelins and a fist took up the whole room, lonely and inviting at once. Then a clatter of replies tossed against the walls. The rumble unified, everyone knocking in time, the entire room becoming one drum under one hand. Geric came up behind Isi, wrapping his arms around her shoulders. She pressed her head against his hands, and when voices joined the javelins, shouting, "Bayern! Bayern!" her shoulders shook with a sob.

The thumps and shouts pulled at Razo's skin and clattered against his own heartbeat. He banged his javelin louder, needing to join that noise, inexplicably afraid of being left out.

3

Burning Again

S pring poked out everywhere. Leaf tips jutted from twigs like stuck-out tongues; dark buds and curly ferns elbowed their way into life. Because the party was journeying forward into spring and south into warmth, the plants appeared to erupt around them, quick and desperate. And the pace of the horses, the pace of the world, seemed to keep time with the pounding of the javelins still echoing in Razo's mind.

Razo often rode near the front with Talone, where Enna led the way by listening to the wind. He knew only pieces of how Enna and Isi had gone to the country of Yasid last year and found a way to share their gifts with each other—the speech of wind and fire. Now in addition to being able to pull heat from the air and send it blazing into fire anywhere she chose, Enna possessed Isi's ability to hear the voice of the wind murmur about what it had blown by and even direct it to change its course. Talone liked to have Enna near the front, listening. She often knew in advance if anything unexpected lay ahead—a damaged bridge, a wildcat.

Other times, Razo drifted in the company, lingering in the rear or trotting through the middle where the soldiers and camp workers tangled and produced the merriest talk. The company avoided the topic of Tira and what might await them, perhaps to keep the tension from burying them all alive. In the strained levity, pranks flourished, and Razo knew to shake out his bedroll before climbing in. Knew it now, anyway. Grass snakes were harmless, but could he help it if he yelped like a pup when that cold, scaly body licked across his bare feet?

Often the laughter was strained; often the dinner songs wobbled and caught in throats. Razo knew he was not the only one remembering the foreboding sound of javelins clamoring in the banquet hall and the stillness afterward that had given him pause to imagine war again.

Four weeks into their journey south, Razo woke in the darkest part of night to weeping. The sound of it seemed wrong, like an instrument played out of tune. The stifling feel of a new-moon night, the air-cracking sob, the early-spring chill riding a breeze—all reminded Razo of the birth night of his baby sister. Four years old, he'd awakened to his mother crying in the night and found her curled up and weeping on the ground as the labor pains bore down. He had crouched beside her, crying, too, begging for a way to make it better, until a neighbor had arrived to shoo him outside with his brothers. The next morning, in the joy of a baby girl, everyone seemed to have forgotten the pain; but Razo never forgot.

He crawled out of his bedroll, taking his sword with him in case there was something he could fight to stop the suffering. He did not have to go far.

Enna slept in a small tent near the ambassador's, and Finn slept before the opening. As Razo approached, he could make out Finn's empty bedroll. From inside the tent, he heard their voices.

"It's all right, Enna, tell me." Finn's voice in a whisper. "It helps to tell me."

"I thought I was . . . was there again. . . . Finn, I was there again. . . ." Enna could barely speak through the sobs.

"You were dreaming, dreaming."

"It was that last battle and I . . . was . . . burning . . . and, and, and a man came at me . . . he was on fire. . . ."

"Shh, all right, it's all right."

"No, listen, he was on fire . . . was coming after me . . . because of what I did . . . and it was so real." She paused, trying to catch her breath. "It wasn't real?"

"The battle was almost a year ago," whispered Finn, "and you didn't mean to hurt anyone, you just had to stop the war, remember? The man in your dream isn't real."

"Oh . . ." She hiccuped and slowed her breath, then it

tightened again, and before a rush of weeping overtook her she said quickly, "But I'm sorry, I'm so sorry. . . ."

"I know, love, I know. Lean into me, I've got you."

Razo's head and hands felt as heavy as night. There was no enemy he could battle, nothing he could do, so he returned to his bedroll and stared up at the empty places between stars.

In the morning, Finn's uniform was not as tidy as usual and Enna's eyes were red.

"How's it, Razo?" she said, cheerful as ever.

"Morning, Enna-girl," Razo said as he fumbled with a horse blanket. It was no easy task to saddle Bee Sting while the mare was nuzzling his pockets for stowed morsels.

Enna left to put out the breakfast fires. She lit them and put them out each day, a small service she was eager to do whenever camp workers were not watching. Outside Bayern's Own, her identity as the fire-speaker was still a secret.

As soon as Enna was out of earshot, Razo turned to Finn.

"Last night . . . ," he whispered. "That happens often?"

Finn rubbed his eyes. "The last few months, maybe once every week or more. Isi believes Enna will get better with time, as the memories fade. I think Enna needs a chance to use her talents without being destructive." He looked back at

Enna leaning over a newly dead fire, then turned and heaved a saddle onto his horse. "It haunts her, Razo, all that she did. I try to sleep near so she needn't wake up alone. In the palace, I used to sneak into her room, sleep beside her."

"Yes, I bet you did," said Razo, elbowing Finn and raising his eyebrows.

Finn looked sharp. "I won't have you thinking that I treat her as a wife when we aren't wed. I sleep beside her to comfort her, that's all. I would never dishonor her."

Razo smirked. "Then you'd better marry her."

"She won't."

"Won't what?" asked Enna, coming upon them.

"Marry me," Finn said with a note of humor.

Enna rolled her eyes. "Is that the only tune you know, piper? Play a different one or I'll take my coin elsewhere. I feel years too young to be having babies."

"Shame," said Razo. "I for one am raring to see what kind of frightening mongrel would be your offspring. Finn's wide shoulders, Enna's black hair, Finn's large hands, Enna's scheming look . . ."

Finn smiled as if he saw the baby in his imagination and thought it beautiful.

The next day, the party crossed Bayern's border and waited for their Tiran escort. Under a shivering sun in a flat landscape, they scratched themselves and played tired pranks so numerous, Talone demanded they cease at once. When the bathing and laundry and shaking off dust peaked from boring to exasperating, Razo escaped into a copse of river trees to hunt.

For Razo, the worst part of journeying was always the bleak, road-weary, stale, and pale food—slosh that was potatoes and meat, somehow; hard little bricks that Conrad tried to convince him were actually bread; disks of salted meat Razo tied to a stick and declared made a mighty fine ax. So Razo's grumbling belly often drove him to hunt for the cookpot. He kept his sling at his hip with a pouch of stones. Some of the soldiers mocked him for wearing a simple Forest weapon so openly, but none protested when he added fresh meat to dinner.

The river beside their camp was spring full, the brushy river trees in heavy leaf, but strangely he could see no squirrels darting about, no fat quail on the bank quivering to hold still. Instead of hunting meat, Razo passed an hour pelting an upright boulder that begged to be a target. When his stomach reminded him that he had not eaten in two entire hours, he picked back up the nicest stones, working his way around the boulder.

Then he saw the body. It was so charred, he could not tell what clothing it had worn, not even if it was a man or a woman. He touched the foot. Cool and hard. It had been there a while.

Suddenly the chirping of insects seemed urgent, warning

of something, pleading for Razo to run away. It struck him ridiculous that after the unmitigated slaughter of a battlefield, just one dead body could frighten him motionless, but still he could not move. He imagined his own skin ached, was aware of the heat of his breath on his lips. His gaze was swallowed up in the white wilderness of the river, and he realized now how loud it was, loud enough to drown the sounds of a murderer approaching, rocks crackling underfoot.

Get going, you numbskull. He forced himself up and sauntered away, very casually, just in case anyone was watching. As soon as he left sight of the river, he broke into a run, not slowing until he had fetched Talone.

"Is it Bayern, do you think?" asked Razo as they crouched over the body. With Talone next to him, the insect chatter lost its menace and the tree shadows seemed to take a step back.

"Not from our party. At noon count, no one from our camp was missing, and you say it's been dead for at least several hours."

It gave Razo a little thrill that his captain trusted his opinion. "Is there a settlement nearby? Maybe some villager . . ." He examined the area, frowning.

"What?" asked Talone. "You have that look as if your mind is working."

Razo smirked. "For once, huh? I was just noticing the ground isn't blackened around it. The body wasn't burned here, and I hope it didn't walk here on its own. So why didn't the murderer dump the body in the river? Or even in that copse? The boulder and trees hide the body from our camp, but we've a good look at the road from here. Coming from the other direction, our Tiran escort would've spotted this body, no question."

"So either the murderer was careless or deliberately placed the body so the Tiran would discover it before we did."

"It's odd, isn't it? I mean, if you want to kill a fellow, why not employ a sword? What kind of person murders by burning?"

As soon as Razo spoke the words, he wished he had not. He squatted and fussed with some rocks on the ground as though looking for something very important and not the least concerned.

"Yes, who burns?" Talone's blue eyes stared at him as if right into his head.

"She wouldn't. . . ."

"She has before." Talone's stoic expression was betrayed by a line of worry in his brow. "I hope not. I hope it was not our Enna."

Razo was remembering the sounds of weeping in the night. *No, listen, he was on fire . . . was coming after me. . . .* And Finn: *The man in your dream isn't real. . . .* Could Enna have done this in her sleep and not known? And if so, whom had she burned? But no, Finn lay each night before Enna's tent. She could not wander away without waking Finn.

Razo looked at the body, his skin squirming. No drag marks, which meant it had been dumped. It would be too heavy for Enna to carry, but not for Finn.

"What are your thoughts?" asked Talone.

"Nothing, I have none," he said quickly. "I'm just wondering what we do now."

Talone sighed, and it had a mighty sound to it. "We send the body down the river before the Tiran see it."

Razo and Talone removed their tunics, wrapping up their hands before lifting the body by ankles and wrists and flinging it into the river. It was frightening to behold how quickly the white torrent grabbed it and pulled it out of sight, how perfectly the water hid all signs of death.

"I hope you make it to the sea," whispered Razo.

Though he was never comfortable with his skinny torso bared, Razo could not make himself put that tunic back on until he could wash off the death touch. He walked back to camp with Talone, his arms crossed over his chest. Wind tickled his skin.

"Don't do anything on your own," said Talone. "Keep your eyes open, and come to me with anything you discover. I'll do whatever needs to be done."

Ahead, Razo saw Enna sitting cross-legged on the ground, jabbering to Finn about something. She was wearing a tunic and skirt dyed dark green, her black braids pinned up to keep her neck free. Razo knew she hated it when her hair touched her neck. She also hated having dry fingertips, music without drums, and potatoes without salt. He knew Enna as well as he knew his own sister and liked her just as well.

Whatever needs to be done.

What would Talone do? Razo whispered a wish that Enna was not burning again.

4

Thousand Years

That evening, the Tiran party made camp across the road. Razo stayed out of the way, bored by all the diplomatic nonsense as Talone and Megina formally greeted Captain Ledel, leader of the Tiran escort, and Lord Kilcad, the Tiran ambassador.

"Look at them, Razo," said Conrad. He was of middling height and lean, his face innocent with freckles, all belying the fact that he was a deadly good grappler. "Don't they look well rested? And bathed, too? Probably moseying along while we killed ourselves to get here on time."

At the word *killed*, Razo could not help glancing at the spot by the river. Puddles of moonlight filled hollows in the river sand.

In the morning, half of the Bayern turned north to accompany the ambassador, Lord Kilcad, into Bayern. Talone's group continued south with Captain Ledel's men, who were there to make certain the Bayern were not harassed while crossing Tira. Or that was the official reason. Razo saw the icy malice in many Tiran soldiers' eyes and thought it would be a miracle if the group could make it to Ingridan without bloodshed.

At night, Razo set up his bedroll near Enna's tent and trained himself to awaken at the least sound. Once he heard her sob at things from her dreams and Finn soothe her back to sleep, but that he could tell, she did not leave her tent.

A morning two weeks from the border, a Bayern camp worker, a girl no more than thirteen years, was pouring water on the breakfast fire when two hulking Tiran passed by. The pot slipped in her hands, splashing water on their boots.

"Trying to get my attention, are you?" said the fiery-haired Tiran. He looked around, as if making certain his captain was not near, then grabbed the girl's wrist and yanked her closer, whispering something in her ear.

"Let off!" The girl struggled, beating her fist against his chest.

"You should be flattered," said the larger soldier, laughing. "You're too ugly to deserve the attention."

Finn was the first one to spring forward. He shoved the Tiran, freeing the girl from his hold, and put himself between them. His hand was on his sword, but he did not draw it yet.

A moment later, Enna was beside him. "Apologize to her, or I'll teach you manners that'd put your mothers to shame." The Tiran laughed. "I said apologize, you filthy, fungus-breathed, privy-licking—"

"What did this Bayern call you?" asked the bigger Tiran.

"You heard fine," Enna said slowly, her glare crackling mad.

The orange-haired Tiran's voice was like grinding stone. "No Bayern woman insults me." He pulled a dagger from his boot.

Razo had stayed put until then, leaving the interfering to those more capable, but there was a Tiran with a dagger, and Enna might burn it from his hand and reveal herself as the fire-speaker, or she might do worse.

Razo leaped forward. "Take a deep breath, everybody." He eased himself between Enna and the Tiran. "Let's just—"

There was a tweak in Razo's side as if someone had pinched him. He looked down and saw the hilt of the dagger sticking out of his body.

Sounds and sights and feelings began to twist together, turn upside down: Enna saying, "Razo, Razo"; the larger Tiran running away; the stab-happy lurch just staring at his hand; a breezy pain zipping out of Razo's middle, tingling all over his body; the air silty as a riverbed in his lungs. He saw the blood, his blood, and just before he fainted, he thought, *Good thing my brothers aren't here to laugh.*

For a few days, things were murky, though that may have had something to do with the sappy substance the camp cook and surgeon kept shoving between Razo's lips. The bitter flavor clung to the back of his throat and made everything he ate taste like ashes.

"Will it leave a scar?" Razo asked the cook when he felt well enough to sit up in the back of a wagon.

"Without a doubt," he said.

"Not in Ingridan yet and already a scar," said Razo as Enna and Finn rode up beside the wagon. "That doesn't bode well, I say. And you two'll be next."

"We don't have your luck," said Finn.

"At least you won't have to worry anymore about dagger boy," said Enna. "Captain Ledel relieved him of his rank, weapons, and clothing and left him to starve days from the nearest village. Pretty harsh, I thought, for just tickling you."

"Ha."

By the time Razo could ride his horse, Bee Sting, again, the Suneast River had split into a massive delta, forming dozens of smaller rivers, and in the long stretches between their banks, barefoot farmers planted in fields so dark, they oozed greenness. As they rode forward, Ingridan stood up taller and taller on the horizon. All the buildings were white, all the roofs red, and the sameness reminded Razo of an army in uniform or some fluffy, frosted dessert that gushes out of its bowl. He liked the idea of the dessert better.

"Where's the ocean?" he wondered aloud.

"You cannot see it from this vantage." A Tiran soldier with hair so pale that it was nearly white rode up beside him. He had removed the blue jacket of his uniform and rolled up his tunic sleeves. Razo wondered if Captain Ledel, who was a terror for order, would notice and reprimand him, but the soldier did not seem worried. He reached out his hand. "I am Victar, third son of Assemblyman Rogis."

Razo hesitated before shaking his hand. "I'm Razo." That did not seem like enough. "Sixth son." Victar appeared to expect more. "Of my ma in the Forest."

Victar had a pleasant smile. "With so many sons, it's no wonder you are a professional soldier. I as well may have little to inherit and must earn my own way."

"Inherit?" Razo laughed. "That word's too fancy by half. In the Forest, everybody's just as poor as everyone else."

"You are very open to admit as much. In the city of rivers, only the dead can close their mouths, so the saying goes. If it crosses my mind, I might reveal what you just said in any tavern or barracks."

Razo shrugged. "Go ahead, though I don't know who'd care."

Victar kept riding beside Razo and appeared disposed to chat, so Razo learned that to be considered for an assembly seat, one must be a noble and have land worth at least four hundred thousand gold fulls (which Razo gathered were a type of coin). When he inquired where Bayern's Own would be housed in Ingridan, Victar spoke of Thousand Years.

"The prince's palace. Its full title is the Palace of the Power That Will Stand for One Thousand Years, so named by the prince who built it."

"And has it?" asked Razo. "Stood for a thousand years?"

"We won't know for another seven hundred."

"Victar!" a Tiran soldier called, anger twitching his face. Razo recognized him as the one who had run away from the stabbing. Razo laid his arm across his belly.

Victar lowered his voice and barely moved his lips. "That is Tumas. He was close friends with the disgraced soldier who wounded you, and I heard him rant that it was your fault, that you thrust yourself on the blade on purpose."

"Ha, that's lovely. I'd hope I've got more sense than that."

"But a man like Tumas won't hear reason. He is not an easy foe, Razo. He has many friends and they will try . . . Just, avoid them, if you understand me."

"Great, already the Tiran want me dead."

"Not all of us. Good luck, Razo."

Victar waved farewell as he rode ahead, and Razo waved after him, then felt ashamed, naive, to have been friendly at all. Just a year ago, Victar was someone Razo might have tried to kill in battle. What a strange circumstance, how unsteady it made the road feel. He patted Bee Sting's neck.

The road spilled into a broad, paved avenue coursing through the center of the city. Half the Tiran soldiers led the way, and the remaining ten brought up the rear, like jailers herding convicts to the gallows. Ingridan citizens eased out of shop doors and leaned from upper windows, arms folded, gazes hot.

They crossed the avenue's second bridge, this one spanning a river four horses wide. Razo liked the rivers, blue tiles covering their banks, giving them a smooth, clean look.

Every few blocks, crowded tenements and grand palaces pulled out of the way of paved squares. Often there were trees, though nothing like the wild, deep Forest that Razo knew. These trees rose slender from planter boxes, their foliage trimmed round on the bottom and pinched off at the top in the shape of a candle flame. Others wore their greenery in perfect balls and shook glossy leaves and tiny white blossoms, their odor claiming both tangy and sweet flavors at once.

Razo was peering into a courtyard's turquoise-tiled fountain as he rode by when something struck him on the cheek.

"Go home!" A group of boys a few years younger than Razo stood in the square, their hands dripping with soggy pieces of orange fruit. Razo wiped the pulp from his face and flicked it at the back of Enna's hand.

"Ew," she said, shaking it off.

Another fruit whizzed past their heads, making Enna alert. A third might have hit Finn, but a wind blew it curiously off course, and it slammed into the nose of Tumas, the Tiran soldier directly behind them. Enna was careful not to smile, staring to the side with an extremely proper expression.

"Good shot, Enna-girl," Razo whispered.

Tumas cursed at the boys.

"What are you going to do, blue jackets?" One of the boys planted his feet and raised his fists. "You lost us a war, and my fists bet you'll lose a street fight."

Tumas wheeled his horse out of formation and cantered at them. The boys pulled their bolder compatriot into an alley, and Captain Ledel ordered Tumas back.

Razo was not particularly eager to keep the seething soldier as a foe and offered him a friendly grin. "My ma used to soak her hands in fruity water. Maybe it's good for our skin?"

"The first chance I get . . . ," said Tumas in the hollow manner of one always congested. He sniffed and rode ahead without finishing the threat, leaving Razo to imagine.

The avenue merged into a broad crossroads, and at last they caught sight of the palace. It nestled between two rivers, far behind iron gates, and proclaimed its magnificence not with towers or banners, but simply by its immensity. Razo counted four stories, forty-four front-facing windows per story, and guessing there were two other wings with a large courtyard in the center . . . he calculated in his head, a trick Talone had taught him for estimating enemy troops from the number of wagons or tents.

"How big?" asked Finn.

"Averaging three windows per room," said Razo, "I would guess over five hundred rooms in the main structure, not including outbuildings, barracks . . ."

"That's too big," said Enna.

". . . stables, gardens and gardener shacks, separate servant quarters, and I'd guess a dairy, animal workers, a mill, all self-sustaining—"

"What do you do with five hundred rooms?"

"It'd only make sense in a siege, though those gates aren't built for sieges, only really useful for keeping out the riffraff."

"Bayern's capital was made for defense," said Finn, "but Ingridan assumes it'll be doing the attacking."

Razo slowed Bee Sting as they neared the gates. "Once we're inside, d'you think they'll just . . . ?" He ran his thumb across his throat.

"They can kill us just as easily in the street," said Finn.

"Let 'em try," said Enna. "I'll gut their city first."

That thought did not comfort Razo much.

The group halted beside a stable as several Tiran emerged from the palace. They wore tunics with a skirt, or leggings for the men, and a swath of loose fabric wrapped around their chests and over their shoulders, all the cloth white, pale blue, or peach. Used to the vibrancy of Bayern dyes, Razo thought the lack of color indescribably boring.

A man in a white robe introduced himself as Lord Belvan, head of forces at Thousand Years. He wore his graying hair slicked back, which drew more attention to his beak nose but also gave him an open, honest aspect.

"I hope to see this arrangement work, Lady Megina," he said. "We lost many good people in that conflict. Let us bury our dead and keep living."

Razo wondered why the prince was not there to talk about peace. Surely Isi and Geric would be the first to welcome the Tiran ambassador at the Bayern palace gates. Razo shrugged internally. His ma always said that fancy folk were as peculiar as pig bladder balloons and not quite as fun.

A flicker of orange color teased Razo's attention.

"May I introduce Lady Dasha," Lord Belvan said, indicating a girl of about sixteen years. "Her father, Lord Kilcad, is Tira's ambassador to Bayern, and while he sojourns in your country, she has agreed to stay at Thousand Years and act as liaison to your people."

She had orange hair. Razo had never seen anyone with that hair color except that swine who'd stabbed him on the journey, and the swine had not been nearly so pleasant to look at. She was wearing a pale peach cloth wrapped around her dress, and her legs were bare at her ankles but for the leather straps of her sandals. If Lord Belvan said anything else, Razo did not hear it—he was completely mystified, or embarrassed, or perhaps enthralled, by those ankles. He had never seen a girl in public with naked ankles before. Now he wondered why. Were ankles bad? Those ankles did not look bad. A mite bony, perhaps, but ultimately intriguing.

He twisted to swat at a fly and found Tumas staring at him, though in a much more uncomfortable manner than he'd been looking at the girl's ankles. He nudged his mount a little closer to Enna and Finn.

A bath and change of clothes later, Razo sat at the welcoming banquet, trolling his fork through his plate, hunting for something appetizing. Everything was fish. Even the leeks and onions were steeped in fish sauce that was thickened with honey until it was cruelly sweet. He bit into a purple vegetable so sour that it made him suck in his cheeks. The thought of home felt emptier than his stomach.

And to irritate him further, there were no chairs. Apparently it was Tiran fashion to lounge on pillows at a banquet table and eat with one hand, but Razo did not lounge so much as sprawl. Finn slouched. Enna sulked.

As soon as they could get away, Razo and Finn sneaked with Enna to her chamber in the palace. Though the rugs and bedclothes were made in drab, unhappy colors, Razo still thought it much more comfy than the barracks where he and Finn were housed. Razo had spent years under one roof with five snoring brothers and was not eager to relive the experience.

"It's a strange city, no mistake," said Razo the fourth night he and Finn camped out on Enna's floor. "In Bayern, it feels like the city wall was built to keep the Forest from marching back in, but Ingridan forgot there was ever anything but city. The only bits of dirt I've seen are the fighting circles near each barracks. Still, you've got to admit that paving everything keeps it clean—"

"I don't have to admit anything," said Enna.

Razo sighed. In the past, Enna had been treated vilely by a Tiran man and apparently still had not healed from it. Razo could not help wondering if that old hurt might not provoke her to do stupid things. To change the subject, he brought out a dry plum cake he had swiped from the dining hall. When Enna pestered him to fetch some milk to wash it down, he threw a pillow at her face.

"I brought the cake! Why don't you or Finn go?"

"Because sometimes Finn and I want to be alone."

"Oh, I see, you two become all lovey and then Razo's left in the cold." Razo meant his tone to be playful, but it was not quite.

"I don't want any milk—" Finn started.

"It's fine, never mind." Razo dragged himself off the floor, opened Enna's door, and bumped right into Lady Dasha of the orange hair and pleasant ankles.

"Oh, excuse me," she said, "I was looking for the ambassador."

"Wrong door," said Razo. "Lady Megina's one room down."

The girl turned away without meeting his eyes. Razo left in the opposite direction and peered back once. She had passed Megina's apartments and continued on.

5

What Goes On Out There

Razo's stomach was squeaking, his intestines knotted and shivering—the Tiran food made his gut as sore as his heart felt when he thought of his ma and Rin and the Forest. He left off keeping an eye on Enna for the first time in a week to report for sword practice and found himself still holding on to a tangerine peel left over from lunch, just to look at some color. Everything else on the palace grounds was so muted—white clothes, white stones.

"You going to play?" asked a sharp-jawed soldier named Veran.

"Oh, yes, sorry." Razo dropped the peel so he could pick up a practice sword. The orange against the pale dirt was as vibrant as the sound of thunder.

After an afternoon of bashing wooden swords with Bayern's Own, and with dinner still hours away, Razo went hunting for a crumb of something familiar lest he cave in on himself. He was wandering near the dining hall when he discovered a passage filled with affable smells.

That could lead to lower kitchens. Or to death, he thought dramatically, then discovered that playing mock terror did not help him shake off the real dread much. He wished Finn and Enna were with him, but he supposed they wanted to be *alone.* Besides, they most likely would not agree to do something as stupid as enter the bowels of the Tiran palace just hours after Lord Belvan had warned about whispered threats to Bayern lives.

Don't be stupid, Razo warned himself. *Taking risks earns you scars, and the next could be the one that ends you.* But Talone had chosen him, and his brain was sore from trying to imagine how he could ever prove his captain had not made a mistake. Besides, how were they ever to make friendly with the people of this country like Isi wanted if they were always locked up and afraid to say "hello there"?

So to disguise the extremely minor tremble in his hands, Razo sauntered in with his hands in his pockets, whistling through the space between his front teeth. (He'd always liked the space, believing that it gave him a roguish appeal.) Several voices gasped at once.

No windows peered into this kitchen with its yellow bricks stained smoke black, squat ceiling, and sulking fires. Nearly half the eyes watching Razo were glittering with glares. Razo shifted his feet.

"You're a Bayern." A freckled serving girl gaped, a smear of something fluffy across her cheek.

"I am?" Razo took the metal spoon from her hand and looked at himself in its silvery bowl. "Nah, I couldn't be. Bayern aren't this good-looking."

She giggled.

He kept the spoon and took over whipping a bowl of cream. Other girls neared, cautiously, like birds toward fallen crumbs. He thought of Isi saying, *It's easy to believe complete strangers are your enemies. If they knew us . . .* He smiled and did his best to exude harmlessness. Several girls stayed working in their corners, their looks as dark as soot stains, but others began to question him.

"So what is Bayern really like?"

"I heard your babies are not born properly but crawl out of the earth."

"Did you bring your fire-breathing horses?"

"Do the Bayern really eat Tiran babies?"

"Where are your horns and tail?"

Razo was sorely tempted to assert that all was true and he'd lost his horns and tail in a tragic childhood accident, but he bit his tongue.

When offered bits of misshapen cakes (he was delighted to discover he'd found the pastry kitchen), he regaled the dough girls and tray girls with details of wintermoon festival, Isi and Geric's wedding, the deeps of the Forest, the muddled pranks he and Enna battled during their animal keeper days, anything of interest that weighed his tongue.

The pastry chef had huge knobs for knuckles, reminding Razo of his own mother who worked too hard. When he dried dishes for her, the chef peeled him a tangerine.

"My first day here," said Razo, "a boy chucked one of these at my face. So how come you don't hate me for being Bayern?"

"The war was none of my business," said the pastry chef. "I've still got blisters on my heels and spasms in my back. What goes on out there doesn't change much down here."

One of the girls in the corner sharpened a knife emphatically, and Razo did not need the chill zipping down his back to know that not all the girls agreed with the pastry chef.

Leaving the kitchens a couple of hours later, Razo played with the skip in his step, his tongue lingering on the sharp, cold flavor of tangerine. His belly was full of cake and fruit, and he was feeling halfway to peace with Tira when a howl ripped the evening air.

Razo was running toward the sound before thinking twice. Others were running, too, soldiers and sentries, all drawn to the noise of death. The movement slammed to a stop at the Bayern barracks, where Brynn, Talone's second-man, was standing with drawn sword over the body of a Tiran. Blood stained half the blade. Slumped behind him lay Veran, one of Bayern's Own, motionless, blood pooling on the pale stones.

Then shouting. So much noise, Razo could not hear

words. The Bayern drew their swords, their backs against the barracks. A mob of Tiran soldiers separated Razo from his countrymen. He cursed himself for leaving his sword at the practice ground and stayed as still as his pounding heart would allow.

Don't notice me, don't notice, he thought, wincing away from the screaming Tiran all around him and for once blessing his unobtrusive stature. He wished for Enna and Finn, then undid that wish with a crossing of fingers. If Enna were there, she might have to burn.

"I said, silence!" Lord Belvan was pushing through the crowd, Talone in his wake.

"What happened, Brynn?" asked Talone.

Brynn's voice was hot, scratched with anger and grief. "That man"——he pointed to the splayed body of the Tiran——"broke into the barracks, shouting, 'Long live His Radiance,' calling for the Bayern ambassador to face him. Veran"——his voice softened on the name, and he gestured to his lifeless comrade——"came forward to reason with him, pulled him outside, said the ambassador wasn't in the barracks. The Tiran screamed, ran his weapon through Veran, and swung at me. I got my sword into the murderer before he could swing a third time."

Shouting again. Curses, weapons raised, shouts of, "Liar! He lies! Kill them!" A Tiran worker had noticed Razo. He elbowed the soldier beside him, pointing. Razo gripped his sling and started to back away.

"Were there any observers?" Belvan shouted, his impressive nose pointed at the crowd. "Any besides the Bayern?"

Please let there be Tiran witnesses. Razo wiped sweat from his forehead. Four Tiran grounds workers were glaring at him, hands hovering over the hilts of daggers. A soldier stood at his back, blocking his escape.

"I saw it, Lord Belvan." A sentry dragged himself forward, then yanked another by the arm. "And so did Weno here. It happened as the Bayern fellow said."

Mournful calls of doubt replaced the shouting, but the witnesses stood firm.

"Thank you for your courage," said Belvan. "I declare no harm done by this Bayern man but in self-defense and order this crowd dispersed."

Razo saluted his new Tiran acquaintances. They glanced at Belvan as they released weapons and stepped back, giving Razo space to tear through the crowd and into the barracks, joining the rest of the Own.

"He wasn't a soldier," one of Belvan's men was saying. "I don't know who he was, my lord. His clothes are fine, but he has no mark of identification on him, just a copper ring."

"Thank you," said Belvan. He turned to Talone with an exhausted expression. "This is a disaster, Captain. I had thought keeping to the grounds would protect you from any armed groups bent on murder, but we met with a fool willing to sneak in and attack on his own. I cannot guarantee

Thousand Years safe from more slippery little fellows like this one."

"We will not be moved," said Megina, arriving, her face full of the fresh news. "We must show that we're here to stay, that despite such threats we trust the Tiran people with our safety."

Enna and Finn trailed her, and Razo saw Enna take in the sight of Veran. He knew her thoughts—if she'd been there, she might have saved him. Then again, Razo thought, she might have not only revealed herself as the fire-speaker, but broken her promise and killed again.

"As you wish, Lady Megina," said Belvan. "But to ease my own mind, I will transfer Captain Ledel's company to the barracks beside yours. Their presence should help deter future attacks."

Lord Belvan did not seem to notice how that news failed to buoy the Bayerns' spirits.

Through the window, Razo saw sentries carrying Veran's body away. Two dead. Razo's throat was too stiff to swallow, and he spat at the ground and closed his eyes. Sliding behind his lids was a memory of the war—the Battle of Ostekin Fields, dead too numerous to bury, bodies stacked together and set aflame. One face in twenty had been a friend.

6

The Second Corpse

azo returned to the pastry kitchen two days later, when the haunting feeling of men slain had started to lift. The mystery behind Veran's attacker had irked him in his sleep, and he had an inkling that the best and truest gossip trickled down to the lowest kitchens.

"Was he a friend of yours?" asked the pastry chef.

"I knew him well enough and liked him, too. Lord Belvan and his men are running around with eyes closed, trying to figure out who it was and if there're more like him, but I told myself, if anyone has any ideas, it'd be the pastry girls."

The freckled girl laughed high and staccato like a marsh bird. "This city's secrets are like a farmer's animals—not a one but will one day end up in the kitchen!"

A few girls volunteered this idea and that, all nonsense, until a usually quiet girl with smooth yellow hair looked up from the washing.

"Any of you heard of Manifest Tira?"

"That a city out east?" asked another.

"It's some group who wants the war back again. My cousin's a part of it. He's war hungry because he didn't get a chance to fight, but I gather the leaders of the group think Tira's destiny is to own Bayern and everything else." She shrugged. "You should watch out for them, Razo. Last time I was at my mother's house in the city, I ran into some of my cousin's new friends, the sort who would skin a cat squealing if they thought it the patriotic thing to do."

Razo stuck his hands in the suds to wash trays beside her. "Do you know who they are or where they meet? Maybe I should warn Lord Belvan."

The girl's eyes widened. "Do that, and I could be their next cat."

"Then I won't say a word about you. I promise."

The girl looked ready to scurry under a table, so he cleared his throat and tried to change topics to something harmless—how wretched his Bayern wool clothing was in the bursting spring. The freckled girl claimed to know the palace thread-mistress, another worked as a morning maid for Lady Dasha, and within hours he had permission for new clothes and an appointment for a fitting.

That night as he entered Enna's room, he felt as splendid as one of the peacocks in the palace garden.

"What on earth are you wearing?" Enna's face scrunched as though she smelled something foul.

Razo raised his hand as if requesting silence. "I'm pretty sure I can guess your opinion of my new wardrobe, but nothing you say'll make me toss it. What we need in all this gloom after Veran's death is a bit of Bayern and Tira playing together nice, that's all I'm saying."

The thread-mistress had made him loose-fitting leggings and a white tunic. The chest cloth most Tiran wrapped around themselves was called a "lummas," and Razo discovered it had some practical purposes, such as wiping sweat or pulling onto his head for shade. Instead of a sash he tied his distance sling around his waist, and he kept his same boots. It was a curious blend of both countries' styles, and he thought it quite natty. He wished only that he could get his hands on the Bayern dyes brought for trading. His eye missed bright colors.

"You look ridiculous . . . ," Enna started.

Razo raised his hand again. "That's not what the girls in the pastry kitchen say."

"Really?" Finn grinned.

Razo laughed suggestively. "Indeed. Well, some I'd give a wide berth while they're sharpening a chopping knife, but others . . . let's just say that my fingers and toes can't keep track of all the winking. Too bad I can't go out in the city tonight and show off my new goods."

Ingridan was celebrating one of its feast days, which the

pastry chef claimed were as common as raisins in a raisin bun. Some of the girls had invited Razo to join them in the streets, draped in flowers and dancing until the moon was high, but Megina had judged it too dangerous yet.

How are we ever going to make them our friends, Razo wondered, *if we can't run out into the streets and dance?*

"I'm sure we're not missing much," said Enna, but Razo thought she sounded sorry not to swathe herself in flowers.

The door burst open. Razo flung himself behind a table while scrabbling for his sword. It was only Megina, and Enna laughed at him.

"A bit jumpy, are we?" said Enna.

"You can poke fun when Tumas and all his friends want *you* dead."

Megina shut the door behind her. "Unbelievable. A maid mentioned she thought two boys were sleeping in my waiting woman's room, and here you are, bedrolls on the carpet as if setting up a war camp. How does it look for my waiting woman to have boys sleeping by her bed?"

"Lady Megina," said Enna, "I'm not really your waiting woman—"

"I know that, but it matters what *they* think. We can't give the Tiran any cause to doubt our character. You two, join the others in the barracks."

Finn argued silently with a firm stance, but Razo gathered both their bedrolls, put a hand on Finn's back, and led him from the room.

"We'll appeal to Talone tomorrow," said Razo. "He's likely to oppose anything Megina says, as they're not exactly grand pals, and besides, I think he'll see good reason to keep someone near Enna."

Finn did not ask why. It made Razo wonder how much he knew.

The snores of the barracks shoved and rattled Razo all night, and on top of that, those crazy Tiran were always ringing bells to tell the hour, as if time were more important than sleep. The twentieth instance he woke, Razo decided to just get up.

The moon slumped low and fat on the horizon. He had been trying so hard to sleep, his body still felt heavy and worried with the idea, and he stumbled on the paving stones and tilted to one side. The sentries he passed frowned at the Bayern sun and crown on his cloak, and Razo felt a warning throb in his side where Tumas's friend had notched him. But he was tired and awake, an unhappy combination, so he decided to ignore his mild dread and practice his sling on the training ground until dawn kicked the day awake.

Besides, Captain Ledel's men are near, so I'm safe, he thought, just to tell himself a good joke.

The night was full of contrast—warm air tingling with a cold chill, dark sky and a bright moon, his sleepy eyes and alert mind. The trees and buildings sloughed their heavy shadows on the dirt, and Razo pushed through them as through a shallow stream, until his boot struck something solid.

One shadow was not shadow. He tapped it with his toe and heard the crackle of burnt cloth. That sour smell gushed down his throat.

Razo looked south, to the dark spot that was Enna's window, and wished for a river at hand.

7

Secret Burial

All the shadows seemed to shift as if the moon were plunging across the sky. The dark parts of the sky leaned lower, and the chill in the air crept closer in, fingering the hairs on Razo's arms and neck. The punching of his heartbeat made him feel knocked about, exposed. Not alone.

Razo flipped around. No one there but a dead body. He could hear his own breathing.

Think, Razo told himself. *You're here, so be useful.*

Again, there were no drag marks on the dirt. Someone must have lifted the body and dumped it. Someone large. Razo knew he himself would not be strong enough to carry it alone. The sound of footsteps in the distance slapped his heartbeat faster. He could drag the body to the Pallo, the palace's slender river. Of course, it cut through the gardens on the other side of the barracks, and he would pass a dozen sentries before reaching it.

He wished down into his gut that he could figure out

what to do on his own, that he would not have to go running for his captain.

Think. Razo. Think for once, Forest-born. No solution tickled
his brain. He flung his cloak over the body before dashing
back to the barracks.

Razo inched through the door of the captain's private
apartment and crouched before the bed. A tree outside the
room's only window crowded out the moonlight, and Razo
could not see. He waited two breaths.

"What is it, Razo?" Talone asked in a voice cracked with
sleep.

"Another body, Captain. Behind the training grounds.
So far as I know, no one's spotted it but me."

A pause.

"Get a shovel from my back room while I put on my
boots."

They dragged the body closer to the barracks, behind
two potted trees. Razo left to keep a watch on the path,
and the sounds of Talone's digging disrupted the night.

"Lovely," Razo whispered as he began to fling stones
against the trunk of a far tree. His skin itched with sweat,
his neck hurt to be twisting around constantly as he searched
for any onlookers. A sentry neared, and Razo swallowed an
exclamation, producing a "haaagh" sound in his throat. It
kind of hurt. To warn Talone of the sentry, he changed targets from the tree to a post near where Talone dug. *Whack,*

his stone lashed the post, and the sounds of a shovel scraping earth paused.

"Morning," Razo said pleasantly, still slinging at the post. "Couldn't sleep, you know? Just practicing my, uh, sling. Here."

The sentry glared as he continued by. Razo held his breath until he was out of sight. Then he sent a stone back at the tree. The digging resumed.

Another sentry passed, and then a third. Razo felt as though he had run up a mountain, his heart speeding, his whole body sore. At last the scraping sounds stopped altogether, so Razo gathered his shot and returned to Talone's room. The captain entered a few minutes later. Dirt rode up his elbows, covered his boots, smudged his beard. He sat on the edge of his cot and leaned his brow against his hands.

"It's fortunate that it rained yesterday. The ground was soft."

Razo slumped onto the floor. "Finn and I were sleeping in her room, all but last night. Lady Megina told us to leave. If I'd stayed . . ."

Talone shook his head, saying it was fruitless to question it.

"Do you think it was her?" asked Razo.

"If the Tiran find burned bodies after our arrival, they'll be convinced we're harboring a 'fire-witch,' as they say, whether or not our Enna is responsible. In sketchy diplomatic situations, the truth matters less than what the other side *thinks* is the truth."

"Lady Megina said as much to me last night."

"Did she?" Talone filled a cup with water and set it on the ground beside Razo. "It's time to tell me everything you know about Enna's burnings."

Razo had been avoiding this very conversation since the end of the war. He squirmed as he spoke, uncomfortable now on the hard floor. "It's been about a year and a half since I first figured Enna had something to do with the reports of random burnings in Tiran camps. When I confronted her about it, she seemed almost relieved to have someone to tell, as well as eager to do more with the fire."

Razo dipped a finger in the water, shook it off. "It was her idea to go on scouting missions with me into the Bayern towns the Tiran had taken, burn tents and stacks of weapons and such. She was aware that her control over the fire slipped sometimes, so she wanted someone to make sure she didn't go too far. After our first burning raid, I brought Finn along, too, but she was already falling fast. When Finn and I realized, we refused to go with her until she was clearheaded. That night she ran off without us to Eylbold, got herself caught by that nasty Tiran captain, and spent a couple of months prisoner. I don't know what-all happened there."

Talone was changing his clothes, washing his hands and face, ridding himself of the residue of grave digging. Razo watched, realizing that whether or not Enna was burning, he and Talone were now elbow deep in these murders. If any Tiran had seen them, if they were found out . . . Razo rubbed his back against the wall. Cold chills always made him feel itchy.

"Finn and I tried to rescue her, as you know." Razo cleared his throat casually. No need to dwell too long on that point. By rights, Talone could have seized their javelins and all rights as soldiers for deserting the army. It had hurt Razo as much as any of his wounds to betray Talone like that. "Captain, you know the rest, how Enna burned our way free and we caught up with the Tiran army before they invaded the capital."

Talone wiped a smear of soot from his boot. "Tell me about Enna during that last battle."

Razo decided he wanted that water now and drank the entire cup without a breath. The cold tingled his empty stomach as though he had swallowed honeybees.

"It was ugly, Captain. It was the worst thing I ever saw, and whenever I find those images in my skull, I kick them out again with a swift boot."

"Go on, son."

At the word *son*, Razo sat up a little taller.

"Well, Finn and I, we stood in front of Enna and fought any Tiran who tried to stop her. They'd started to catch fire, whole groups of them. I tried not to watch, but I could hear them scream. When I . . . when I turned back once to look at Enna, she was lying on her stomach, holding herself up on her elbows. She sobbed, but her face was smooth, as if she didn't know she was crying. She just stared at the field, at the burning men."

Razo scratched his face with both hands. "Times I saw her set fire to tents and things, and I could tell she enjoyed it, but that dead expression . . . I didn't look back again. Before long, some Tiran villain got a sword between my ribs and I didn't see her again for months, not until she and Isi had returned from their trip south."

"Do you know what happened there?" asked Talone.

"Finn told me that in Yasid, Isi was able to teach Enna wind speech and Enna taught Isi fire, so now they both have both talents, and somehow that made Enna better."

Talone did not even blink, and what he did not say seemed to hang above Razo's head. *Is she better?*

"What do you think?" asked Talone.

"I don't think much, Captain. You know that."

Talone did not laugh. Razo wondered if that meant he agreed, if he did think Razo was as witless as a startled hare. Razo slumped. "I hope it isn't Enna."

"We need to be sure."

"You want me to keep sleeping in her room?"

Talone shook his head. "Megina is right. And Enna's safety relies on the fact that no one knows who she is. If we look like we're protecting her . . . No, it's better to watch her from afar."

"Finn'll go back," said Razo.

"I know."

What if he's carrying off the bodies she burns? Razo wanted to ask.

A knock jumped Razo to his feet, javelin in hand. Talone opened the door, his face as emotionless as ever.

"Good morning, Captain Talone."

Captain Ledel's hair was a dirty yellow, tied back at his thick neck, the tip flung over one of his warrior shoulders. His eyes looked tired, but he smiled pleasantly into the impressive scar that ran down his jawline. Razo generally approved of facial scars. Sadly, all his own battle marks were on his torso where girls could not easily catch sight of them.

"You are occupied, Captain?" Ledel asked, looking at Razo. He had a peculiar rasp to his voice that made Razo wonder if he had been up all night.

"One of my soldiers is here to receive his daily orders," said Talone.

Ledel nodded once, an approving gesture. "You are an early riser. I always say, a captain should never sleep."

"Not when anyone is looking," said Talone.

"I hope you will postpone any engagements this morning. The men need amusement, and tension often yields under the power of some friendly bashing. What do you say to mock combats at the training grounds?"

Talone barely hesitated before nodding. "I'll wake my men."

"Good. It's natural for recent rivals to feel animosity. We are all military men, and the war is fresh in our ears, but

I won't tolerate disorderly violence. There is nothing I despise so much as professionals in the art of war who think they can stomp upon its rules."

Ledel spoke with a trembling earnestness that raised goose bumps on Razo's skin. Why was Ledel so desperate to assert his fervor for following the rules of war? It made Razo wonder.

8

The Own's Worst Swordsman

edel's men were waiting on the patch of uncovered soil between the two barracks, still bleary-eyed and wincing at the sharp disk of the sun. The morning light exposed every scar on their faces as well as every heap and dip in the dirt. Razo fiercely, desperately avoided looking at the spot where the body was buried.

Ledel tossed two wooden swords into the fighting ring, matched the first pair, and combat began. Razo squirmed as he watched, thinking of eleven different ways a wooden sword could kill. When one soldier managed to touch his opponent anywhere between waist and neck, one of the captains would call out, "Match, for Tira," or, "Match, Bayern."

A couple of rounds into the exercise, Razo caught sight of Ledel muttering to his secondman, his jaw scar looking pink and raw and his manner intense. Razo shadowed them in time to hear, ". . . we'll see how well they perform as soldiers without the fire fighting for them. If only they do not . . ."

Razo kept walking and joined Finn.

"Do you get the feeling they're just waiting for the chance to poke out someone's eyeball?" Razo whispered under the din of clacking swords.

Finn nodded. "Everything about this feels like the war, only without the killing."

"So far." Razo looked for Tumas and squinted against the morning sun, his eyes tearing. "That big brute of theirs, every time he looks at me, I get the crawly sensation that he's spittin' eager for the chance to slice me pigwise."

"Tumas," Ledel called the soldier into the ring.

Razo snorted. "There he goes. I wonder what poor sap Talone'll call to face—"

"Razo," said Talone.

Razo gaped—at Tumas leering in the ring, at the other soldiers staring at him, at his captain, who was sending him against an opponent who wanted him dead, or at least wounded as painfully as possible. He wondered if it would be worse to run away now or lose an eye to Tumas's wooden sword.

Finn grabbed Razo's arm and whispered, "What's the captain thinking? You can't do it."

At that, Razo shook off Finn's hand and strode into the ring, taking position on the large shadow of Tumas's head that the sun dropped before him. The man was tall and impressively imposing in every way but his large, flabby ears, which reminded Razo of nothing so much as a pair of pork chops. Tumas grinned, and Razo felt his side throb where the soldier's friend had carved a scar. *I can do this, I can.*

"Begin!" Ledel shouted.

Tumas moved. Razo swung. He felt a jab in his gut.

"Match, for Tira," said Ledel.

Razo fell to one knee, pushing against the pain in his ribs, and stayed down. No blood. He would be all right when the sharpness ebbed, but the Tiran soldiers were laughing, and Razo did not want to look up and see a flicker of shame in the faces of his comrades.

You've still got both your eyeballs, Razo thought with hopeful cheer. He grabbed for a breath and scooted out of the ring, feeling as though he dragged a very heavy shadow behind him.

"Come, I was expecting some sport!" Tumas's voice squealed through his congested nose. "This is a child. I demand another turn."

"You demand nothing, soldier," said Ledel. "Stand properly."

Tumas straightened. "Yes, Captain."

Ledel turned to Talone. "What say you? Shall we see if any of your boys can beat our Tumas?"

"Fair enough," said Talone. "Finn."

Tumas noticed the smiles of the Bayern soldiers that indicated this opponent was different, and his expression stiffened. The two challengers faced each other, sword tips resting on the ground in ready position. Then, without warning, Tumas pounced.

The first move Finn made was to step aside. And the second. And the third. Tumas's lower lip began to twitch.

Razo had watched Finn fight a thousand times, in practice and in wartime. What never ceased to catch his breath was Finn's expression of acceptance, almost of surrender. He wasted nothing, letting every motion matter. And although Razo was just leaning against the barracks wall, watching Finn made him feel as though even he himself mattered. He watched with energy, muscles taut, face aching, as tired as if he were the one fighting.

Tumas's swipes began to have a vicious slice to them, seeking not just to touch Finn, but to bruise something, rip something. Then he hit Finn's sword, and Finn was not able to bounce the strike away. They faced each other, weapons crossed. Finn opened his mouth to breathe. Tumas spat in his face. Ledel shouted Tumas's name in disapproval but did not stop the match, and that quickly, the myth of a friendly bout evaporated. Shouts exploded from both sides.

Razo had run to the edge of the fighting circle without realizing it. Right here, he realized, the war could start again.

Tumas pushed off and attacked again, harassing Finn with strikes on his sword that would ache in Finn's arm tomorrow. Then Razo saw the opening, just before it happened. Finn was drawing Tumas closer, getting him comfortable in his attacking, letting him fall into a routine of strike, strike, strike—then gently, almost like a step in a dance, Finn lowered his sword and moved his inside foot back. Tumas stumbled. Finn turned and tapped his sword on the Tiran's back, lightly, as though he were getting a stranger's attention.

"Match," said Talone. "Bayern."

Tumas's chest heaved. A drop of sweat fell into his eye, but he did not blink. "I'm not fresh. If I had been fresh, the outcome would be different."

"Perhaps you're right." Finn put out his hand to shake. Tumas's face contorted. He pulled his arm back and swung.

"Watch it!" Razo shouted, but Finn had anticipated Tumas's fist and leaned away. Ledel and others rushed forward to grab Tumas, who was cursing and shouting. Other Tiran joined the uproar, shoving Bayern soldiers in the chest, waiting for someone to draw first blood, for that permission to fight. Shouting from both sides now, muscles tensed, hands in fists. The moment spun around and around, and Razo felt twisted and backward, his eyes murky with the memory of a battlefield, men plunging swords through bodies, blood on his clothes that was not his own, killing and wondering why, expecting pain, anticipating dying, questioning if he were already dead . . .

"Enough!" shouted Ledel.

The Tiran soldiers quieted at the bark of their commander, a touch of fear evident in their obedience. Tumas seemed to tremble with the desire to keep hitting but pulled his arms to his sides. Razo breathed for the first time since Tumas had swung at Finn.

When Talone spoke, his tone was civil, calling no attention to the Tirans' bad behavior. "Thank you for this exercise, Captain Ledel. I hope we may meet here again."

And Ledel made no apology, not as though he did not care, Razo thought, but more that the quick chaos he'd witnessed so offended him that he could not even admit it had happened.

"Indeed. Good day."

Razo noticed Enna standing on the path, watching. Finn saw her, and his entire demeanor changed. Razo tried to determine if he had stood up a little straighter or stuck out his chin or chest, but he could not figure any one thing.

"Well fought, Forest boy," said Enna, approaching.

Finn shrugged. "It was just an exercise."

"You exercised him quite nicely, I thought."

"Does that mean you'll marry me?"

Enna laughed.

The way they seemed wholly absorbed in each other made Razo certain they wanted to be alone, so of course he hustled his way over. Tumas and another soldier passed by Razo so close that they pushed him between their shoulders and dragged him along a few steps.

"Why ith thith one here?" asked Tumas's friend with a lisp so severe, it seemed feigned.

"He's their errand boy," said Tumas. "What a good joke to give him a sword."

Razo writhed, wanting out, too ashamed to shout for help, when Ledel growled for Tumas to come.

Tumas lifted Razo by the arm, bringing his ear to the soldier's mouth. "You're not safe," he whispered before dropping him.

Razo ran behind the barracks. He shoved his sword into its sheath and clenched his javelin, wanting his weapons in hand, just to feel them. He realized he was standing on the secret grave, and he edged away.

Enna and Finn had disappeared. The rest of Bayern's Own were heading out to find breakfast. Conrad called to Razo to join them, but Razo pretended to be too far away to hear.

Again and again, he wondered, *Why is this one here?*

9

Tree Rat

he third afternoon after the match, Razo, Enna, and Finn rambled through the palace gardens, speaking longingly of Bayern potatoes, almond cakes, and venison stew and feeling caged inside the iron fence like animals in a traveling menagerie. They had been in Ingridan for three weeks with little to show for it. And now, only days before the assembly adjourned for the summer, Razo could not help feeling that the mission was failing. But they did not speak about the mission; they talked about potatoes.

When Finn left to take his turn for Megina guard duty, Enna sprinted in the opposite direction, mumbling a quick farewell.

"Slippery girl," said Razo, racing after her. He thought he saw her black hair entering the Bayern stable, so he made his way around the far side. A row of potted trees lined one wall, and he walked inside them, listening through the stable windows for anything out of the ordinary among the wheeze, nicker, and whuffle of horses.

He had come to the end when he saw that girl again, the Tiran ambassador's daughter, pressing her back to the stable as if she did not want to be seen. She brought her cupped palm to her mouth and drank from it. There was a bucket of water on the ground, and Razo supposed she had dipped her hand in it, though he had not seen her do it. She turned and startled when she saw him.

"Oh, hello," she said.

"Hello. I bump into you again." Razo eased out, hoping that he made creeping behind potted trees look as normal as dipping bread in gravy.

She picked a leaf out of his hair. "Yes, that's because I was . . . looking for you."

"Here I am." He tugged casually on his hair to make sure it stood up properly.

"My name is Dasha." By way of greeting, she crossed her wrists on her chest and inclined her head.

"Uh, Razo." He tried to do the nod-and-hands thing, too, though he must have done it awkwardly, for she smiled.

Her smile was peculiar—it made her nose wrinkle, not as though she smelled something unpleasant, but more that she was so amused, her whole face wanted to be a part of the smile. It affected him strangely, and he stared at her longer than was probably polite. Her hair was not so much orange as the color of rust on iron, and her eyes were blue like the tiled fountains in the public squares. Though she was of his height, she was such a skinny thing, he could probably fling her over a shoulder. He was contemplating this appealing notion when he realized she had spoken.

"What was that?"

"I said, I am the liaison to the Bayern at Thousand Years, if you require anything."

"Ah," seemed like an appropriate response.

Her mouth twisted in a half smile. "*Do* you require anything?"

"Oh, you're asking me. No, not really. Well, except the ocean."

"You want the ocean?"

"Yes, fetch it for me!"

She blinked, and Razo laughed. "No, you nit, I don't want the ocean. I just want to see it. Everyone was going on about seeing an ocean, and here I've been in Ingridan for almost three weeks and not a peep. But I know we're not supposed to leave the palace, so I guess I'm out of luck."

She stared at him, as though mentioning the ocean were as insulting as showing his bum to the world.

"What?" he said.

"You called me a nit."

"Oh. I did! And I hardly know you. I mean, I'm sorry."

She laughed and tugged on his sleeve. The touch made him want to stand on his toes to be taller.

"You can call me a nit anytime you want, and you can most certainly see the ocean."

"I can? I mean, I can't. It's not safe."

"I was speaking with Lord Belvan and Lady Megina this morning, and they agreed it's time Ingridan observes the Bayern presence. I think a visit to the shore will be a perfect first outing. We'll leave after second bell tomorrow, Lord Razo."

He was about to protest that second bell was pretty early, just an hour past dawn, and then he thought he had better set her straight about the "Lord" thing. But it did feel rather comfortable just before his name like that, and while he was hesitating, Dasha had turned to go. She bumped into Enna emerging from the stables.

"Oh," said Dasha, seeing Enna.

"Oh," said Enna, seeing Razo.

Dasha did not wait to apologize and was gone in her smooth, hurried gait.

"What're you up to, Enna-girl?" asked Razo.

Enna smiled innocently. "Nothing. Let's go eat."

He suspected she was trying to distract him, but eating did sound like a reasonable plan.

The next morning, the second bell rang with a bone-vibrating noise, as though the brass ball were rolling inside Razo's head. He startled awake, his heart thudding with the reminder that he would be leaving the palace gates today.

At the stables, the Bayern drank cups of tea and mounted their horses. One of the tea girls wore her fluffy yellow hair in two separate bunches, looking like a rabbit with large, drooping ears. When she approached Razo, he recognized her as Pela from the pastry kitchens, one of the glaring girls who seemed to fantasize about cutting out his Bayern heart with her own fingernails.

"Morning, Pela. How's Cinny?" Trying to be friendly, Razo asked after one of the tray girls who had sprained her ankle two days before.

"Lounging in a chair, doing all the easy jobs, and not nearly as pretty as me." Pela put a cup of tea in his hand, stroking his fingers a moment longer than was necessary.

Huh, he thought, *that's a change.* Her touch made him want to look serious and manly, and he downed the stinging hot tea in one gulp. To hide the pain, he turned to mount his horse and botched his whole image by having to scramble up just to stick his foot in the stirrup. Once in the saddle, he discovered his stirrups were so high, his knees were sticking up level with the saddle rim.

"What the—?" He had to dismount and adjust the length. By then Pela had moved off, serving tea to Tumas. They appeared to be chatting intimately.

"New saddle?" asked Finn, riding up.

"Finn, do you see the lias—whatever, the orange-haired girl?" Razo gestured ahead without looking. "Do you think she's pretty?"

Finn glanced Dasha's way, then returned his attention to his horse. "She's all right."

"Really? Just all right?"

Finn shrugged.

Razo rolled his eyes and tapped Bee Sting to a walk. "What am I saying? He doesn't think any girl is pretty but Enna."

"Are there any girls but Enna?" Finn called back.

"There'd better be."

A memory of Bettin came unbidden—a night in Bayern's capital four years ago. Isi had been sitting by the fire, telling a bed tale to all the animal workers. It had been a romantic one, the kind that usually made Razo sniff in boredom, but he'd liked it because Bettin had been sitting beside him. That night, all that stuff about a man and a woman and hearts and vows of forever had seemed as real as the fire in the grate.

"Stupid," Razo muttered. Saying the word made him feel a touch better.

Bee Sting trotted briefly as they passed the palace gates. Razo gripped the hard rim of the saddle, anticipating an attack from angry Tiran citizens, but the streets of Ingridan were sleepy. The dawning sun polished the stones to a soft gold, making the city feel warm and friendly, and street after street, nothing jumped out at them. Still, Razo could not relax.

"Take a look at that," said Conrad as they passed a palace a quarter the size of Thousand Years. "A feather bed and private room for every guard and maid, I'd bet, and fancy chairs for the dogs and cats, while they're at it."

"But what good's a fancy house like that for the likes of you, Forest-born?" said Razo. "You'd get lost in the corridors and barely survive by eating leather chair covers."

"That so, squirrel meat? Well, you'd mistake the kitchen for the privy and scare away the pretty maids."

Victar rode nearby. "That is Lady Dasha's home." He wet his lips as he nodded in her direction.

Conrad wagged his eyebrows. "Lives like a princess, and pretty, too."

"Yes, she is considered a more than adequate match for any noble bachelor of Ingridan." Victar's smile was mischievous. "Her father has extensive holdings."

"With her father in Bayern," said Razo, "you'd think she'd have plenty to do managing everything. So why'd she volunteer to stay at Thousand Years with the Bayern?"

Victar shrugged slightly, as if he did not know or care.

The party left the main avenue for narrow streets where the houses crowded on top of one another, and the air changed—it swept over Razo as though it were more river than wind, the smell sharp and so briny that it seized the top of his throat.

Then there was the ocean.

The white buildings of the city stopped just shy of the bay, as if afraid of getting their toes wet. In the distance, he could see the harbor and dozens of ships, some grand and long, their masts a forest of trees smoothed of their branches.

Dasha led them to a slim section of shore, as quiet and clean as the morning streets. Razo left Bee Sting at a post and walked across a field of sand.

He knew the ocean was huge because he had been told so, but he could see only the thin line of it before the horizon clamped down. There was no grandeur, not like seeing a mountain; nothing to surround him and make him feel changed, as when he entered a wood or stood in the midst of a snowstorm. Even so, the sea felt bigger than weather, older than ruins. The sight rustled at his soul.

He stared, and his unease lengthened inside him, as though it stretched after sleeping. Up the waves rolled, back they fell, like breath pushed out and pulled back in. The hushing noise made his bones feel soft, his eyes drowsy. He thought he could lie in the sand and forget who he was, let the water and the sound of water unstitch his soul from his body and send it floating away to see what the dead see.

"Do you like it?" asked Dasha.

The sound of her voice startled him. Something about an ocean made him forget he was not alone.

"I don't know that it's up to me to like," he said. "It's not really a people thing, is it? Not like a city or a farm. It's got more wilderness about it than anything I've ever seen."

He thought that was a very apt observation and congratulated himself, waiting for Dasha to agree. She was staring at the water, her lips parted, her eyes losing focus to the crumbling surf, almost as if she were trying to catch a glimpse of someone she knew far out on the waves. He watched her watching the sea and had the peculiar impression that she *knew* the ocean, the way he knew his sister, Rin, or the Forest, or his way around a roasted chicken.

He cleared his throat and spoke again. "It's pretty, even though it's so empty."

She pulled her gaze back to him. "Just under the surface it teems with fish and plants."

"So, it's a forest for fish."

"Exactly! Except, I've never seen a forest."

"Never seen a forest?" Razo shook his head. Now Dasha seemed stranger than a sea. "There was a time I thought my Forest was the world."

"All those trees. And animals, too, right? Is it beautiful?" She rocked on her feet as though too excited to hold still.

"It's home, and I guess I think it's just what it ought to be. Think of it as an ocean of trees, if you want."

"And what do you eat from a forest instead of fish?"

"Sometimes red deer, but that's a big quarry and rare to catch. I hunt some birds, but mostly rabbits or squirrel."

"What is 'squirrel'?"

"It's like a chipmunk, but with a long, fat tail."

Dasha wrinkled her brow, indicating she did not understand.

"Squirrel and chipmunk, they're about this big, furry, kind of like, I don't know, like rats that live in trees."

"Rats? You eat rats?"

"They're not really rats, I was just trying to think of something that—"

"You eat tree rats. That's one rumor of Bayern habits I hadn't heard."

"They're not tree rats really, they're just . . . ugh, I shouldn't've said *rats*, I meant . . . Wait, what rumors have you heard?"

"You eat babies," she said blankly.

"No, you eat babies!"

"I do not!"

"I don't mean you personally. I mean, that's what I've heard about the Tiran, but I never believed it."

"And I didn't believe it about the Bayern."

"So what are we hollering about?"

"What *are* you hollering about?" asked Enna as she and Finn joined them.

"We weren't," said Razo. "Well, maybe, but . . . Dasha, what was I saying?"

Dasha did not seem to take his question seriously. She turned to the newcomers and introduced herself.

"Finn of Bayern's Own," said Finn.

"I'm Enna, waiting woman to Lady Megina."

Razo caught the barest flinch in Dasha's expression, a dart of her eyes, a subtle indication that perhaps she did not believe what Enna had just said. But she conversed in a friendly manner with Enna, eagerly even, and did not seem the least aware that she was talking to Tira's great enemy the fire-witch. He discovered his hand was gripping the hilt of his sword and he slowly let go.

Enna said something Razo did not catch, most likely some disparaging comment about him, and Dasha smiled. The way the sun hit Dasha's eyes, they were so light in color, they appeared translucent. Razo stared.

"Are you all right?" Dasha asked. "Your face looks pained. Did you bite your lip or something? . . . No? Well, we should return. It was a pleasure, Enna, Finn, tree rat."

She walked away.

Enna and Finn looked at Dasha and then at Razo.

"Did she just call you tree rat?" asked Enna.

"Did she?" said Razo.

"I think she just called you tree rat."

"No."

Finn nodded. "She did. She called you tree rat."

"Why would she—" Enna started.

"Because of squirrels, I guess," said Razo, still watching Dasha walk away. Negotiating the sand, she took small steps, and her hips kind of swayed. He found it curious.

"Squirrels?" asked Enna.

"Rats in trees," Razo said distractedly. Dasha seemed to find her walking rhythm from the sound of the surf, almost as if she were not a girl but water upon the sand. His soul whistled an easy tune.

When she had disappeared into the group of Tiran, Razo looked back at Enna and Finn. Both were staring at him, mouths agape.

"What?" he said.

Enna laughed and started back up the beach. "Razo, you're a picture."

"I am?" He turned to Finn. "Is that good or bad?"

Finn shrugged. "I'm still trying to figure out *squirrels*."

On the ride back, Razo contemplated being a picture, and being a tree rat, and the way Dasha had walked up the beach, and the rustling of the ocean. He was feeling pretty good, which made the scene at Thousand Years all the more abrupt.

It was a hornets' nest.

Clusters of Tiran citizens mobbed outside the palace gates. When they saw the returning Bayern soldiers, the excited shouting turned to anger. Fists pounded the air.

A mounted Tiran guard rushed through the gates and toward the Bayern. Razo loosed his sling and urged Bee Sting closer to Enna and Finn, saying, "I'm sorry," because he had promised his horse that he would keep her out of another war.

Lord Belvan rode at the head of his own group of soldiers, holding up his bare hand. "Quickly! Captain Talone, let's get your people into the safety of Thousand Years."

Talone cantered his horse forward, shouting, "Follow Lord Belvan!"

"What's happened?" Conrad asked.

No one answered. Lord Belvan's soldiers surrounded the Bayern, separating them from the citizens on the streets, and led them through the gate. The sun, glaring above the horizon, fumed in its sizzling spring heat.

Inside the grounds, sentries stood with drawn weapons and courtiers and palace workers with unsheathed glares. The Bayern rode past the stable where Razo had followed Enna the day before. Amid a throng of watchers, three men carried something heavy wrapped in a blanket. One man was jostled by the crowd, and he leaned to the side to catch his footing. From beneath the blanket a blackened leg dropped into view.

10

The Captain's Spy

azo could not catch his breath, and his jaw tightened as if he would throw up. *How can she do this?*

Lord Belvan's men led the Bayern to a back stable, where they tumbled off their mounts and fled into the palace. They ran down a corridor, Belvan barking commands, splitting the Bayern into smaller groups, stuffing them into various rooms and posting guards "until it quiets out there."

"What do you think's going on?" Enna asked.

"It's pretty clear," Razo whispered. He would not look at her. "Talone and I found the first two, Enna. Or were there more? I should've been watching better, but I never could stop you. You'd run off a cliff if the idea took you."

"What're you talking about?" asked Finn.

"That was another body they just found out there. Burned brittle."

"And you think Enna—"

Razo glared. "Who else, Finn?"

Lord Belvan urged Razo into the next room. Razo glanced back at Enna—she was neither furious nor devastated. She was dazed. Stunned to silence. The door shut.

Razo sat on the floor. In memory, her look pierced him like the long, thin thorns that slip deep into skin. He knew now that if Enna had burned those people, she did not know she had.

Razo shared the space with three of Bayern's Own, who spent an hour chewing over the ugly situation.

"If a war starts and we're here . . . ," said one.

"Prisoners for the duration, if not executed on the spot."

"Do you think Lady Megina's to blame? Who is she, anyway? I never heard of the king's cousin till she was suddenly ambassador."

Razo kept quiet, picking at the wood grain. Enna's face had sent him tilting, and he seemed to rock as though unaccustomed to still earth after hours on horseback.

After a second hour, the noise outside their window lost its urgency and dwindled to the hum and rub of every day. When his three companions left to find Talone, Razo stayed.

He was sitting in an abandoned chair before the hearth when Enna burst into the room, slamming the door behind her. She set a fire blazing in the hearth, spitting sparks.

"Watch it, Enna!" Razo leaped from his seat and hopped about, slapping at his clothes.

"You think I didn't know you were there? You think I'd burn you by accident?"

Razo brushed off his lummas, petulant that there were no burned spots to account for his yelping. "You could've—"

"You're fine, Razo."

He barely breathed the question. "Enna, *are* you burning again?"

"No."

"I saw you sneak into that stable yesterday, and I thought—"

Enna put back her head and laughed, but it came out hard, as though the laugh burned her throat. "I was short-ening the stirrups on your horse's saddle!"

"My stirrups . . . that was you!"

"Of course it was, you dolt." She tried to sound casual, the kind of voice she used for throwing around insults, but her words were strained. "I didn't burn anybody."

"Are you sure? Not by accident? Not in your sleep or . . . or anything?"

She sat on the floor before her fire. Her fingers rubbed the hem of her tunic, her eyes followed the flames, and Razo thought how Enna, like fire, like wind, could never hold completely still.

"What happened with me and Isi on our journey—I never told you much. Maybe if I had, if you'd understood, you'd know that I've changed, that I . . ." She paused as though she struggled with words. It made him feel proud, that Enna would care what she said to him, that she worried what he thought.

"Isi and I went to Yasid," she continued in her artless voice. "We learned how to share our knowledge of fire and wind languages with each other, so that we'd have balance. I form fire out of the heat that rises off living things, and during the war, that heat was gathering around me constantly, pressing in, demanding. But now that I have wind speech, too, the wind's always nearby to blow off the heat so it can't overwhelm me. Same with Isi—the wind used to hound her with its speech, with the images of what it had touched. But now that she understands fire speech, too, the heat's always there to break up the wind."

Enna cleared her throat. The sound made her seem young, just a little girl. "What I'm trying to explain is, I'm not the fire's puppet. I can't lose control anymore. So if you still think I'm burning people, you'd have to believe that I'm doing it on purpose. That I want to." She looked now at Razo, and he imagined that because she had been staring at the fire so long, her gaze was hot on his skin. "I don't want to, Razo. And I'm not. And I won't. Burn another person. Never again."

Razo's hands were orange and strange in the firelight. He turned them over, looking for an answer. Something to say. He settled on, "I'm sorry."

Enna frowned. "I guess if people suspect me, it's my own fault."

"But, Enna, if you don't burn, if you won't let yourself, then what good . . . I mean, why are you here? Why'd you demand to come when——"

"During the war, it took me just a few moments to burn down homes that took weeks to build. I ended lives like snapping a twig in two. That can't be all I am, Razo! There's got to be ways I can help without . . . without hurting."

"Isi thought it was too dangerous."

"She worries too much for me, but she believes I can do it, too." She bit her lip. "Do you?"

I want you to, he thought. *I hope you can. I'll help you try.* He just nodded. "If it's not you burning people, that means it's someone else."

"Brilliant," said Enna. "You always were the brightest sheep boy I knew."

Razo gave her a playful knock with his elbow and tried to enjoy the moment, but he had just accused one of his best friends of murdering three people in her sleep.

Finn was waiting outside the door, his hand on his sword hilt, and Razo greeted him without meeting his eyes.

"I'm sorry, Finn. I'm a wooden-headed dummy."

"Don't be so hard," said Finn. "You're just a straw-brained scarecrow."

Razo left hurriedly, claiming an urgent need for a privy, and went to find Talone on his own. It frightened him a bit to face his captain. What could he possibly do to earn his place among Bayern's Own after being so wrong about Enna?

He'd turned a corner in the quiet corridor when he saw Tumas. Razo cursed into his teeth, wishing Finn and Enna would come this way, and in a hurry. He started to turn back, but Tumas grabbed his shoulder.

"Well, if it isn't the knee biter," Tumas said in his stuffed-nose whine. "Care for a rematch? Come on, right now, you with a sword and me with a feather."

Razo kept his eyes down, as he would if running into a Forest wolf. He stepped to the side, and Tumas followed, blocking his way.

"Don't think I forgot how you pushed my friend Hemar into scratching you. He didn't deserve a slow death in a desert."

From behind a closed door came muffled voices laughing, and Razo let himself believe they were laughing at him, too. He took those laughs like punches, absorbing their impact, feeling the ache they left behind. He side-stepped again, and Tumas blocked.

"If you wanted to dance, you could've asked," said Razo, eyes still down.

"Bayern scum." Tumas glanced around as if afraid that others might come this way any moment, and he let Razo sidle by.

Razo was going to let it go, he should have let it go, but he was so tired of rolling over for the bullies, belly up like a puppy. As he walked away, he said, "You still sore that a Bayern boy whipped you with a wooden sword? Pathetic."

The strike hit Razo's back. A fist? A boot? He crunched to the floor, his breath in knots. Tumas picked him up by his tunic and yanked him into a dark room.

"Pathetic?" said Tumas.

A punch to the belly. A deep, groaning kind of pain.

"Pathetic?" said Tumas.

A jab to the nose. A shattering pain, piercing, blinding.

Razo's voice was caged—he could no more yell for help than he could stop the low moaning in his gullet. He thought he'd been knocked around enough by his brothers to take any good pummeling, but there was murder behind Tumas's strikes that left Razo breathless. He tumbled to his feet, pitching about, desperate to hit back before the next blow killed him. Laughter rumbled through the walls, and a single set of footsteps passed by the door.

Tumas spat a curse. "This is not over," he said.

It was many dizzying moments before Razo realized that he was alone, slumped against a wall in a dim room, and, if the pain was any indication, still alive.

"Pathetic," he whispered, wiping blood from his nose.

Talone was in his chamber with three soldiers when Razo burst in. After a glance at Razo's face, he told the men to leave.

"What happened?" asked Talone.

"Nothing." From a very young age, Razo had learned that tattling was a way to invite a worse thumping. "Just send me home."

"No."

Never before had Razo wanted to strike Talone.

"Why'm I here, Captain? To humiliate myself at sword practice? To go crazy thinking my best friend is a murderer? Which she's not, by the way. I was wrong. This whole city is crossing its fingers for war, and I'm just tinder for the fire. Why me when you've got Enna and Finn and Conrad and all the best of the Own? I'm just . . ." He punched a wall. "I'm not deaf, I hear what everyone thinks of me, and they're right, I'm no Bayern's Own. My brothers always told me I'm slow in the head, my arms are wet rags, I'm only imposing to a bunny rabbit, I'm—"

"Who has ink-stained hands?" Talone interrupted.

Razo could not have been more stunned to stuttered confusion than if Talone had danced a jig. "I'm telling you that I'm pathetic, and I'm through here and . . . Ink-stained hands? What're you—"

"Don't think, soldier, just answer my question. Who has ink-stained hands?"

"Uh, Geric does, sometimes, on his right hand. But why do—"

"Who often has candle wax dripped on her dress?"

"I'm not in a gaming mood, Captain."

"Candle wax."

Razo threw up his hands. Talone was a boulder too heavy to push out of the way. "Isi's waiting woman, the one who wears her braids in loops."

"And who wears sandals far too long for his toes?"

"I guess that squat-nosed page does, the one who brings you messages from Lord Belvan."

"Not everyone has such observation, or such memory, and you do it without seeming to pay attention to anything beyond dinner."

Razo sniffed, and a grating sound and prickly pain made him wish he had not. "I don't think it's such a big thing. You noticed those things, too."

"I had to probe my memory pretty thoroughly to come up with something to challenge you." He'd been cleaning his boots and only now looked up. "You always were a good scout, Razo, and I have long believed that you have the makings of a very good spy."

"Spy?"

"You fell into that role without my prodding. To answer your question—you are here, Razo, to continue the work you did for me during the war. Instead of scouting Tiran camps for troop numbers and locations, you will scout information: Who is trying to respark the war? Who is burning bodies?"

"You've had me in mind as a spy all along? Since Bayern, even?"

"I waited to give you your assignment until the need presented itself. In the sword match, I set you up against Tumas because I don't want the Tiran to think of you as a threat. If you seem weak, your invisibility increases."

"You humiliated me and could've lost me an eyeball, and on purpose?"

Talone nodded.

Razo made a sound of exasperation and fumbled for words. "You . . . you know . . . back home, that kind of underhanded trickery would get you wrestled facedown in goat dung."

Talone smiled. He actually smiled. And Razo smiled back. Foolishly, no doubt. He felt as though he had brought a fat hare back to his mother's stewpot and been cheek kissed and head patted. This was usually the part where his brothers would jump him as soon as her back was turned, but there were no brothers around.

Here, Razo was a *spy*.

"So, you believe Enna is innocent? That is good news," said Talone, accepting Razo's assessment without further inquiry. "I suspect you have already latched on to new suspects."

Razo realized that he had. "There's Tumas, old porkchop head."

"Pork-chop . . . ? Ah, his ears. Yes, that firebrand has not been coy. There's not a body in the city who doesn't know he hates Bayern."

"He had opportunity." Razo played with a javelin, digging the tip between the tiles. "With the first murder, he could've ridden ahead of the Tiran escort and left that body by the river. But his captain, Ledel, he's a strict fiend. I don't think any of his men would scoot a toe over a line without his consent. Except maybe Victar. He doesn't seem to give a rat's tail for anybody's authority. And then there's Manifest Tira, that group I told you about who think Tira ought to return to war. Lord Belvan turn up anything about them?"

"Not yet. Any other suspicions?"

"Well, um, maybe, it's not likely, but maybe...Dasha, the Tiran ambassador's daughter?" Razo sniffed to show that he was not in the least convinced it was she, and his nose throbbed anew. "Ow. Once I found her prowling outside Enna's room, and she was sneaking near the stable the day before they found the third body. She'd have to be working with someone else to have arranged the drop of the one by the border, and no way she could carry the bodies herself."

"Hm," said Talone. "Belvan mentioned that she was eager to volunteer as our liaison and live at Thousand Years. If it is Dasha, then she and her father might be conspiring together to sabotage peace. Our queen and king could be in peril. You said she was interested in Enna? If she knows that Enna is the fire-speaker, she may be targeting Enna herself."

Panic swooped in Razo's belly. "Isi was right, it's too dangerous for Enna. I mean, I'm her *friend*, and I thought she was a murderer. If any Tiran even suspects that she was the fire-witch, she'll be trussed and hanged by sundown."

"You're right," said Talone. "Which means Dasha may not know."

"Send Enna home."

"No. We may need her. Besides, she won't go."

No, she would not, curse her. Razo knocked the bag of stones against his leg and swore to himself that he would do anything to help Enna keep from burning people again.

"Anyone else?" Talone asked.

"The day of our match, I overheard Captain Ledel say he was anxious to see Bayern soldiers fail without fire fighting for us. But then again, he placed a death sentence on his own soldier who stuck me with a dagger, so it seems like he doesn't have a grudge against Bayern. And, well, the prince hasn't made a hair of an effort to get to know any of the Bayern, and he'd have the power to order murders himself, I imagine. Besides, remember how the crazy assassin who killed Veran in the barracks was shouting, 'Long live His Radiance'? I heard from the pastry girls that 'Radiance' is what everyone calls Tira's prince."

"The prince . . ."

"But the more I think about it, the more I see that we don't know anything, not even if there's a genuine fire-speaker on the loose or just some crazy who burns victims in a bonfire to make it look like the work of a fire-witch. I almost liked it better when I thought it was Enna. Now I feel like I saw a spider drop under my bedcovers and I don't know where it is or when it'll bite."

"And what would you do with the spider?"

"I'd get out of bed."

Talone shook his head. "We leave Tira now, we look guilty. No, too much is at stake. The real threat of war is greater than the uncertain fear of assassination."

"That's basically what Megina was talking about when she wouldn't let Belvan move us somewhere safer."

"Sometimes she seems surprisingly wise, doesn't she?" Talone looked out the window. "Razo, I have some misgivings about this assignment. We both know you're not the most . . . subtle . . . person. Don't throw yourself into trouble you can't handle. Just observe, and always come back to me with what you know. And I want you to work this alone. The more people who know what you're about, the more danger you'll be in, besides the fact that the murderer could be anyone—even one of our own."

"So, although Enna could be in danger, or Lord Kilcad could be plotting to kill Isi and Geric, or fanatical Tiran citizens might try to slit all our throats, we're staying."

"It sounds to me, my boy, like you had best get to work."

That night, the Bayern folk took their evening meal in the barracks. The bread was rubbery and the soup cold (on purpose, apparently, another inexplicable Tiran custom).

After refusing to tell Enna and Finn why his nose looked like a pickled beet, Razo stood alone by the window and practiced identifying people from a distance. He watched two men cross a courtyard and successfully named Tumas and Ledel before their faces became clear in the folding dusk. Tumas saw Razo, but instead of smirking at his swollen nose and black eyes, the soldier glanced at Ledel, edgy and uncertain. Apparently Tumas did not have his captain's approval to pounce on a Bayern and was afraid Ledel would find out. A man like Tumas afraid. The thought made Razo itchy.

He plunked down beside Enna, begging for a back scratch, and asked, "Do you two know someone who has ink-stained hands?"

"Razo," said Enna, scratching lazily, "yet again, I have absolutely no idea what you're talking about."

"I mean, have either of you ever noticed someone we know well who's always got ink stains on his hands? Uh, hand actually. Just one ... No guesses? But if I say Geric, now you'll remember, right? ... No? But if you had to guess *which* hand is always ink-stained, you'd know that? The right one? You probably knew it was the right one and I just said it too fast."

Enna continued her stare. Finn's brows raised, halfway between surprised and amused.

Razo laughed self-consciously. "I'm just ... I ... Never mind." He turned back to his soup. Still cold.

Maybe Talone *was* right about him. And except for the threat of immediate death to him and his closest friends, this spying business might be something of a lark.

11

What the Kitchen Girl Found

azo woke feeling strangely eager to get up and see the day happen, as though he were ten years old on the morning of the wintermoon festival. Then he remembered.

He was a spy.

The other soldiers ate breakfast sullenly, but Razo whistled a dance song. He stopped after a few glares warned that he was either too jovial or just plain out of tune.

"At least the Tiran didn't murder us in our sleep," said Razo.

Conrad snapped a boot lace pulling it too tight. His eyes were heavy with sleeplessness. "If they're going to, I wish they'd get it over with already."

"This whole mess is a bit more complicated than watching geese or sheep, isn't it?"

"Sometimes I miss our old animal keeper days, and then I remember." Conrad looked directly into Razo's eyes and whispered, "We're in Bayern's Own." He laughed, as pleased as a gaggle of geese on a spring morning. "I still can't believe our luck."

Talone came midmorning with unexpected orders. "Lady Megina will go out into the city and dine with the chief of assembly today."

A few soldiers chuckled. "She's bold, that one." Others raised eyebrows, questioning if it was wise. When Talone named Razo part of the guard, he thought he detected an uncertain flicker in several of his comrades' faces.

I'm a spy, he wished he could explain to them. *I'm not completely useless. At least, I won't be. Eventually. Hopefully.*

They rode in closed carriages to the chief of assembly's palace, smaller than Thousand Years but more decadent, its capstones and pillars twisting with stone vines and plaster flowers.

"Lovely place for a massacre," Razo whispered to Finn as they climbed the steps.

The door guard let Megina and Enna pass but stopped Razo, Finn, Talone, and the five other Bayern soldiers, demanding they leave their weapons at the door.

"Do it," said Megina.

During the meal, Razo watched the ambassador carefully as she devoured slimy sea creatures cooked in their shells, appearing to relish every bite. And the talk . . . Razo's eyeballs itched with annoyance. She did not even mention the burned body or assert Bayern's innocence. She just gabbed—about the weather, about food, saying things that made the chief of assembly laugh.

"What do you think about Megina?" Razo asked Finn. They stood on the far side of the room and under the noise of dining could speak without being heard.

"You don't think she's trustworthy?" asked Finn.

"I don't know. . . . Geric thought she was, but . . . well, I guess lately everyone's looking squirmy to me."

"I wish she'd negotiated about our weapons." Finn patted his belt. "I don't like being without my sword. Feels like I've lost a limb."

"Lost a limb? Not hardly. Javelin's all right for reaching a back itch, and a sword's a good prop, but no weapon feels easy in my hand."

"What about your sling?" asked Finn.

Razo blinked. A sling was not really a weapon, not unless you were a squirrel.

The third hour of the dinner hobbled on, and Razo was almost wishing for a brawl with the chief of assembly's guards, just to break the boredom.

"Finn, do you think I can hit Enna with a pebble from here?"

"Not a chance," said Finn, though there was the suggestion of a smile around his mouth.

Enna was sitting behind Megina, leaning back on her hands, staring at the ceiling. Razo eased a small pebble out of his pouch, and keeping his arm down straight at his side, he flicked it, striking Enna on the shoulder.

"What . . . ?" Enna sat up.

Razo bit his lip to throbbing to kill his laugh and stared straight ahead. Finn breathed out an almost silent chuckle.

"Did you ask something?" said Megina.

"No, my lady," said Enna. "Just a cough."

Razo felt a sting on the side of his neck and slapped it, thinking it was an insect. Until he smelled burning hair. He looked at his palm. She had singed a single hair from his neck.

By the time they dragged into Thousand Years, the sun was making a show of setting, the sky all rust and gold and heaving with clouds. After hours of standing at attention, Razo thought he could eat his saddle raw. The pastry kitchen was empty, the only sound a low fire snapping at a log. No sooner had he started to poke around for a treat than Pela hopped through the door, her shrubs of yellow hair flopping. Instinctively, he moved toward the door, not feeling safe alone around a girl like Pela with so many sharp knives about. *But she's become friendlier,* he thought, remembering how she touched his hand when giving him a cup of tea.

"There you are." She set down an empty tray. "I have something to show you."

"You do?" Razo hoped it was something to eat.

"Yes, but it will cost you."

He was about to protest his poverty when in some slur of movement, some hitch of skirt, leg wrapped around leg, hop, and a trip, Razo found himself sitting on a stool against the wall, Pela on his lap, her legs bestride his.

"Oh," he said. Or perhaps grunted. She was pleasantly robust. He squeezed his arms against his sides in case she tried to tickle him.

"I don't want much," she said, affecting a shy face and toying with his lummas.

Enna often declared that when it came to catching innuendo, Razo was as slow as a dead hare fleeing, but he thought he had a handle on this.

"What is it?" He was appalled to find that his voice had tangled in his throat and came out less of a manly inquiry and more of a squeal. He did not want her to think that she was the only girl ever to climb onto his lap, so he grumbled his throat clear and asked again, "What is it?"

She leaned in closer, her lips just separated from his.

"A parchment," she whispered. Her breath tickled his face, and he tried not to squirm. She smelled nice, like salted meat, and that made him want to hold very still so that she would not go away.

"What's on the parchment?" His hands were still tight to his sides. Should he put them on her waist or back or something?

"I don't know, but when I entered Lady Dasha's room, she stuffed it away, hiding it all suspicious-like, and since you were nudging for any information on her the other day, I pinched it for you this morning. And all I want for it is—"

"You took a parchment from Dasha's room?" He bolted upright, sending Pela tumbling to the floor.

"I'm sorry," he said, leaning over her, trying to help her upright. "Whoops, that was awkward." She reached for his hand, but he was trying to lift her from under her shoulders, and she fell on her rump again.

"Never mind, I'm fine," she said, finally gaining her feet on her own and shaking her skirt clean. Her entire face glowed red.

Razo picked up a folded paper that must have fallen from her pocket. "Is this it?"

The door banged open and a parade of girls with empty trays poured through. Pela and Razo took a few guilty steps away from each other, Razo stuffing the parchment into the waist of his leggings.

"Hello, Razo."

"Evening, Razo."

The freckled girl came in laughing. "Did Lord Rogis's son Victar propose to anyone else at dinner or just me?"

"Stay away from that one!" said another. "Acts as if he'll drape amber around your neck, but the word is he and his rich father aren't even talking. . . ."

Razo said hello to all the girls and kissed the pastry chef's cheek, telling her she worked too hard and to let the girls finish up so she could go soak her feet. When he left, Pela followed him out the door, pressing herself against his back, her mouth on his ear. He could feel some nice parts of her body touching his.

"If you don't return that before Lady Dasha notices, my skin will pay for it," she whispered. "Her chamber door is unlocked. Read it quickly, then go stick the parchment back beneath her lamp. She won't be back tonight, so you could look around a bit too, if it helped."

Razo nodded and left, but not before she patted his bum.

Thoughts of Pela chased after him down the dark corridor, inching over his skin, wriggling so that the hairs of his arms stood up. She was a pretty girl. And, well, she was any girl. He had not thought much of anyone since Bettin.

He paced outside Talone's dark apartment in the heavy huff of night, flicking pebbles with his thumbnail to hear them pop against the door. With every moment his anxiety tightened, a rope twisting. Getting caught with a parchment stolen from Lady Dasha's room would not do much to ease the political tension.

Some hour later, the captain returned, emanating the salty fish smell of Tiran dinner.

"It's about time," said Razo. "If there's ever any doubt of my commitment to Bayern and peace, know that I missed a meal to wait for you."

"There was never a doubt." Talone ushered him inside and lit a lamp.

"Found in Dasha's room and I've got to get it back quick, but I don't know reading."

Talone scanned the parchment. "This looks like notes taken while studying some books. She cites several sources that mention 'fire-witches.'"

"Uh-oh."

"Indeed." He studied it, his brow furrowed. "She seemed interested in the fire worshippers from Yasid, people who know how to work both fire and water. Here's a note at the bottom that says, 'Apparently live healthy all their lives,' underlined twice."

"You think Dasha is the . . ."

Talone shook his head. "After Enna, we won't make the mistake to assume anything, not without definitive proof."

So Razo set off to find proof. He scurried down the servants' walkway until it climbed into the lamplit main corridor of the palace. A dusting girl passed by, and Razo ducked into a side hallway just in time, grinning at the darkness. Skulking around a palace was quite a bit more exciting than hunting squirrels. The fear of being caught gave speed to his blood and made his pulse click in his ear.

He'd followed Dasha once before and remembered which door was hers. He knocked, peered inside, then jumped in and shut the door, quiet as brushing two feathers together. He smiled at his own stealth, then swaggered right into a chair, banging it against the wall.

You oaf. He cut short his swagger and began to move

with exaggerated sneakiness. There was a certain pleasure in that, too.

Three large windows opened to the central courtyard, allowing the pale moonlight to creep in and over everything, marking the chairs and tables with rims of silver. He did not know what he was looking for, but clothing streaked with soot might be a handy implication of guilt.

He slid the parchment beneath a lamp on a table. Various bottles, jars, and wooden boxes were arranged in pretty little groups. He peered into a few—powders, mint leaves for chewing, a yellow cream that had no odor. He shook a silver tube, heard the muted slosh of liquid, and raised the cap to his nose. A perfume of tangerine blossoms teased him with uncertain intimacy. What did it remind him of? He closed his eyes, and the scent pulled him into a memory of the ocean, his feet uneven in the sand, the lulling hush of waves, and Dasha standing close.

Razo sorted through the wardrobe—no burn marks, no scent of smoke. So he shrugged at the moon, slipped into the corridor, and stood a moment by her door, wondering what to do next.

"Tree rat!"

Razo jumped back at least two steps and hit his back against a wall. His heart banged so hard against his ribs, it felt bruised.

"Dasha . . . Lady Dasha . . . I . . ."

"Oh, what happened to your nose?"

"Nothing." He sniffed. "Ouch. I mean, it broke. Accident."

"I'm sorry. Were you looking for me just now?"

He nodded, not quite ready to give up the support of the wall. "Yes, um, how are you?"

Dasha smiled, and her nose crinkled. How did that one expression make him feel as helpless as if two big brothers sat on his chest or Pela straddled his lap?

"So I guess that means you heard." Dasha opened her door and handed him her lamp. "There was no one here, but I wouldn't mind having you look around again."

What is she talking about? Razo wondered, but he played along, holding the lamp aloft and walking through her rooms.

"Of course," she said, "it was probably a lie all along. The door *was* unlocked for some reason, but why would a Bayern hide in my rooms and wait to murder me? I told the soldiers that when they came for me an hour ago, but they insisted on escorting me to my rooms. Said they'd had a very reliable tip. Nonsense, I said, and sure enough, the soldiers didn't find anyone lurking about. I've just now come from Lord Belvan's chambers, convincing him that the Bayern aren't a threat to me no matter what some troublemaker claimed."

Razo realized that if he'd come here as soon as he'd left Pela instead of going to Talone first, he would have been the one stalking Dasha's rooms, just in time for soldiers to burst in. The light in Razo's hand swayed, sending shadows zooming across the walls.

"Nothing appears to be missing." She removed her lummas and laid it directly over the parchment Razo had replaced. Coincidence, or was she hiding it?

"All . . . all clear," he said, pleased his voice betrayed only a petty tremble.

"Thank you." She took the lamp and smiled at him, right into the ghostly light. "I've been meaning to tell someone from your party that I'll be leaving tomorrow, back to my father's estate. In the summer, the assembly is in recess, and most people return to their lands in the country. I will be away for three months, but Lord Belvan will be here to aid you. Look at you! You seem crushed."

He did? "I'm not." That seemed rude. "I mean, I'll miss you." What was he saying? "But I hope you have a good time." He was a spy; he should be trying to find out information. "I guess you have business to deal with in the country. Well, have you, you know, taken care of everything you need to here?"

"I have tried. . . ." A shiver of uncertainty crossed her face, as though she'd stepped on something sharp and tried to hide the pain. "Why do you ask?"

"No reason."

Her stare pinned him, and he had the sudden and unhappy conviction that small though she was, this Dasha was as dangerous to play with as a well-sharpened dagger.

"You wouldn't just ask for no reason. What would I need to take care of?"

"Just . . . stuff. I mean, I was just wondering if I could do anything for you while you're gone."

"I'm in a real muddle, Razo. I wish . . ." She looked at him, so hard that it made him squirm. "No, I don't think you can help me."

"Are you sure? I'm pretty smart." That sounded stupid. He inhaled through the space in his front teeth as if he could suck those words back inside.

"You don't . . . Never mind. But thank you."

Her thanks seemed so genuine, he had a passing stitch of guilt for pretending to offer help after prowling around her chambers, searching for a sign that she was a murderer.

"Um, uh, you'll be wanting to get sleep, then, I guess, if you're on your way tomorrow."

He left, congratulating himself for coming up with the weakest good-bye ever spoken.

In short order, his guilt was overcome by a cramp of hunger. He found a tangerine tree in the courtyard and looted the leaves for the last of the season, eating the stingingly sweet fruit in its branches. The ground felt too dangerous, the place where Tiran like Tumas walked, eager for a chance to skip the nose breaking and move on to Razo's spine. Rubbed between the sensation of fear and the pleasure of food, he watched Dasha's window.

A lamp flickered on her windowsill. Had she lit it without spark or flint? She knew something, Razo was certain.

Her gaze often shifted, her fingers twitched. Her bearing declared too heartily that she was happy, fine, all openness and nothing to hide.

So what did she hide?

The lamp sputtered; the window went dark.

12

The Best Sling Finn Ever Saw

azo woke to the guttering snores in the barracks, sat up, yawned, and gasped for air. Heat weighed down his body, slick and damp, crawling into his mouth and down his throat with each breath. It seemed the change of seasons had accosted the city of rivers overnight.

The Bayern soldiers staggered into their boots and outside, hoping to find breathable air, but out was as stifling as in, shade as scorching as sunlight. The air was heavy with ocean, the invisible drops of water clinging to everything. Razo wondered if he might drown.

"Welcome to an Ingridan summer," said Victar, joining Razo on the way to breakfast.

"This heat's cruel mean."

"No meaner than a Bayern winter." Victar recounted winter nights during the Tiran invasion, runny noses forming tiny icicles on upper lips, raids canceled because the men could not lift a spear for shivering. He flung his words casually, laughing and gesturing with no hesitation. He seemed completely unaware how his talk of the recent war tightened the mood around him.

"My elder brother is already at our father's estate in the country, but I'm a military man now and must stand the heat like any Ingridan lad. The rich and squeamish flee the city summer. The hearty stay behind."

"Stay and sweat," said Victar's friend.

The two companies breakfasted in a dark, first-story room in the north wing of the palace, all the windows open, holding their breath for a breeze. The cheese was salty, the bread gristly, and Razo missed his ma's stewpot with a cruel ache. But he was becoming crazed for those spicy Ingridan olives. He liked how when he bit them, they bit back.

He had filled his plate and was about to join Conrad when Victar waved him over. *Might be good to make friends with some Tiran,* he thought.

Razo was gabbing with Victar's friends when Tumas entered, as big and angry as the heat. He looked at Razo, and his lips twitched in what might have been a smile, though it resembled more the snarl of a feral dog. Razo returned an openmouthed grin and waved with mock glee.

"Tiran Fifth Company," called Ledel's secondman, a lean, tall soldier with skin tanned dark brown. He stood in the doorway, waiting for the room to quiet.

"Where's your captain?" Razo asked Victar in a whisper.

"On one of his many jaunts, I suppose. Yesterday was a

feast day, and the captain always disappears on feast days. Beat me with a spear if I know where he goes."

"I have news from Lord Belvan," said the secondman. "Our summer assignment has changed to the Tacitan province. We leave in the morning."

The Tiran cheered and slapped the tables. Razo guessed Tacitan was a cool, windy place.

"For once, birdface Belvan does something right," said a young, squinty friend of Tumas. The raucous laugh among the Tiran made Razo feel as though he'd been insulted but was too thickheaded to see.

"What'd Belvan do so wrong?" Razo asked Victar.

"He was opposed to the war from the beginning and was not demoted after the failed invasion. Nowhere outside his own company is that man much loved."

"Do you like him?" asked Razo.

Victar shrugged. "I don't concern myself with him."

"What say we have a last bout with these Bayern boys?" asked Tumas, his glance sliding over Razo. "Stretch our backs before the long march?"

Talone was having his weekly meeting with Lord Belvan, so Brynn was in charge of the Bayern. He looked around, gauging the eagerness in the expressions of his countrymen. Finn had been the sound victor at the last scuffle, and none of Bayern's Own seemed opposed. Razo wondered if he could sneak away unnoticed.

"Heartily accepted," said Brynn. "Bayern's Own don't turn down a challenge."

Yes, yes, all right, curse them, thought Razo. *I'm an Own. I won't flee.*

He grumbled as he followed the others to the training ground, tapping his javelin against his backside, herding himself like a sheep to the slaughtering shed. Enna and Finn caught up with him.

"What's all this?" she asked.

"Mock combat. You going to join us, Finn?"

"Sure, I'll play."

Razo snorted. If this was *play,* the game should be called Humiliate Razo with a Wooden Sword, not unlike many of his childhood games: Five Brothers Wrestle Razo, Little Man Underfoot, Razo the Rug, Razo Our Tiny Foe. His mother never had guessed why her youngest son spent so much time tromping alone through the trees with his sling.

They arrived at the training ground before Razo had been able to formulate any plan. He stood on the sidelines, cheering and jesting with the others. Inwardly he crouched and shuddered and felt that bowl of olives in his stomach start to churn.

Ledel arrived, carrying a bundle of something under his arm. "What is going on?" His voice was raspy again from lack of sleep, and his jaw scar was an unpleasant purple color.

"Another bout, Captain," said the secondman, "before we prepare to leave. Your permission to continue?"

The Tiran soldiers held still, waiting. Victar yawned.

"Proceed," said Ledel, though he seemed particularly grumpy about something.

Brynn set up two fighting rings, and practice battles began to swirl and clash, Tiran and Bayern stepping in and out. With each defeat the sun scorched hotter.

Waiting for his first turn, Razo bounced on the balls of his feet, chewing on his bottom lip. The heat made his eyelids sticky and lungs heavy. Though not as heavy as his stomach. He burped extravagantly.

"Razo," Brynn called.

"And Victar," said the Tiran secondman.

Razo hopped into the ring, wiped the sweat from his palm, and gripped the wooden sword. He was so relieved it was not Tumas, he winked at Victar as though he were having a lark. Like Finn, Razo dodged the first swing and the second, made a few jabs, and dodged again. His focus was so taut, a rope could have tied his gaze to his opponent. He swung and dodged, rolled and hopped up again, and felt he was really doing well.

"Match, for Tira," said the secondman.

Razo had not even felt the sword graze the middle of his jerkin. A few of Bayern's Own shook their heads.

Two failed matches later, noon was nearing, and the heat fell straight down, pushing his shadow into a pool around his feet. That spit of shade did nothing—his toes were hot and scratchy. Razo thought there might be just one more chance to redeem himself.

When Brynn called his name again, he strutted into the ring, calm and confident, and took his stance opposite Tumas's red-nosed, lisping friend. The Tiran swung, Razo dodged, swooped. And met a sword hilt in the stomach.

He stumbled forward, shuffling on his toes, and vomited cheese and olives beside someone's sandals.

"Was that necessary?" asked the Tiran in slightly stained sandals.

"Sorry," said Razo. He straightened and saw that the other ring's match had ended and all eyes were on him.

Tumas was elbowing his friend. "I told you that little one is a joke, and if you ask me, he makes the whole lot of them laughable." He glanced at Ledel as if checking for his permission to keep speaking, then said to Brynn, "When my horse didn't do the job, I put him out of his misery."

"That's enough," said Brynn, because Ledel, for some reason, did not.

Razo shambled a few more steps away and flung the wooden sword at the ground. Words were churning in his belly that he was ready to belch up. He almost said, "That's it." He almost yelled, "I'm through. I quit. I'm an embarrassment, a scarecrow, noodle-armed, sized for tossing. I'm gone."

The words burned like stomach acid on the back of his

tongue, and if he had spoken them, he would have lived by them—he would have gone home to the Forest and spent his days solitary among his brothers' families. At least, in the moment before he spoke, he envisioned that future. It was a prospect he would not have to test out, because Finn spoke first.

"Try him with a missile weapon."

Finn had been sitting on a stone, his sword upright in the dirt, his hands resting on the cross. He had been silent after each of his three victories and silent as he watched. When he spoke, his unruffled voice was loud enough to cut through the noise.

Some of the Tiran laughed.

"A game of spears would be the cake to this meal," said Tumas.

Finn shook his head. "Razo's sling to your spear."

Some of the Bayern looked away, as though embarrassed that Finn had brought a sheep boy's plaything into a soldier's battle. The Tiran laughter pitched and climbed.

Razo sidled up to Finn, swatting at the sweat trickling into his eyes. "What're you doing? Trying to humiliate me further?"

Finn stood, tapped the dirt off his sword tip, and put it in his sheath. He met Razo's eyes, and his expression was as sincere as that of a child too young to lie. "You're the best sling I ever saw."

"I am not. Why're you making up stuff? I'm just . . . Never mind, the captain wouldn't want me flaunting my sling around anyway."

"Why not? Talone didn't tell me to pull back during sword bouts. It'll be good for the Tiran to have a little respect for us."

Razo laughed through his nose. "I'm not good enough to cause fear."

"Then there's nothing to worry about," said Finn, but a glint in his eye said he thought otherwise. It made Razo want to go prove him right.

Ledel was giving orders for their march east, soldiers were sheathing swords, gathering idle javelins and spears. Finn walked right into their midst.

"Captain Ledel, we're not done yet. Let Razo sling."

A couple of Bayern groaned. Ledel met Finn's eyes without blinking, reminding Razo of some lidless creature, a snake, a spider. His voice rasped. "We are not sullying a match of men with a peasant weapon."

That smacked of insulting Bayern, and a few soldiers, especially Conrad and Luzo, who were also Forest-born, put up a fuss.

"That is enough," said Ledel, his voice sharp enough to split skin.

"Hello!" Dasha bounded up the path, waving and smiling.

"Lady Dasha." Ledel inclined his head respectfully, and his men stood at attention.

"Captain Ledel, good morning." Behind her trudged six men loaded down with leather satchels and clothing bundles. Her orange hair was loose, wisps tickling her face. She brushed them away with a smile as though they were playful kittens. "And all my Bayern friends. I am off and wanted to say farewell and tell you . . ." She paused, seeming to notice the chilly mood. "What's happening?"

"Razo's challenging the Tiran to missile weapons," said Finn, "his sling to their spears, but Captain Ledel won't have it."

Dasha laughed, thoroughly amused. "And why not, Captain Ledel? You aren't afraid?"

The muscle under Ledel's face scar twitched. "Go on, Antoch," he said to his secondman, "but I will not stay to watch. We leave at eighth bell."

The Tiran did not wait until Ledel was out of sight before they began to draw lines in the dirt and hold tug matches to determine who got to face Razo first.

Razo hefted his pouch of stones like a merchant guessing weight and price. What if he lost? Certainly his mark as the greatest failure in Bayern's Own would be indelible. But if he succeeded, could it spark another clash like the one after Finn's victory? Or something worse? The stifling heat was the kind that smothered good judgment.

Then Razo noticed that Dasha was watching him, her smile full of marvelous expectation. He stepped up to the line.

The secondman indicated a tree trunk some twenty paces away as the target. Razo frowned.

"Losing heart, are you?" Tumas yelled.

If Razo had not felt so hot and wretched after losing three sword matches, he would have laughed. That target was a mite easy. He put his toes behind the line in the dirt, inserted a stone into his sling's leather pouch, spun once, and released. The stone hit the center of the trunk with a noise like a long whip cracking.

Most of the Tiran wanted a go, some hitting the tree with their spear, grazing it, or missing altogether. Razo's stones smacked against the center, again and again.

"Put other thlingerth at the mark," said Tumas's lisping friend.

The best Tiran slingers fetched hemp slings and almond-shaped lead bullets from the armory. Now the targets were three metal pails sitting atop a log forty paces away. Razo put three stones in his left hand and turned his left side to the pails. He placed the first stone in the leather pouch, swung and released, heard the *whiz* of stone cutting air and the metallic *clang* of the pail even as he placed another stone in the pouch, released, *whiz-clang*, never stopping the circle, and a third *whiz-clang*. Those sounds felt as satisfying as cold water in an empty belly.

Out of the ten Tiran slingers, only the squinty-eyed soldier hit three for three. The Tiran soldiers cheered him until Finn said, "Move the target back."

The pails now waited sixty paces away, and the Tiran missed twice. Razo's turn was a song that rang out in threes.

The Bayern were getting restless and bunched together, keen for their turn at the pails. After a couple of rounds, only Conrad and Luzo had hit all three.

"Move the target back," Finn said, smiling.

Brynn placed the pails at seventy paces. It was a respectable distance. Two pails chimed for Conrad, one for Luzo. Razo readied three stones and noticed a slight tremble in his hand.

Easier than a squirrel who scampers, he thought. *Easier than a twitching hare.*

He swung and released three times. Three pails lay on their sides.

There was a general gasp and chatter that did not have time to build before Finn's clear voice cut through.

"Move the target back."

Some of the men laughed. Brynn, with a mischievous look, took one pail under his arm and walked on. And just kept walking.

"That was far enough five minutes ago," Conrad yelled.

Brynn set it down and jogged back. "One hundred and fifty paces, Razo. Miss already so we can get out of this sun."

Razo stared at the pail, a dark glint on white stone, and felt the heat pressing on the top of his head, insisting itself into each breath. A short sling could never reach that distance. He shook his head and looped up his sling, fastening it to his side.

"Coward," said Tumas, standing very near.

Without pause, Razo pulled his long sling from his waist. It was a small target for the distance sling, but everyone was watching. Dasha was watching. He felt clamped in and squeezed inside the moment, and the only way out was forward.

He tried pretending that he was alone, that the heat was the pressure of Forest shadows, and the whispers and shifting of boots were just the trees moaning.

He placed the shot in the pouch and whipped the sling at his side, angled to the ground. His body leaned with the motion, tipping forward, slanting back, pulled always toward the stone as it clung to the sling's pouch. The weight of the stone felt good, the length of the sling just right. When the stone completed the third circle, he let go his thumb, his right arm stretching forward. He could hear the stone cut through the air, a hum that lowered in pitch until it exploded in a metallic crash.

He breathed hard as though he had run a league and turned slowly to face the others. They were silent, staring at his downed target. The Bayern started to smile.

"What about Razo," Conrad whispered, his breath full of awe.

A few soldiers chuckled, laughing as though they could not believe.

"What about Razo!" Conrad spoke louder, inviting a cheer.

"Bayern!" some shouted.

"Bayern's Own!"

"Razo and Bayern!"

Razo shivered in the heat, waiting for the Tiran reaction. Dasha was the first to respond. She was smiling.

"Ledel was right to have been afraid."

Victar laughed his deep belly laugh. "He schooled us well. Excellent."

The Tiran who had shared Razo's breakfast table that morning smothered him with congratulatory jabs. Hands clapped his back, shoulders lifted him aloft, then dumped him back into more backslaps. He laughed nervously, feeling at once large as a mountain and small as prey. Finn was beside him.

"Why didn't you tell me before that I was so good?" asked Razo. He found he was almost angry about it, except that he felt like crowing.

"Didn't seem to matter before," said Finn.

Enna was sitting in the thin shadow of the barracks, wiping laugh tears from her eyes. She seemed surprised to be laughing and so pleased with it as to keep it up as long as possible.

Brynn and others were anxious to go lunch in a nice, shady place, and they pulled Razo along with them. Tumas made a point to leave in the opposite direction with several of Ledel's soldiers, their lips moving as though they grumbled. The secondman had disappeared.

"Never saw such slinging," said one of Victar's friends. "Good show. I hardly thought it a weapon, but I see that a sling can be deadly in the hands of a master."

A master, thought Razo. *He means me.*

"Razo."

Razo's skin shuddered under sweat at Talone's voice. He ducked away from the group and went to his captain.

"I did something wrong," said Razo.

"Yes. I wish you had not shown an entire company of Tiran soldiers how handy my spy is with a sling. You're supposed to be invisible."

"I didn't know I was that good! I swear, Captain."

"Neither did I." Talone frowned. In a way that Razo could not explain, the frown remained a frown but also became a smile. "Be ready with that sling. You may have to use it."

13

The Season of the Prince

Summer tightened its burning grip. The air was dense and wet and followed Razo around like the hot huff of some large creature. The city was half-empty, making everything feel naked, stripped down to the skeleton, the whole world stone hard and dangerous.

At least the Tiran food was growing on Razo. The pastry chef had taken to him like a mother, plying him with bowls of cold beans and red bacon, chilled fish soups, and fig cakes. That was something. For a week he ate, lounged, and waited for something to happen. The diversion from tension was a relief.

Then it got boring. So Razo decided to get sandals.

"Do you think it wise to lose all your Bayern garb?" asked Talone.

"When Lady Megina saw my new clothing, she thought it paid a compliment to the Tiran, said I looked like walking peace."

"She did? Sometimes she surprises me." Talone rubbed his chin. "So far, it seems our presence hasn't made a

dent in the hatred for Bayern, and I don't like the thought
of you out there in the city alone. But you're right, we can't
do much good locked up here. Be careful."

Razo found Enna and Finn holed up her room, enjoying
a curious little wind that spun around them like a beast
pacing its cage.

"Are you sure you two won't come? Think of it—*sandals*,"
Razo said provocatively.

"Why step into that blaze and be drenched in sweat?"
Enna leaned back on her hands and smiled. Her black hair
swirled, her tunic and skirt flapped as though with glee. Over
the past month, she had spent nearly every day as Megina's
attendant at scores of dinners with assembly members, and
she had declared that if the summer heat chased away all
those droning fancy folk, then it was welcome. Of course, it
was easy for her to smile at the heat when she had wind on
hand to shoo it off. Razo let the breeze suck the sweat from
his brow before dragging himself away.

Out in the streets, the morning heat struck him like a
blacksmith's hammer. He held the edge of his lummas over
his black hair as the Tiran often did to protect themselves
from the sun, though he did it to hide.

He had never been alone in the city. For the first few
blocks, the freedom was exhilarating, but the farther he
walked from Thousand Years, the more exposed he felt. By
the time he reached the heart, his sick stomach and tired
pulse made him wish he had not come.

"The heart," Ingridan citizens called the assembly build-ing and surrounding squares. It was the center of Ingridan, the hub of order, business, and law, and it thrummed with activity at any hour. Victar had claimed that a member of each Ingridan household passed through the heart at least once each day, if not on business, then just to gather gossip.

The cobbler's stall reeked enough to make his eyes sweat, so Razo jumped into business, choosing deep brown leather and a style that wrapped up his ankle. Soon he was shod in fresh sandals and wriggling his toes, terribly pleased, until he recognized the man browsing the front of the shop from one of the formal banquets at Thousand Years. It was the prince.

He was around Geric's age and had a round face and thin arms. His neck was laden with ropes of amber beads, his fingers alight with rings, the kind of showy richness that made Razo sniff. Several men and women surrounded him, young and old, their hair darker than most Tiran, their skin a richer tone.

Long live His Radiance, Veran's murderer had exclaimed.

The city seemed massive and the palace painfully far away. He was just one rather squat boy alone in his enemy's city. What did he think he could possibly do?

Isi was just one girl, he reminded himself. *And she changed Bayern.*

"Excuse me, you're the prince," said Razo.

The prince smoothed the embroidered edge of his tunic.

"So I am! And if I'm not mistaken by your accent, you are Bayern."

Razo's heart sped up, his blood felt slippery in his veins, but he let the lummas drop to his shoulders. "Yes, pleasure to meet you. Um, should I bow?"

"Most people do. On second thought, why bother now? Let us pretend that you already did."

"All right." Razo paused. "That was a nice bow I gave you."

"Indeed it was," said the prince with enthusiasm. "And what luck! I have been itching to talk to a Bayern for weeks, and here you are. I have a certain question I must ask. Have you or anyone you know ever . . . eaten a baby?" His eyebrows twitched up with interest.

"No, Bayern don't eat babies." Razo spoke loudly enough that all the prince's companions might hear. "Not baby *people*, at any rate, though I don't mind a chicken egg or two, cooked right. . . ."

"Ha! I didn't think so. Rupert owes me a tithe. He bet me, you see."

"I've been asked about the baby thing a lot."

"I'm sure you have. Well, farewell." He turned away from the shop.

"Wait, um, uh, prince? Do you mind if I walk with you? Around? For a bit?"

The prince paused, and his innocent surprise made Razo believe no one had ever made such a request of him before. "I . . . I suppose so. What is your name?"

"Razo. Of Bayern's Own. And thanks, Prince . . . um, I don't think I've actually ever heard your name."

"I don't have one. My mother gave me a nursery name, but no one else will call me anything but Radiance until I wed and my wife grants me a household name."

"Truly?" A man without a name. Razo's thoughts were lost in that maze.

They emerged into the vicious sunlight, the prince's entourage pushing them forward on the breeze of their fans. Razo kept glancing back, worrying that one of the prince's guards would cut his throat in the first shady alley, until he saw that none bore a sword.

"Why don't your guards wear weapons?" he asked, too curious to play cautious.

"The Wasking are my friends, not my guards! No one will harm the prince's body. It would mean shame and ruin to them, their children, their grandchildren, their great-grandchildren . . . Celi, do you remember how many greats? Hm? . . . Well, no matter. Unless, that is, *you* mean me harm. Have you ever used that sword of yours to kill?"

The prince looked at him, his eyes a sudden intense, cold blue.

"Yes, in the war," Razo said, adding hurriedly, "But I'd rather not do it ever again."

"Is that so? It was a shame, that whole war business."

Razo schooled his expression to the sleek indifference he'd been practicing.

The prince leaned forward, concerned. "Are you all right? Your face appears to be turning red, your eyebrows twitching—"

"I'm fine, just the heat, you know." Razo cleared his throat. "So, um, what did you think about that whole war business, anyway?"

"Mm? Seems a waste, but of course, it's not my concern."

"But you're the prince . . ."

"So I am." He smoothed his tunic again, looking newly pleased, as though he had fallen into the title only that morning. "And I am not a member of the assembly. Only they have the power to pass laws, execute criminals, and declare war. Across centuries, the assembly has whittled down the prince's power. Now all I do is bits of public finery, open and close assembly sessions, and such and so. . . ." He stooped to inspect a merchant's display of inlaid wooden boxes. "Oh, and I may choose my own bride. Tiran princes have always used their choice to maneuver current politics. My grandfather married a noble widow from Circuna, an eastern province that rumbled of secession—Circuna is still unified with Tira. My mother was the sister of an assemblyman, and after she married the prince my father, her brother became chief of assembly."

"Or you could marry for love," said Razo.

The prince smiled at an elderly man and woman, both squat and pleasantly round, walking hand in hand. "But how could I waste my only political power? Ah-ha, you think I am being overly candid, don't you, Razo's-Own?"

"It's actually just Razo, of Bayern's—"

"But I speak nothing that is not voiced in Ingridan's taverns. Not that I frequent the taverns. Too cramped, too crowded." They were strolling the amber market, and merchants held up bits of jewelry, offering gifts to the prince. "My people love me from afar. I hire as my companions people who are not *my* people." The prince gestured to the group walking in two neat lines behind them. "They're from the Wasking Islands and have such musical accents. Simply splendid!"

Razo glanced back and lowered his voice. "Do the Wasking hate Bayern, too?"

"Hate Bayern?" the prince said too loudly. "Of course not. And Tiran don't hate Bayern, either. The war was just some nonsense thought up by disgruntled nobles. Ah, I can tell from your twitching face that you don't believe me. I'll prove it to you, Razo's-Own. Tomorrow night you will celebrate the feast of the watermelon harvest with us. When my city sees its prince with a Bayern lad, they will embrace you."

"But, Radiance, someone did kill one of my comrades on the palace grounds, and—"

"Yes, yes, I heard." The prince waved his hand impatiently. "But that was last spring. Summer is the season of the prince."

The prince turned his profile as though posing for a portrait. Behind his Wasking friends, Razo spied a couple of Tiran men, following close, their eyes on the Bayern lad.

14

Watchers in White

It rained the next day, rinsing the dust from the air and shoving all the heat indoors. Razo squandered several hours playing sticks with Conrad and wondering, hoping, that the weather might delay the festival and keep him alive a few more hours. But that afternoon, the rain stopped suddenly as though the sky had swallowed. The storm-cleaned city looked sharp enough to prick a finger.

"Nothing for it," Razo told Talone. "I said I'd go with the prince, and if I don't stick close to him, how'll I ever find out if he ordered the murders?"

When the sun set, Razo fell in with the prince's party at the palace gates, and they flowed down the streets toward the heart. Wet stones glistened silver under starlight, and the heat held its breath. People opened their doors and shutters, pulled chairs and tables outside, and gossiped with neighbors as they ate, serenaded by a crooked moon.

The prince was called to every table, and he grinned

and huzzahed, waved and wished all well, stopped to sample every fish and soup, each cake and melon, praising them as he would a lady's beauty. And the people's gazes worshipped him. Most avoided looking at Razo at all. A few glared.

Razo's stomach cramped against the food, and he kept circling as he walked, watching for knives in shadows, hints of violence in strangers' eyes. Often he saw someone dressed in plain white, watching him from across the street. As the night progressed, the watcher changed, but someone was always there. Razo eyed the prince. If His Radiance noticed the watchers, if he knew them, Razo could not tell.

Eventually the idea of dawn poured dark blue into the black sky. The prince regaled café diners with outrageous stories Razo had told him, and Razo slumped in a chair, drunk with sleepiness and exhausted from being afraid. The watcher had been absent for an hour or more, and Razo had relaxed his spine, so it took him too long to notice the new men gathering on the fringe of the prince's party and the wildness in their eyes.

"Radiance," said Razo, standing up. "Radiance, I think I'd—"

"What's a Bayern boy doing at a sacred Tiran festival?" When the man spoke, the laughter cut short. Glances shifted to Razo. "He's of a murdering kind. Who among you opens the chicken coop and invites the fox in?"

The owner of the café shifted guiltily. "He came with the prince."

"Lies!" said another, a man of middle age with the look of a professional soldier. "Even if you've all gone soft, we won't forget. Manifest Tira!"

"Manifest Tira!" the other men shouted. "Long live His Radiance!"

Razo fumbled for his sling, but the men pounced too quickly, two standing at his sides, pinning his arms down, one at his feet to keep his legs still, the other behind him, his hands squeezing Razo's neck. Razo's breathing broke, and soft black shapes crumbled around the edge of everything.

"Stop!" said the prince.

The hands relaxed, and Razo's breath screamed back into his lungs.

"Radiance, this is your enemy," said the strangler, his voice passionate but eerily calm. "Let me exterminate your enemies. Let me cleanse this city."

"He is my friend." The prince was standing, but he did not move forward, made no aggressive gesture. He appeared almost relaxed.

"The Bayern boy has tricked you, Radiance. He plots your death." Again, his hand squeezed air out of Razo.

"I said, he is my friend!" The prince spoke with urgency now, looking around at the people. "And the prince's friend requires your protection."

There was the barest hesitation, a trembling of indecision, before the crowd sprang.

"Get your hands off!"

"What do you think, attacking the prince's friend?"

"You shame us."

They tore Razo free and beat back the Manifest Tira fanatics until they fled into a side street. The café owner shook his head.

"I am sorry, Radiance."

The prince patted his shoulder. After a moment his face changed, brightening with the rim of the sun crossing the horizon. "Well! That was a feast day to remember. A good tussle in the streets pumps the blood, doesn't it?" He laughed heartily. "I think my city needs sleep now. Thank you all! Huzzah!"

A carriage opened, and the prince gestured to Razo that he should ride with him.

Razo sat in silence, rocked nearly to sleep by the motion, the gloom of staying out all night weighing his head. He wondered if his throbbing neck would bruise impressively and if the pastry girls would notice. The thought did not cheer him as much as he thought it should.

"In front of me, right in front of me they attack you." The prince rubbed his eyes, dazed, as if wondering if he were dreaming. "I never imagined . . ."

Razo shrugged. "It's probably my own fault. I'm always trying to wiggle into narrow places."

"But *with* me . . ." The prince shook his head. "I wish I knew of a way to make a change."

Razo wondered if he should just let this go, just walk away as he should have with Tumas. The city was too dangerous, the prince not easy to trust. But what if the prince could do something? What if Razo could help him bend Tiran opinion? He swallowed his fear and said, "Maybe I could keep going out in the city with you, maybe if the people get used to seeing a Bayern with their prince . . ."

"Yes, of course! Well thought, Razo's-Own." The prince snuggled back in the carriage seat, already cheered out of his dejection. "You will see. Ingridan will yet show her true colors."

Colors, thought Razo, and began to hatch what he hoped was a very promising idea.

15

Brighter Colors

The next morning, Razo asked Talone if he could be assigned to the prince for the summer.

"You think he may be ordering the burnings," said Talone, slicing his sword along a whetstone.

"I don't know. After Enna I don't dare think twice in the same spot. If he tells the truth, then he doesn't have enough power. Most of the time his thoughts don't go deeper than his tongue, but maybe he'd be useful. . . ." Razo tried to wrestle impressions into words. "Everywhere we went, everyone was looking at him like he was an almond cake. He mayn't have power, but . . ."

"But the people love him and watch him. The people's opinion influences the assembly, and when they renew session for autumn, the assembly will vote if Tira returns to war. Very well." Talone's sword screeched in sharpening. "Lady Megina has tried to meet with the prince, but he seems to avoid any activity that smells of politics. Go see what you can do."

The prince's apartment was one open chamber,

claiming the entire fifth story of the main palace wing. Razo passed Wasking men and women, dodged pillars, ducked beneath torrents of hanging fabric, and cawed back at a caged bird that screeched, "By your leave! By your leave!" He finally found the prince in a courtyard at the chamber's center, surrounded by potted fruit trees and flowering vines.

"It is Razo's-Own!" said the prince, jumping up. "I told Nom, I do not think he will come, and Nom said I might send a messenger, and I said I did not know how and never mind, let's go out on the porch, and if he does not come today, then he won't be welcome, because I am not a patient man and I cannot wait a week. It is my season, after all. So let's be off!"

Within half an hour they were strolling the restless market.

"Rupert, my old tutor, bet me another tithe that if the Bayern don't eat babies, at least they don't keep their word. And, ha-ha! He was wrong again. How I love it when Rupert is wrong."

"Me too," said Razo.

"Rupert cannot come to the market with us, for if he moves too much, his bones might break. Look, a new shipment of amber is in!"

Razo spent several hours in the numbing heat of the market, anticipating his own sudden murder, and questioning if this mindless outing really was ensuring peace.

At last he spotted what he'd been hoping to find—a merchant tendering pouches of Bayern dyes. He was Wasking, bearing a shaggy head of black hair and skin like honeyed wine. The merchant sat in a sad little cart with a rodent-gnawed cloth to screen the sun, its legs so crooked that if it had been a horse, its owner would have offered it a quick and compassionate death.

"No demand for goods from the north," he said, avoiding even the name of the kingdom.

The prince frowned. Razo purchased a few pouches.

Razo spent two weeks accompanying the prince to the docks and market, theater and music hall, and no burned bodies popped up. The heat seemed to have chased the murderer into hiding, but Manifest Tira stayed like the stones. Often he could hear one of their number orating in Speaker's Corner. "Why should we roll over and lick Bayern's hand? Their presence here dirties us and distracts us from our destiny. Tira is the greatest country in the world, and one day our borders will stretch north and west. . . ."

The summer heat built like the tension before a tavern brawl, until it finally exploded into rain. Razo gathered his Tiran-made clothing and Bayern dyes and ran through the storm to the kitchen to borrow their pots.

"You've been away," said Pela with pouting lips.

"I've got this new friend. . . ."

"We know," said the freckled girl. It's the prince."

"And all of Ingridan knows you were attacked," said the girl with smooth hair.

"What's all of Ingridan saying?" Razo asked.

"That Bayern or no, people had no right attacking any-one under the prince's protection."

Progress, Razo thought.

He pulled a thin, pale blue scarf out of his stone pouch and wound it around the pastry chef's neck. "The prince was going to toss it, said I could have it if I wanted. It's called silk."

The chef fingered the fabric and blushed, and the girls oohed and whistled. When she saw Razo's bundle of clothes and packs of dyes, she insisted on helping him, and soon many of the girls were lending a hand, though none could fathom why he would want to ruin the beautiful white fabric.

A few hours later, Razo climbed into the freshly dyed and dried orange pants, long yellow tunic, and red lummas. He felt like the birds for sale in the market, the ones from Wasking with different-colored heads, wings, and tails, and he was betting that the prince would be intrigued.

The afternoon still thundered when Razo climbed the stairs to the top floor of the main palace wing and the prince's personal apartment. He said hello to his Wasking friends reading by the door, swiping from them a piece of cracker bread for his favorite caged bird (the one he'd trained to shriek, "Razo the great!"). All the windows were covered in thick-slatted shutters, allowing air in and keeping most of the rain out. The prince was lazing on a peach-colored pillow, looking horribly bored. As soon as he saw Razo, he bolted upright.

"What are you wearing?"

"My clothes," Razo said impressively. "Touched with the Bayern dyes. Now they look proper, except they pinch. . . . Maybe the dyes shrink fabric a bit? Don't know why everyone in this country drags themselves along in white all the time. White's only good for funerals and weddings. No Bayern right in the head feels at home in—"

"I want that, Nom." The prince pointed at Razo and spoke to the tall Wasking man.

"You wish your clothing dyed like the Bayern boy's, Radiance?" asked Nom, his accent smooth as water over stones. "Very well."

The prince beamed. "What a noise we'll make among the drab and dull, how we'll . . . Wait, I want more green. I hope I did not imply I only wanted your colors. We can't turn a cold shoulder to green, and blue, and purple, for the sake of all ordered things, how can you dismiss purple? Celi, call Nom back and tell him of my need for purple!"

That week, Razo brought Enna and Finn into the city for the festival of seven rivers, and with his friends by his side, he felt safer than he had in weeks. They laughed and ate all day aboard the prince's boat on the Tumult, the river so crowded with wooden crafts banging and scraping one another that they could scarcely spot any water. The prince was elated to have three whole Bayern in his party.

"Look at their hair!" the prince shouted to passing boats. "Black as pitch. And such salty accents. Marvelous!"

Enna took Razo aside, whispering in his ear, "He's kind of odd, isn't he? I mean, are you the only friend he doesn't pay?"

"He pretends not to be lonely," Razo whispered. "Enna, when you write to Isi next, tell her the prince here needs a wife. If he marries a Bayern woman, it might help sway more Tiran to our side."

"Huzzah!" the prince shouted from the deck of the boat. He was dressed in one long tunic, purple from shoulders to ankles, with a river-blue lummas running across his chest and flung over his forearm. Every time someone remarked on his new clothing, the prince mentioned "those dashing Bayern dyes."

The prince kept wearing his colors all summer. Razo's heart thumped the first time he noticed a Tiran woman in the market wearing a bright green lummas over her hair. A few days later at the music hall, Enna counted five dyed lummas cloths in the audience. By the next feast day, the rickety stall of the Wasking merchant had transformed into a sturdy structure—steps up, a planked floor, extravagant shade. The merchant had combed his hair and broadened his smile.

By the time the summer heat got lazy and let the wind

from the ocean tear it into strands, and the nobles tottered back dusty and bored of country life, one in ten citizens had cast off their white and pale hues for the darker, richer tones of Bayern.

"There's number twenty-two—yellow!" said Megina, watching the street from a window and counting dyed lummas cloths. "I can send our traders back for more dyes and other Bayern goods at last. The queen was right—trading will make peace more plausible. You surprised me, Razo."

Razo squelched a pleased grin. "I watched you that time you had dinner with the chief of assembly, how you didn't try to convince him that Bayern's good and innocent. You were just friendly. At the time, I thought you weren't so smart, but that's all I tried to do with the prince. Look, there's twenty-three. . . ."

Razo stopped, realizing the orange he saw entering the palace gates belonged not to a dyed lummas, but to a girl's hair.

A queer crush in his chest felt both painful and exciting. Dasha was back. Summer was over. The darkness that had clutched at him all spring and been stifled by the summer heat now seemed to crouch and wait, ready to pounce again.

16

Razo's Luck

The banquet hall rose three stories, and the shadows swayed and crept under the light of a thousand oil lamps. To Razo's mind, the crossing and snapping of light and shadow made the walls feel alive and crawling, the room tangled in spiderwebs.

Then the food arrived, and Razo was distracted from dread—pork skewers, bowls of sweet onions, cucumbers, and watermelon deliciously chilled. Would that the assembly renewed session every night to celebrate with such a feast.

"Ingridan food isn't so bad," he said. "Or am I just getting used to it?"

"You'd eat a plate and call it pleasantly crunchy," said Enna.

Finn just nodded. His mouth was full.

Razo's idea of paradise was a place where the pigs ran around already roasted, and that night he wondered if he might actually be dead. The pork was tender in the middle and seared on the outside, the chunks of fat crispy. It almost brought a tear to the eye.

Razo was on his ninth skewer when the chief of assembly called out for music. Dasha complied, sitting on a cushion in the center of the hall, a harp on her lap, and coaxed a song from the strings. Razo stopped eating. The music jabbed and tugged as though she plucked at his organs. It seemed a lullaby, but one that made the hairs on his neck feel like pressing needles. He hated for it to stop.

How could she know which string she touched with her eyes closed? Razo stared, fascinated, until Talone approached Razo's table and knelt behind Megina.

"Lady . . ." He spoke just loudly enough that Razo could catch his words if he leaned forward. "Lord Belvan just informs me that his men found two burned bodies outside our barracks. They have taken the bodies away from Thousand Years to be buried secretly."

Razo's eyes roved the room—Ledel's men back from the country and lounging at their banquet table, Dasha at her harp, Belvan near the prince, and the assembly members in white tunics crossed with red sashes like long scratches on pale skin.

"Thank you, Captain." Megina's voice was steady but full of breath. "Lord Belvan must indeed be a champion for peace."

"As well, he told me something curious—a merchant complained about a ruckus in the warehouse district during the festival yesterday when all business should have been halted. Belvan's men investigated this morning and found the place empty but for heaps of freshly burned crates. They know of no reason for the oddity."

Maybe it's not a fire-speaker, thought Razo. *Maybe the murderer's burning his victims in a warehouse bonfire before tossing them outside our barracks.*

"Captain, was Lord Belvan able to identify the bodies?" Razo asked.

"No. And though he hopes to keep the public unaware of it, he'll have to report to the assembly. We have just two weeks before they vote about a return to war."

Razo set down a ceramic mug, cracking the handle, and realized he was spitting angry. *Why kill? Just to frame us? And who's the burner burning? Murders don't make sense. Why not just cause random fires and blame them on Bayern? Why go so far as murder?* His head felt bloated and throbbed with too many questions. So what that he knew who had ink-stained hands when he could not shake anything into sense?

While most of the banqueters stretched and staggered out, Razo lingered over watermelon rinds and dishes of minty honey crystals. He was keeping an eye on Dasha, who after chatting with two ladies in the hall at last strolled his way.

"Hello, tree rat." Dasha sat beside him and began to pick through the remains of the feast. "I wondered when you were going to come talk to me."

"You did?"

"Mm-hmm," she said as she finished a slice of cucumber. "You do drag your feet. I have been away for weeks and weeks, and all you can do is sit there and stare."

"I wasn't staring at you. . . ."

"You weren't? I thought you were." She studied an empty bowl. "So you were ignoring me."

"No, I wasn't." His head felt even thicker than before, and he rubbed his eyes. "I was looking at you a lot, just not, you know, *staring*, necessarily."

"And . . . ?"

"And what?"

She sighed. "And what did you think?"

She wants a compliment, he thought, pleased that he was catching on so quickly.

"*And* you look really pretty with your hair up like that, prettiest girl in here tonight."

Dasha's smile took a long time spreading from one corner of her mouth to the other. "So, you were looking. Well, thank you, but I meant, what did you think about the song I played?"

Razo stared hard at the short rope of pearls around her throat, commanding his face to be still, not to show any color, not to betray his utter humiliation with so much as an eyebrow twitch.

"What's the matter?" she asked. "You look as though you're in pain."

"Just a strained . . . toe. *Ahem.* Anyway, that's what I meant, that you looked pretty while playing the harp. You *sounded* pretty."

"Thank you." She hooked a finger in her pearls, the action reminding Razo to look up. "I wanted to talk to you about the Bayern and how the situation has been over the summer. Do you have time tomorrow morning?"

"Yes," said Razo without hesitation.

"I thought we could go riding through the heart."

"Good," said Razo, thinking that riding in a public place would be safer.

"On second thought, how about by the ocean?"

"You're right, that would be better," said Razo, now realizing that anywhere too public might be even more dangerous. He straightened for whatever she might say next, and no matter what it was, he was ready to agree.

Then he went cold, as if all his blood drained out of him from his head through his boots. He was ready to agree. No matter what she said. *She has people-speaking.*

Isi had told him about people-speaking, how it was a talent like Enna's fire and wind speech. He had been around people-speakers before—they were charming and persuasive, yet they planted an uncomfortable sensation in Razo's mind, made him itch where he could not reach. And they had been safe only once they were dead.

"Perhaps if you liked we could—"

"I, uh, I should go," he interrupted, standing and knocking an empty platter to the floor. "I'll see you tomorrow."

Razo scuttled away. He had barely fled the uncertain lamplight of the banquet hall for a dark corridor when a hand grabbed him and pulled him against a wall.

"Pela," said Razo like a sigh of relief. "I thought you were Tumas at first. What're you doing?"

"I baked this special for you." Pela stood close to him, holding a pastry in both hands. She smiled, her two bunches of yellow hair bobbing.

"Uh, thanks, but I . . ." He was about to make an excuse why he could not take it, but she looked so much like a rabbit, cute and pathetic at once, he could not bear to hurt her. "But I don't have anything for *you*. But thanks."

He examined it as he walked away, and despite having just gorged at a banquet, his stomach burbled gleefully. It was his favorite kind of turnover—flaky crust, pears and syrup oozing out, with some dark red berries he'd never seen before. He raised it to his lips but stopped. Somehow accepting a gift from lap-sitting Pela felt like lying behind Dasha's back.

Probably her people-speaking power over me, thought Razo. He was passing by the kennels and tossed the tartlet to a large brown dog, who snapped it out of the air and gulped it whole.

The next morning, Razo wheedled Finn and Enna up early, begging their company, and they followed him to the stable, yawning, pillow marks still imprinted on their cheeks. They sat on their horses and waited at the Bayern stables for Dasha.

"Enna, you've spent more time with a people-speaker than I have—"

"Ick. I really don't want to think about that. Ever again."

"I know"—Razo craned around, trying to spot Dasha among the early-morning errand runners—"but if Dasha's one of them, then it might explain how she's able to move the bodies around, you know, persuading others to do stuff for her. She doesn't seem like a murderer, but the people-speakers I knew can seem so friendly and innocent and pretty and—"

"Hello!" Dasha rode up on a gray stallion, her orange hair in two neat braids. She wore white trousers with her tunic, and her lummas was dyed a dazzling Bayern turquoise, making her eyes appear the same bright color. "Are Enna and Finn joining us? What fun! I brought plenty of victuals"— she patted a basket tied behind her saddle—"so shall we go?"

She tapped her mount forward. Razo glared at Bee Sting when she followed without a prompt.

They rode through twisting side streets, Dasha begging details of what the city had been like during the blistering summer months. Razo could not speak fast enough, could not leap forward quickly enough whenever she wanted a thing, and could not pass Finn and Enna enough meaningful looks over his shoulder.

They were sitting on a blanket in the sand, watching the surf stroke the shore, when Dasha held up her hands and laughed, as pleased as a fish in a stream. "I am stickier than a stickle bush, I'm so drenched in peach juice." She hopped up to rinse off her hands.

"So, am I right?" he whispered as soon as Dasha was beyond earshot.

Finn shrugged.

"There's something wrong with her, no doubt," said Enna.

"I knew it!"

"No, no, I mean something else.... Ugh, I wish I were better at wind-speaking. Isi would be able to tell. I don't think she's a fire-speaker. The heat *is* different around her, somehow.... But nothing makes me think she's a people-speaker. What makes you—"

"How could you miss it? Just the sound of her voice makes my chest feel tight, and my face gets hot and my mouth goes dry whenever she's near. It's getting so bad, all I have to do is see her and I'm already thinking, What does she want? What can I do for her? She's got some power over me, there's no question, and what else could it be?"

There was a heavy pause, then Enna burst out laughing. Finn smiled at his boots.

"What, what?" Razo looked back and forth wildly. "What did I miss?"

Enna rolled her eyes. "This is delicate, and I'll admit that I'm not at my best when things are delicate." She stood and stretched. "I'll go help Dasha scrape off the stickiness. Finn, would you ...?" She gestured at Razo with her head.

"What is it?" Razo asked when Enna was gone. "If you

and Enna knew that Dasha was an enemy all along and kept me ignorant for your own amusement . . ."

Finn balked at speaking, even more than normal, and kept running a finger on the inside of his collar as if his shirt scratched his neck. "It's just . . . have you thought, Razo, that maybe what you were talking about isn't because she has people-speaking, but might be that you're, you know . . ." He looked at Razo hard, his eyes unblinking.

Razo was about to explode with impatience because he did not know and this game was getting dull and . . . then he knew. The thought rushed him like wildfire hitting an autumn wheat field. He felt his face burn, and he shook his head casually as if he did not know, then wished he had not, because Finn was forced to actually say it aloud.

". . . falling in love with her."

Razo's voice stuck in his throat. He coughed. "I . . . uh, that's just, that's . . ."

"I found another in my saddlebag!" said Dasha, returning with a fig-and-egg cake in hand.

Enna was behind her, and whatever expression Razo had plastered on his face made her turn her back and double over in hysterics.

"Are you all right?" Dasha's look skipped to each person. "What did I miss?"

"Didn't you hear it?" asked Razo with some pressure in his voice. "Enna just let out some serious gas. That was coarse, Enna-girl, and not funny a whit."

Finn snorted once as though trying very hard not to laugh. Enna's chuckle stopped short, and she glared back at Razo.

Razo shrugged, his mouth miming, "What?"

Only when the party was mounted and returning up the beach, Finn and Enna in the lead, did Razo let his attention return to Dasha. She was watching the sea, her gaze lost where the horizon was misty. With the conversation hushed, the sound of waves pierced him again as it had the first time, whispered an ache of loneliness, made him feel full of secrets. The way Dasha watched the water, he thought she would understand.

In love. That'd be just my luck.

Razo grumbled to himself as he stabled Bee Sting and ambled back to the barracks. There was a commotion around the kennels, and something was lying on the ground. Razo thought if it was another burned body, he might as well cut his own throat. As he neared, he heard one man say to another, "Dead. Just up and died in the night. Wasn't even sick yesterday."

Razo slithered through the throng and saw—it was a large brown dog.

17

Daggers in the Assembly

F our days after the death of the dog, Razo paced outside the barracks. He had not returned to the pastry kitchen and had so far avoided Pela, though lately everything he ate tasted a little off. He hoped it was just his imagination. Now Thousand Years was abuzz with the gossip that two of Ledel's men had deserted after the last feast day. According to Ledel, the men had been enamored of a group called Manifest Tira. With new blood in their ranks, Razo suspected Manifest Tira would creep out and bite soon.

He should try to chase them down. But how? Were they the burners? Was Dasha involved? And how could he find out without hanging around her and confirming to Enna and Finn that he really was infatuated? The problem became harder and crunchier the longer he chewed, and he feared he might crack a tooth on it.

"Hello!"

Startled, Razo took two steps back, his heels hit a stone, and he fell on his backside. Dasha stood over him, as pleased as if she were looking at a litter of bunnies.

"I scared you! I never scare anyone."

"No?" Razo hopped back up and adopted a posture that said he was completely unruffled, never had been, and in fact was ready to do something manly like lift boulders or swallow live worms. "You frighten me regularly."

"Would you say I'm terrifying?" She lifted one eyebrow.

"Alarming, at the very least."

"Oh, good." She hooked her arm through his and began to walk, easily knocking his composure off its feet, until he noticed that her shoulder was touching the top of his arm and he could see the part in her hair. He was taller than Dasha. His gait turned into a swagger.

"And where're we going?"

"The assembly. They asked for Lady Megina today, and you're the first Bayern I came across."

"Is something wrong?"

"I don't know, but when the chief of assembly calls, you don't dawdle."

It was past midday when all the Bayern gathered, entered carriages, and made the slow, bouncy ride into the heart. The scene around the assembly was calm and quick in the supple heat of early autumn, the sky a bottomless blue. The ambassador promenaded across the plaza, smiling and waving.

Razo felt raw and exposed, missing the protection of the prince.

The door guard outside the assembly collected swords, daggers, and slings. A Tiran man pushed his way in front of Dasha. He was perhaps twenty years old, with hair cut short, his robes sharply white. Razo took him for some assembly member's aide who had taken too long on an errand. When the door guard asked for his weapon, the man held up his arms to show that he wore no sword. There appeared to be something darker than his white robes at his waist beneath his lummas, but Razo decided it was just a fold in the fabric.

Talone ordered Enna to stay with half of Bayern's Own outside. He did not trust the assembly door guard to keep back any armed fanatics who might try to come in after the ambassador. Finn, Razo, and the Own's best grapplers, including Conrad, accompanied the captain inside.

The walls of the assembly were curved, high windows piercing the white stone dome. The sixty assemblymen and -women in white robes and scarlet sashes sat on rows of steps that wrapped around the chamber. When the door minister announced Megina, the current debate paused. All faces turned to see the Bayern, then outcries arose like birds startled from a wheat field.

"Something's not right," said Talone, reaching for the sword that was not there.

The chief of assembly stood in the speaking circle at the lowest point of the room. "Quiet, please. Lady Megina, why have you come?"

"Lady Dasha gave me a message, saying you requested my presence."

"I am here, honored chief," said Dasha, stepping forward. "The message came from your aide, Tophin, just after the third bell."

"I apologize, Ambassador, for your inconvenience," said the chief of assembly, "but I sent no message."

"How odd. But as I am here, may I take this opportunity to address the assembly?"

The chief stepped aside, offering the circle.

"Lady Megina, we should go," Talone said in a low warning.

"We have less than two weeks before they vote," Megina whispered. "I can't pass up this chance." She began to descend the wide, shallow steps.

No sooner was she beyond Talone's reach than two men rushed forward, coming between the ambassador and her guards. One shoved Talone, knocking him back against the steps. Razo reached for the man, his fingers just grazing his tunic. The other man had already gained the circle, and he pulled a short dagger from his side, seizing Megina around her waist.

Talone hollered, and the Bayern leaped forward. The first thug pulled his dagger and shook it at them.

"Stay back! We will speak, and you will hear us or she dies."

It was the young man who had pushed through the line. Razo cursed his own stupidity. The assassination of an ambassador was something even those Bayern eager for peace would not be able to ignore.

"This assembly is disgraced by harboring enemy spies and kissing our brothers' murderers," said the first villain.

They were walking Megina up a set of stairs, apparently seeking a wall at their backs. Razo scanned the chamber. When the ambassador and her captors reached the top, they would be directly below a ledge. Razo started toward it till he glimpsed Talone with Conrad and another grappler, climbing a pillar. Razo stayed back, thinking he would only get in their way.

"We will be heard! We will not allow Tira to fall in with thieves—" One of the men's sandals squeaked on a marble stair that was suddenly wet. He slipped, regained his feet, and slipped again. Razo wondered how that particular stone came to be wet but thought it awfully lucky. The slip bought Talone a little more time. Razo peeked toward Talone, gauging the progress in their climb, and caught a glimpse of Dasha. Her face was intense, almost pained.

"The vile enemy . . . ," the villain screeched. "Our murderers are not our neighbors. . . ."

His voice was building, higher and louder, as though he would come to some climax, and soon. Talone was still out of sight. Razo did not think Megina could wait.

The door guard had taken his sword, his javelin, his bag

of stones, and his short sling from his side, but his long-distance sling still cinched his waist like a belt. An elderly assemblyman beside him was clutching a cane topped with a wooden ball as big as a fist.

"Excuse me," said Razo, snatching the cane. He broke it over his knee.

The assassin was canting in a voice rubbed raw, building in pitch, coming to the end. "We make this sacrifice . . ."

The sling felt cumbersome with the cane knob in its leather pouch, the target too close for a distance sling. His hands shaking, he wrapped a length of the sling around his wrist to shorten it. The villain was angling the dagger to Megina's throat. Razo swung once and released.

The knob hit the assassin on the cheek. He screamed, let go of Megina, and fell over, his hands cradling his face. The second villain's dagger did not have time to fall. Talone dropped from the ledge onto the man's back, shoving him to the ground. Conrad followed, wrestling the dagger from Talone's man, the other grappler securing the wounded man. Finn rushed forward, putting Megina behind him.

"And on the very steps of our assembly chamber . . . ," whispered the old man.

The Bayern were quiet as they rode back to Thousand Years. Razo watched Dasha, and she watched the carriage window.

The assembly guards were hunting Tophin, the chief's aide, who had disappeared. Razo wondered if his body would show up burned.

Lord Belvan and Talone led the bound, would-be assassins to the bowels of the palace for questioning, where the only light seeped from oily torches dripping smoke. Razo was at their heels. He needed to hear those men admit to the burnings.

At the door of the dark, stale chamber, Talone put a hand on Razo's chest.

"I'll help," said Razo.

"No, son, I'll do this myself."

Talone shut the door.

18

A Ram's-Head Ring

azo found Talone two days later sitting on his bunk at the barracks, his forehead resting on his fist.

"Are you grayer than you were?" asked Razo, rubbing his own temples.

Talone smiled grimly, and Razo decided he would rather not know what had happened in that cell.

"I do not believe that they're the burners."

"Ah, Captain, don't tell me that. They've got to be!"

Talone shook his head. "I don't think so. They belong to that Manifest Tira group. One was former military and from a moderately wealthy family, the other a poor boy who felt cheated when the quick end to the war stole his chance to fight. Their confidence was frightening—they believe all of Tira will hail them as heroes for even attempting to kill the ambassador. They hate Bayern, no doubt, but a bungled assassination of the ambassador in the midst of the assembly is juvenile, desperate, clumsy. The burner is following a much more sophisticated plan."

"Aimed at the same results—a repeat of the war."

"Perhaps." Talone's voice was too tired to have emotion. "Manifest Tira claims that Tira is destined to inherit any nation that touches its borders, and war is the sacred means to claim that destiny. They are brash, fearless, like the soldier who flung himself into the Bayern barracks just to kill as many as he could before being killed himself. But the burner is shrouded, slow, and secretive, and seemingly murdering fellow Tiran just to incite hatred of Bayern. That's a different kind of evil. Smells like revenge to me, vengeance for a deep, ugly wound.

"This does not bode well for Megina, or any of us," said Talone, rubbing his eyes. "The burner attacks from the shadows, secretive, calculating. But Manifest Tira . . ."

"People know them," said Razo. "They're cousins and neighbors, and they're out in the market saying vile things about Bayern. They couldn't be a secret if the people of Ingridan didn't choose to protect them."

Talone nodded, his eyes closed. "Those two would not give up the names of their cohorts, but one did reveal the location of their meetings. Belvan's men will have cleared out any lingering members of Manifest Tira by now. Even if they're not the burners, they're still a threat to our mission. I want you to take a look."

Talone gave him directions to a warehouse on the western edge of the city and was half-asleep when he told him to be careful. Razo clicked the door shut under the sound of a snore.

He wore plain Tiran garb, the only bits that had as yet escaped the dye pots. The sky was vague with clouds still disputing the question of rain, but Razo shaded his head with his lummas and hoped no one would wonder why. He hopped in the back of a penny wagon through the heart, then made his way on foot past the pungent luxury of the spice market and the sour, stifled air of the slaughter district.

Sometimes his sandals flapped on the stones, echoing in alleyways, invoking the sound of someone following. Razo earned an ache in his neck from looking back so often. He was negotiating a fringe area of the city—weeds cracked through the cobblestones and tough green moss crawled under shadows, hinting that not all in Ingridan was scrubbed clean.

He thought he was lost and used that excuse to run, shake off the feeling of being followed. He scampered over four or five streets before discovering the Rosewater, the river that formed the city's western border. It was thick with rubbish this far south, and the blue-tiled sides did little to brighten the waters. An occasional boat slid past, but all business was halted for the feast of cedar fires, and the day was as slow and sluggish as the clouds.

A couple of Belvan's men milled outside the warehouse

and gave Razo a nod of permission to enter. It was a one-story, thin structure and smelled like sodden wood, cheap and sad. The floor was littered with grubby straw, a few empty crates the only remnants of business before the warehouse became the meeting place of angry politics. Nothing looked burned. Razo pocketed a few scraps of paper and besides that found only a copper ring, cut straight and stamped with a ram's head. It fit his left middle finger, so he slipped it on for safekeeping, recalling one like it on the man who killed Veran. And now that he thought of it, he believed those two assassins also wore—

"Psst."

Razo had not expected to hear someone from behind. He held still, the hairs on his neck rising to listen. His left hand was up, the ring visible.

"Psst, there are guards out front. Where is—"

The voice cut short, perhaps doubting for the first time whom he was talking to. Razo turned, met eyes with a man of thirty, hair shorn, a copper ring on his left hand. When he saw Razo's face, he pulled a knife from his belt and charged.

Razo lowered his shoulder and rammed into the man's gut, forcing him to stumble back and giving Razo time to draw his sword.

"Hel—" Razo began to holler, but the man was upon him again, slicing the air with his dagger. Razo thrust with his sword; the man dodged, grabbed Razo's sword arm, and slashed his skin.

Razo exclaimed and dropped his sword at the slicing pain, but he managed to grab the man's arm, gripping fiercely until his arms shook with the effort of keeping that dagger one thumb away from his belly. He stepped back into his foe and bit down hard. He tasted blood before the man dropped his dagger. Razo elbowed behind him and heard a grunt but soon had two arms around his neck. He was brought down, unable to breathe.

He thrashed, he screamed, dry and silent. Through a crack in the door, he could see the back of one of Lord Belvan's men, casually standing guard. Tiny black dots played across his vision. Panic clawed at him, bony fingers pulling him down.

If you're going to win one blasted wrestle in your life, he thought, *this should be the one.*

Razo relaxed his whole body and closed his eyes so he would not have to see the going-black that meant he had no air. Then, pulling all his strength together, he whipped his head back. There was a crunch, and Razo laughed breathlessly that he was the one breaking noses for once.

Intoxicated by the air in his lungs, he leaped to his feet and stormed into the man. They locked arms. The man tried to trip him with a leg behind Razo's knee—an old trick. Razo managed to stay on his feet by crouching down, then shoved his head up into the man's chin. The man's jaw snapped shut. As he fell back, he kicked Razo in the gut. They both hit earth, Razo gagging at the pain in his belly, rasping for breath to call for help. The man was crawling for his dagger. Razo lurched forward, throwing himself on the man's back, scrabbling to keep his foe from reaching the weapon.

"In here," said Razo, his voice chafing. He gulped for more air. "In here!"

Belvan's men peeked through the door, then ran in when they saw. The soldiers seized the attacker by his arms, allowing Razo to roll off his back onto the floor, slump against a crate, and breathe. Slowly, the black dots swam away.

"Another one?" asked one of Belvan's men.

"Climbed in a window, I guess," said Razo. "I thought I'd bought it, but I bested him in the end. Me, Razo, grappled down a bigger foe. Don't keep this one a secret, fellows."

The soldier sniffed. "And what should we do with him?"

"Uh, take him back to Captain Talone and Lord Belvan, would you? I'm going to keep poking around."

"You're bleeding."

Razo twisted his forearm, trying to get a good look. "That fellow had teeth, sure enough." The cut was not deep but might leave a striking scar. He tore a strip of his lummas cloth and wrapped the arm.

For some time after the soldiers and their prisoner left, Razo stayed put, his eyes half-closed. His solitude fastened around him.

Something rasped. Something else squeaked. Razo snatched up his sword, holding the weapon before him as he scoured the warehouse.

"Anybody home?" he called out, swinging at every mouse scratch or board creak. "I'm so lonely," he said in mock-timid tones to make himself laugh, but he glanced at the door once or twice, wishing he'd thought to ask one of Belvan's men to stick around.

He was sorting through the detritus of broken crates when movement outside made him look up. Fifty paces off, on the bank of the river, stood Tumas.

Razo dropped down, breathing so loudly that he was put to mind of his brother Jef snoring. His calves began to tremble from crouching, and he knew if Tumas found him here, far from watchful eyes, he'd break bones bigger than his nose. The waiting made him ache with impatience. After a time, he gave up thoughts of self-preservation as boring and scuttled to the doorway. No one there.

Calling himself a fine spy to hide instead of hunt, he ran toward the river, looking down every alley, glancing at every window. Near the place where he had first spotted Tumas, a narrow stairway tumbled into the water, joining a small dock. Had he rowed away?

Razo kept a careful three-pace distance from the edge while he walked, scanning the water, not watching where he stepped. His boot stuck something yielding.

The smell of burned bodies was becoming uncomfortably familiar to him now, a foul mix of baked meat, garbage fire smoke, and weakly built privies. He could taste the smell, and he spat over the side of the river.

The face was burned to black indistinction, the body nearly as brittle as charcoal. No jewelry, no indication of who the poor fellow was. In a second-story warehouse, Razo thought he saw the pale sheen of a face staring out, but when he looked, no one was there. He had to get rid of this in a hurry, before someone discovered a Bayern and a burned body together. With his feet, he rolled the corpse toward the water and sent it hurtling into the river below.

"Sleep well," he whispered. He hated the burner for forcing him to bury another person like that, with no family knowing where their child or sibling had gone to, with no mention of great deeds and loving friends, the body not embraced by earth but tumbling into the unsteady sea.

The squeak of a sandal brought Razo up. There she was, Dasha, standing so close that he was startled by her blue eyes when everything else was so dull—a leaden river under the sunless sky, a smudge of ash on gray stones. He took a step back from those eyes.

"Razo," she said.

There was something tight in her voice, and he wondered if she would admit it all. Just then, he could not bear to hear.

"It was you." He backed away from the thought and, like a fool, moved closer to the river. His heel bumped a stone, he stumbled, and then came the astonishing sensation of falling.

19

River Fingers

The tumble seemed to take hours, giving him time to realize he was falling a long way, to wonder if hitting the river below would hurt much. He imagined being carried away to the sea and meeting up with scores of burned corpses and generations of dead Tiran, all sitting on the sea floor, grinning their bare grins, motioning for him with naked hands.

Then the water struck his gut, and he could not have breathed even if there had been air. He flailed, wishing a scream. The water seized him and pulled him down.

Razo thrashed his way up once. His face scraped the surface, and he sucked in air and water. Dasha was running on the bank above him, not quite keeping pace with the river, and yelling at him to swim to the lower bank on the other side. Now he wanted to laugh. As if he could swim two paces, let alone across a river.

His clothes, his sword, and his bag of stones were as heavy as the world. His head went under. The water sang in his ears.

As the dark and cold and confusion lulled him, rocked him, he thought to feel embarrassed to be dying so easily, and in front of a pretty girl no less. His arms and legs still wrestled with the deep, but his mind was falling asleep.

A sudden lift startled him to gasp. He was on his back staring at the gray sky, wrenching air into lungs, coughing out water. Then he noticed that he was not floating downstream but gliding toward the opposite shore, like the waterbirds that propel themselves with wide, flat feet. Razo glanced at his own feet and saw his toes peek through his sandals. At least he was not a duck.

He thought he saw Dasha swimming some distance off, but when he turned to look, water gushed over his face, so he kept his face up and focused on making certain he had plenty of that wonderful air.

His head bumped something hard, and he twisted around, somehow keeping afloat until his fingers grasped a tiled edge and he could pull himself up. The far bank of the river was built into a series of wide steps, so as the river rose and fell it would always meet an easy dock. Razo crawled away from the water and lay on a step, coughing his breath, his legs trembling. He could not quite believe he was alive.

A hand reached out of the water. Another. Dasha pulled herself up and sat where she was, her legs knee deep in the river. Her hair was straight and dripping, one tiny silver star clinging to a strand, the others washed away. She looked at him, her lips parted.

"Did you pull me?" Razo asked. "Is that how I made it across?"

Dasha did not answer. She turned to the river as if considering jumping back in.

A heavy gust wrapped around Razo's face and warned of more than wind to come. Darker clouds pushed through the gray ones, swirling and undulating as though the sky mirrored the river's waves.

"It's going to storm soon." Standing up, he felt like a newborn colt, shaking on unfamiliar legs. He searched for a bridge to take them back across the Rosewater and into the city, but no arch interrupted the slate water. When he started to climb the bank steps, Dasha did not follow. Now she was watching the sky.

"Come on, noble girl." He put his arm around her waist to lift her to her feet. "We've got to get away from the river. If it rains much and this wind gets tougher, we could be swept away."

She let him lead her. The wind grew more insistent, pushing them from behind. He scrambled up the steps and saw dark fields, the laborers absent for the feast day. A squarish shape in the distance was the only destination. Dasha's steps seemed reluctant, so Razo put his arm around her shoulders and made her run.

It was a small hut, rattling in the wind like chattering teeth and likely to crumble in on itself any day, but it was empty and had a roof, so Razo tore the knotted rope off the door and pulled Dasha inside.

Lightning sliced the gray; thunder hurled itself across the sky. There was a pause, as if the world took a deep breath, and then rain struck. The thin metal roof shuddered, the walls groaned once, and Razo leaned toward the center of the room, uneasy with a storm that seemed intent on clawing its way inside.

He shrugged and chuckled at himself. It was just weather, nothing to get his boot straps tangled about. Then he looked at Dasha—pale, crouched on the floor. She was staring straight up. He could not help but follow her gaze, but nothing hung in the air above them.

"What ails you?" he asked.

"Did I do it?"

Razo's heart seemed to fall a long way. It *was* her. She had killed those people. The question in her voice encouraged him somewhat that she was innocent, in a way. In the way that Enna had been during the war, in the way that Finn forgave Enna.

"Did you mean to do it?"

Dasha looked at him. In the dim light, the blacks of her eyes nearly crowded out all the blue, giving her a startled expression. "Sometimes I do." She returned her gaze upward, opening her face and neck to the sound of rain. "I want to, the desire pulls me, and I can't help it . . . or I don't want to help it. I love it, though I didn't mean to do it this time."

The room seemed to slant now. Razo was backing away. "What do you mean, you love it? You love killing people?"

"Killing people?"

"I thought that you . . . I can't believe you enjoy it, I just didn't think . . ." An icy shiver scratched at his back, like the warning before he went too far taunting his big brother Brun. "So, you going to kill me next?"

"Kill you next? Razo, what—"

"Those bodies, that one by the river, you burned them."

"I did not! I found it there, just like you did."

"You said you loved it, but you didn't mean to—"

"I was talking about something else, just forget about it. . . ."

"What was it, Dasha? What didn't you mean to do?"

"The rain!" She stood up, her arms straight, her fingers straight. "I was talking about the rain." Her voice went low, and she turned her back on him, resting her forehead against a shuddering wall. "Never mind."

Razo was done with tiptoeing around slippery places. He grabbed her shoulders and turned her to face him. "Tell me."

She blinked fast, as though she were battered by sharp rainfall; then the release of her shoulders spoke of defeat.

She held up her hand, and her forefinger and thumb met, pinching the air. She put her finger out and showed a drop of water hanging from its tip. It got fatter and heavier, sagging until it dropped.

Razo gaped. "What're you . . . ?"

She did it again and again, plucking drops of water from the air like berries from a summer bush. Her expression was calm, rapt, pleased.

"My grandfather taught me this. He called it river fingers. After I got the hang of it, he taught me this, too." She grabbed at the air, and water hung from all five of her fingers like long, luminous nails. She shook them off. "And this." She cupped her hand around nothing. Her palm filled with water, and she sipped it dry.

"It's easy on days like today, so much water in the air, not just the rain, but the invisible damp. The world is full of water we can't see. But I can . . . *feel* it." Dasha stared at her open hand as drops of water gathered on her fingertips and rolled into the cup of her palm.

"You know the language of water," Razo whispered. "You can draw it to you, like some folk can with wind or fire. You got the river to carry me, didn't you? Ho there, now, I just realized something—that day in the assembly! You made the stair wet so the assassin would slip."

She nodded. "I try not to use it much, but I wanted to help. That was all I knew how to do from that distance." She shrugged, the gesture a self-criticism.

"I'll bet you could do more than that," said Razo, re-membering how Isi had once pushed back five goose thieves with the wind, how Enna . . . Enna had done a lot of things.

Dasha tilted her head, crinkling her nose without smil-ing. "On days like today, I can feel how heavy the clouds are. My skin aches, and I know if I just feel it, just close my eyes and hear the clouds release, the rain break apart, the world sigh in relief, it will happen. But I don't." She touched her breastbone. "There's a funny tickling inside me when I'm near the ocean, near a river, itching me to leap in and try something more. What I did with you today in the river, I had never done before."

"Well, I thank you, then. Your, uh, river fingers saved my life. My friend Isi would call it the gift of water-speaking."

"It does not seem like a gift. It killed my grandfather."

"What? Killed your . . . How?"

Dasha searched Razo's eyes, and he straightened, tried to look as trustworthy as possible. The walls of the shack groaned again, a creak of wood as hard and distinct as a word. Dasha led Razo to the center of the room, sat beside him, and told her story.

"When I was six, after the death of my mother, I lived in the country under the care of my grandfather. That was the year he first told me about river fingers. He told me one had to be born to the talent in order to learn, and he sensed that, unlike my father, I had ability. His own mother had taught him; then before she died she forbade him to use it. He had obeyed her until he had a companion in the art."

Dasha harvested another water drop from the air, and she watched it sadly, as if it were a dead thing. "Grandfather could touch the dry creek shore and call the water to flood the banks or on a cloudy day ask the rain to fall. How it used to make me laugh!"

Razo became conscious again of the torrent on the roof, like fingernails scratching metal.

"When I was ten, my father brought me to Ingridan, where I was always afraid someone would guess what I could do. Even then, I sensed the wisdom in Grandfather's insistence on secrecy. Three years later, I returned to the country to find Grandfather looking haggard. At first I thought he was simply sad because he missed me." Dasha's laugh was bitter. Her fingers plucked at her skirt.

"One morning I sat at my window and saw Grandfather sneak away toward the creek. I thought he was off for a bit of fun!" Her voice cracked.

"So I followed . . ." She cleared her throat. "I followed him. Quietly, in bare feet. I stayed behind a bush, excited to catch him at some new river fingers trick. I remember he was sweating, or at least his face and arms were drenched, and he was muttering, 'Coming, I'm coming. . . .' He did not hesitate, just walked right into the creek and let himself fall. Not like he was going swimming, more like he was going to bed. The current pulled him down.

"I chased after him, Razo, I did, and when I couldn't find him, I ran into the water to listen—it sparked images in my mind of an otter upstream, of fish and crawfish and grubs, and trees that bowed themselves into the creek. No whisper of Grandfather. At the time I didn't understand. Now, I believe the river could no longer detect a difference between him and water."

Razo put his arm around her shoulder. She leaned in to him, her head resting against his neck. It made him sigh in relief— he did not like listening to someone else's pain without doing something to make it better. "Did you ever find him?"

"Downstream," she said blankly. "His body had washed ashore, drowned. The water had lied. He had sought to join it completely, but dead, he was still just a man."

Razo listened to the rain trying to find a way in. "Could that happen to you?"

"Yes."

"Soon?"

She shrugged. "I don't know what happened to Grandfather. Maybe he used his talent too much, so I avoid it. But I want to use it, all the time, and it feels so natural when I do. A relief. But I'm afraid, too." She sat up so she could see Razo's face. "I know it's Enna, Razo."

Cold rushed from his belly up into his face. It was hard to play casual there in that scrap of a shelter with the storm tearing at the roof, Dasha's story still slumping around their shoulders, sad and strange, a tired ghost.

"What's Enna?" he asked.

"Enna is the fire-witch. I'd hoped your fire-witch might come with the Bayern, and so I volunteered to be the liaison. When I get close enough to touch, the water in the air can tell me who has a peculiar heat swirling about. I wanted . . . Please, Razo, don't think ill of me, I can see that little frown between your brows and your thoughts full of doubt now. . . . I wanted to meet the fire-witch, I thought she might give me a chance. Am I a fool?"

That was not a question Razo was eager to answer. Dasha sighed.

"My grandfather collected books with any mention of river fingers. I've been studying them and found out about the fire worshippers in Yasid, people who could spark fire from air. One author believed they could also call rain down."

The parchment in her room, he thought.

"They lived without struggling against the call of water, in harmony with water and fire. I thought if Enna could teach me . . ."

"You want Enna to teach you fire?" He did not try to deny it anymore.

"These past months, I have been hoping to make her friendship. I try to be where she will be, but I also fear that she will sense in me the river fingers as I sensed the fire in her. It's funny, I feel at ease addressing the assembly, but around Enna I am all shaking knees and dry mouth. It's easier when you're around. You make people relax, you know that?"

"Really?"

First Talone tells him that he has the keen eye of a spy, then he is the best slinger Finn ever saw, and now he makes people relax. Why did everyone take so long to tell him these things? The best any of his brothers ever said was that he did not stink as sour as their third oldest brother, Thein, who after a day chopping wood reeked like a twice dead skunk.

"I was so happy when she came on that beach ride with us, but I guess . . ." Dasha shrugged. "For many, the war is hard to forget."

"So what *were* you doing by the river today?"

"Following Tumas. One night when I was trying to get up the courage to go to Enna's room and talk to her, I saw him climbing a tree, peering into her window. I fetched a palace guard, but when we returned he was gone. His intent might have been pure lechery, but I was afraid he might know what I know. I daydreamed that if I could figure out what Tumas knew and was able to tell Enna, then she might be grateful, she would think me . . ." Dasha shrugged, shy. "I was in the heart today and saw him heading down a side street alone. I'd lost him and was walking back up the Rosewater when I came upon you. Did Tumas kill that person?"

"I don't know." He had never told Finn and Enna his

mandate from Talone, but inside that small, dry space, surrounded by an invasion of rain, telling Dasha felt like the safest thing in the world. "It's the sixth one found like that, burned, abandoned, though usually they're left near the Bayern, to cast suspicion, I think. To incite the people and push the assembly to vote for war." He sighed. "I'll talk to Enna. I'll ask her to teach you."

"Thank you, tree rat."

Razo leaned his cheek into the top of her head, smiling at how nice it felt, trying to ignore how his stomach pinched together at the thought of his intended conversation with a certain fire-witch.

In the sundown after rain, the eastern horizon was pale yellow and the clouds rich blue, as though the sky had pulled inside out. Razo walked home, his arm still around Dasha's shoulders, and thought he rather knew how the sky felt.

"Are you insane?"

Enna paced. The night air that blew through her slatted shutters was cool with the memory of the rainstorm. It did not calm her much. "She's Tiran! They're trying to kill us, already succeeded with Veran."

"Enna, please," said Razo. "Dasha figured out you're a fire-speaker on her own, and the fact she hasn't told any-one's a good sign, right? She could get overwhelmed by the water speech, just like you were with fire. She could die. If she had the balance of both water and fire like you do with wind and—"

"Razo, I spent weeks prisoner to a Tiran who had a prettier tongue than your Dasha, and he flattered me and took care of me and made me believe I was his friend, his . . ." She glanced at Finn, then hurried on. "What he wanted in return was to learn fire speech, said it would make the Tiran general trust me, that it was for my good, for Bayern's good. I almost did it! He didn't really care about me or Bayern, none of them do. If you're set on being the fool, Razo, I'll not stand by and watch. I can't"—her voice broke—"live that nightmare again."

Finn frowned. "Maybe she could go to Yasid. . . ."

"What, do you want a Tiran to learn fire and come burning down our doors? Besides, the people I met there, they were very particular about who they would teach. Go ahead and send her to the desert and tell her good riddance."

Finn took Enna's hand. "Enna, you don't have to teach her anything, but if you just talk—"

Enna ripped loose from Finn's grip and stormed out the door, Finn at her heels.

"That went well," Razo muttered to himself.

He met Dasha in the courtyard under the grasping sweet scent of lime trees in their autumn bloom. She stood when he approached, clasping her hands.

"And?"

Razo rubbed his hair. "Dasha, Enna is, she . . ."

"She is not going to help me," she said, her tone empty.

"Enna's not a bad sort. It's just that she's been hurt before, betrayed in a foul way by a Tiran fellow—"

"I understand. How can she trust me? Of course she can't. Well, it was just a hope. Maybe there will be some other way."

Her tone was light and sincere, her smile full of enthusiasm. Razo knew Enna had been overcome by fire nearly to the point of death before she and Isi could get to Yasid and find balance. He did not have much hope for some other way.

"Listen, Enna may change her mind...well, maybe she'll...that is, if only..."

Dasha laughed lightly. "Razo, you're a mess! Don't worry about me."

But he could not help it. Besides, if Dasha was innocent, a murderer was still out there, unknown. He felt an unpleasant, squirmy prickle, not unlike when his brothers dropped a fern spider down his shirt.

"Enna's loyal, deep as her bones' bones," said Razo. "If she knew you, she'd trust you. Help me figure out who's behind the burning and stop them, and Enna'll change her mind. She'll believe then that you're a friend to Bayern."

Dasha's eyes flashed in the moonlight. "Will it be dangerous?"

"Oh, I guess, now that you mention it, that it might—"

"Sounds like fun."

When Razo reported to Talone in his chamber the next morning, he ended his story after rolling the body into the river, omitting the part where he confided his role as spy and the discovery of six bodies to the most likely suspect, who also happened to have water-speaking and knew about Enna and quite possibly was Bayern's biggest threat. Razo swallowed nervously, then belched air. He knew he was a terrible liar, but Talone seemed too preoccupied to notice.

"The assembly has decided to vote on the war matter in one week." Talone stood, resting his arms on the windowsill. "Despite a shift in public opinion with those who remained in Ingridan over the summer, the majority of citizens are still angry about the end of the war, still chanting for a second chance. There have been six burned bodies so far. Unless there's a dramatic change, unless the public turns against Manifest Tira and the body burner is found and stopped, Lord Belvan believes the assembly will vote for war."

Razo opened his mouth, but nothing came out. Talone nodded, agreeing with what Razo did not say.

"And if in the meantime another body is discovered," said Talone, rubbing his eyes, "Belvan suggested we depart Tira in the night."

"One week?" The cost of telling Dasha the truth just rose, higher than Razo could pay. He stood beside Talone, resting his elbows on the sill, and stared at the strips of outside activity he could see between the shutter slats.

His fingertips and toes were tingling. Usually this would be the moment where he would tell Talone everything and sit back while the captain decided what to do. Was it only yesterday that Razo had won a wrestling match against that Manifest Tira dagger boy? He felt the possibilities of other victories ticking the pulse in his neck, making his muscles long to run.

"One week." Razo looked Talone dead in the eye. He felt excited and hopeful, and at the same time terrified and unsure, but for once he knew his expression betrayed nothing but confidence. "I'll do it, Captain. Before they vote, I'll figure it all out."

It was a ridiculous promise, and he felt like a little boy sticking a ring of pinecones on his head and declaring himself king. But he'd said it, and now his blood sped with the hope of, *What if I really can do it? What if I do?*

He left without another word and went to find Dasha. An ache like a lead ball in his gut told him that Dasha could be playing him like a harp, nudging him to sing out just the tune she wanted, making him think he was creating his own music. But he believed she was innocent. He had made his choice.

Razo took Dasha to the most private place he knew in Thousand Years. While trailing Tumas last spring, he had discovered an empty barracks. The inside smelled fusty and sour, of spilled wine and bedclothes abandoned in a rush, a patina of dust drowsing over everything. The building stood white and cold and barren, a memorial to some of the hundreds of Tiran soldiers who would never return from the battlefields of Bayern. *Had they been burned?* Razo scratched his calf with a toe. A footstep in the dirt of the training circle meant someone had been here recently, but on looking again, Razo thought it might have been made by his own sandal.

On the abandoned training ground, he began to teach Dasha the sling, having noticed that people talk more easily when their hands are occupied. While she tried out a few stones, he stayed behind her, his arm across her back, his hand around her wrist. His chin touched her hair. The first time the stone left the sling in a more or less straight line, Dasha screeched with joy.

"You're not doing something tricky?" asked Razo. "Making it fly straight by using water . . . somehow?"

"No." Dasha's fingernail traced the middle of the braided sling as she thought. "I wonder if I . . . if the water . . . No, I don't see how. I might be able to do the reverse—weigh down a stone with water, make it go off course."

"That was a pretty good shot, then. Try it on your own." Razo kept his hand on her waist a moment before stepping back. "I'm uneasy about the body we found by the river. Usually they're dumped near the Bayern barracks or stable, and once by our camp. Seems like Tumas—if it was Tumas—got interrupted. That means he'd some other plan."

"You don't think it was him?" Dasha winced as her stone slumped out of her sling.

"Seems likely, but neither of us actually saw him with

the body. Do you know him? Any reason why he'd want to pin burning deaths on Bayern besides that he's just a nasty-fingered, putrid-breathed, nose-breaking mud eater?"

"None that I know of, though that list of attributes alone might be enough to convict him."

"The location of the bodies, especially the first one, makes me think it might be someone in Captain Ledel's company."

"What about the captain himself? Fly straight, you stupid stone! He lost a brother in the Battle of Ostekin Fields."

Razo sat up. Dasha's stone hit a tree stump. "Good shot! A brother? Was he killed by soldiers or burned?"

"I'm not certain, but that was not all. Captain Ledel was the leader of the southern forces in Bayern and stood to advance considerably when Tira occupied. I had heard some rumors that he would be second in command over all occupation forces—that was, of course, before the war was lost. The leader of Tiran forces in Bayern, Captain Tiedan, was executed for his failure. I suppose Captain Ledel is lucky he was just demoted to a twenty captain."

"I wonder if he'd consider himself lucky." Razo scratched marks into the dirt. *If it smells like bacon, it'll taste like bacon,* his ma used to say. "But Ledel swears by order, following the proper rules of war and all that. Wouldn't sneaking and murdering during peacetime be against his rules?"

"I would think so," said Dasha.

"He just doesn't strike me as the kind who could murder people, burn them like that. And he's got a tight leash on his men. Even Tumas seems afraid to jump without his approval. I can't imagine his soldiers would do something as involved as burn other Tiran and blame it on the Bayern without their captain's permission. It all doesn't click together in my head."

"What about Victar, Assemblyman Rogis's son?" said Dasha. *Thwack!* went her stone against wood.

"Uh, are you aiming for that particular tree?"

She looked at him over her shoulder, one eyebrow raised. "I am now."

"In that case, excellent shot. Why'd you ask about Victar? He seems like a good sort, and he's been friendly kind with me."

"I don't know him myself, but my father mentioned once that Rogis was one of the loudest voices in support of invasion."

"Aw, not Victar. I like him," said Razo, jumping up to put more stones in Dasha's outstretched hand. "But he does have a touch of the radical in him, does Victar, goes his own way, never looks at Ledel for approval." Razo scratched his chin a bit harder than needed. "Wait, um, he didn't go to his father's country estate this summer, did he? I think I heard that he and his father are estranged. Maybe they disagreed about the war."

Thwack! "That actually was the place I was aiming for! Heard it from whom?"

"One of the girls in the pastry kitchen."

Plop, her stone fell to the ground. "Heard it how? Did you just ask them?"

"We talk, me and the pastry girls. We're friendly." Not that he'd been there recently, what with pastries that killed large dogs.

"Friendly?"

"As in friends. I'm friends with the girls in the kitchens, friendly kind of friends."

"Oh, I see." Dasha flicked the sling over his shoulder. "Thanks for the practice. I'll ask around, see what else I can find out about Captain Ledel and his men."

"Just take care that you don't give yourself away."

"Oh, I can be *subtle.*" She gave him a significant look and left without waiting for him to pick up the fallen shot. He clinked the stones into his pouch and wondered how the mood had plunged from summer to winter inside a moment. Could she have been upset just because he frequented the pastry kitchen? It did not make any sense.

One week, he thought.

Come night, he planned to climb a tree beside Ledel's barracks and spy a bit, but there were still hours of anxious daylight. He was standing in the skinny shade of a tree beside the barracks, deliberating what to do next, when he saw a young man with short hair weaving through the relentless traffic of the palace grounds. He caught sight of a copper-colored glint on his hand before the young man disappeared into the palace.

Razo did not need a closer look to guess it was a copper ring, marked with the head of a ram.

21

An Ambassador's Assassin

Razo ran, his breath fuming in his lungs. The young man had been moving toward the south wing of the palace, where both Megina and Enna lived. When he shimmied through the crowds and into the palace, the *clack* of sandals on stone stairs was just fading out of hearing. Up he hiked to the third floor, relieved to find two Bayern sentries still posted outside the ambassador's room.

"Has anyone come looking for Lady Megina?" he asked Conrad.

"Not in an hour. Why?"

"Is she in there?" Razo gestured to the door, looking over his shoulder to watch for anyone coming from behind.

"Yes, she's there."

"And Enna's in her room?"

"No, she's off with Finn and Lord Belvan in the city. Razo, what's going on? You look like—"

"Make sure Megina's all right, then don't let anyone in. I'll be back."

Razo fled to the stairs, slid down the rails, and raced to see if he could spot the potential assassin outside. Talone was approaching the palace, and when he saw Razo's face, he ran to meet him.

"Manifest Tira in the palace . . ." Razo sputtered words, his breath disheveled with anxiety. "Maybe looking for Megina. I lost him—"

Then they both saw—a man scaling the outside of the palace, climbing from a second-story window to the third story, straight toward one of Megina's windows. Her shutters were open, inviting in the cool air as well as any assassins who cared to call.

"I'll go in," said Talone, veering toward the door to the palace. "You—"

Talone did not finish his sentence, but Razo knew what he was going to say. He was already pulling free his distance sling, drawing a stone from his bag. The target was too far away, so he kept running as he put the stone in the leather pouch and swung it round. The moment he was close enough, he let it free, the shot ripping the air as it circled. The man dropped into the window, the stone striking the space where his head had just been.

Razo cursed and kept running so hard, the back of his throat ached and tasted of blood. When he reached the place where the young man had climbed, Raz leaped onto a windowsill and shinned up ledges. Palace guards were running at him, shouting.

"Assassin!" Razo pointed up. "I'm trying . . . stop the assassin . . . the ambassador!"

He swung an arm over Megina's windowsill and heard metal whack metal. Pulling himself onto his elbows, he saw Talone raise his sword in defense against the Tiran's swing. Megina stood behind Conrad and the other Bayern sentry, one sleeve of her dress ripped, cloth hanging open like a wound.

Razo scrambled into the room, rolling out of the way when the fight got too close, and grabbed a javelin lying on the floor. He crouched and waited for a clean shot at the Tiran man, hoping to nab one of his legs, but the opponents tangled and pulled away, circled and sliced, swung fists when swords locked, never offering Razo an opening.

Come on, come on. Razo was not fond of bare swords swinging in small spaces. They often managed to slice a bit of skin or lob off limbs and heads. Suddenly the Tiran lurched, and his leg curved behind Talone's heels, tripping him back. Talone hit the floor.

"No!" cried Razo, leaping forward.

But the Tiran sword stopped short. Talone's own sword thrust up through the Tiran's white tunic. It was quickly turning red.

Talone yelled with effort, pushing the sword and man away. The Tiran fell dead to the side.

The room was filling with Tiran soldiers—Lord Belvan's men, Razo was relieved to see. Had it been Ledel's, he might have drawn his own sword. Soldiers climbed through the windows and burst through the doors, exclaiming and demanding answers until Megina's clear voice cut through the noise. Within minutes, the Tiran soldiers carried the body away, bolted the windows, sent men to search the rest of the south wing, and set up guards on every floor.

Razo sat in a corner, playing with a cut on his hand, a result of clambering up the wall too quickly. He ripped a corner of cloth from one of the ambassador's tunics (*don't think she'll mind, as I helped save her life and all,* he thought), tied up the cut, and discovered himself alone but for Talone and Megina, who stood in the center of the room, facing each other, apparently having forgotten that Razo existed.

"You're not hurt." Talone looked over her body as if making certain, his hand lifting a flap of her torn sleeve, letting it fall.

"Thank you, Captain." Her hand kept fluttering to her heart and back to her side, as if she did not know where to put it.

"That was quick thinking," said Talone. "You kicked him solid, gave me a chance to get between you."

Megina's eyes widened. "I did kick him, didn't I?"

Her lips tensed, his tensed, and then, unexpectedly, they both laughed. It spooked Razo to goose bumps.

"The king spoke for hours on your many talents, Lady Megina, but he neglected to mention the kicking."

Megina was laughing until she squeaked. "Don't tell him!

This entire enterprise has been failure and terror and bad news, and I don't want to give him any more reason to laugh at me. Though I don't mind if you do, Captain."

The laughing stopped, her eyes still teary. "I suppose I'll have to keep a guard with me now, on both sides of the door."

"I will see to it," he said, though his voice was husky, seemingly saying different words altogether. He looked at her face, her hands.

"If you're to assign me a constant guard," she said, wincing as though confessing a bad deed, "I would that it was you."

Razo held his breath, afraid that any moment they would remember his presence. He crept to the exit and had almost escaped unnoticed when his javelin tip caught the doorjamb and clattered to the floor. He swiped it up and ran off.

His ribs itched inside him where he could not scratch. Seeing them made him see himself. He had been the one in the room who stood alone, whom no one looked at, who dropped his javelin and ran away. He knew he should be laughing at it, but just then he could not. No one had ever *looked* at him in the way Megina had looked at Talone, as if she never wished to look away.

Bettin had made him feel that the world was a laugh, that he was a bucketful of fun, that his heart zigging in his chest was the only way to feel. But in the end it had been a lie.

He thought of Dasha.

Nothing sounded worse to Razo just then than being alone, so he climbed to the fourth floor. The prince was challenging Nom to a game of Tempests, carved marble pieces played on a round board. At a glance, Razo could see Nom was beating him soundly.

"Razo's-Own! What a pleasure. We see you all too infrequently since the summer's end. I hope your captain is not working you too hard. But see how your face is red, and you are sweating. Celi! Please bring cold drinks and grapes, and I recall Razo's-Own enjoyed a good strip of bacon, well crisped, or is that too heavy for afternoon? Well, bring it anyway, and, ooh, see if there are fresh peaches, not the pockmarked ones, of course, nor those hard little yellow ones. I would rather go without, wouldn't you?"

Razo leaned back against a heap of pillows, too tired to care about sweating on the fine fabric. He was aware that the prince had asked a question but could not recall what it had been, so he offered a noncommittal, "Mm."

"Precisely so," said the prince.

Razo waited to gulp down some water before sharing the news of the ambassador, the assassination attempt, and his captain's quick sword. The sight of Talone and Megina looking at each other still made his heart rattle strangely in his chest, and he could not cork up that feeling enough to hold back a gusty exhale.

The prince frowned in his way, which was simply the

absence of amusement around his mouth. "You are worried, my friend, about your presence in my country, about the hope of your mission of peace."

"The assembly votes in less than a week, and it's not looking good for us. I'd hoped all those people using Bayern dyes meant that Tiran opinion was improving. I guess we just won over the summer folk, and the rich and powerful haven't changed their minds." Razo played with the fringe on a pillow, accidentally pulling several strands loose. He stuffed them under another pillow before anyone could notice.

The prince was quiet, eating grapes as a merchant inspects coins. Razo's eyes had just closed when the prince shouted, "I have it! A way to support your cause. I'd already considered marrying a Bayern, but the only noblewoman in your party is the ambassador. It is a shame your king does not have a sister, but just as well—marrying a Bayern woman at this time of crisis might cause more harm than good, giving impetus for others to rise up and oppose. No, the situation needs a more subtle solution. Just now I hit upon it—the ambassador's daughter!"

Razo did not want to argue, the prince seemed so elated with the idea, but he had to say, "Radiance, Lady Megina doesn't have any children."

"No, no, you mistake me. I mean the *Tiran* ambassador, Lord Kilcad's daughter, the fiery-haired girl. Is that not perfect?"

Razo wanted very much to sit down and then realized that he already was.

"She is a little thing," said the prince, peeling a grape. "Strange hair color in that family, but very respectable. Lord Kilcad is the Tiran most actively campaigning for peace, and she is the liaison to the Bayern. If I chose her, no one could mistake where the prince sides on this issue. I shall write to her father for permission at once, and I'll do it just for you, my friend."

Razo forced himself to lean back, act casual. He bumped a pillow fringed with tiny bells, and it tinkled sadly.

"Razo's-Own, you do not seem pleased."

"I . . . uh . . ." A turning stomach struck him as an extreme reaction to such news. So what if the prince was going to marry Dasha? They were all nobles, and it was just the sort of thing fancy folk were wont to do. A poor Forest boy and a noble Tiran girl would be a ridiculous match, and he would not cross three days of Forest in two days to tell her what he thought, never again. No, he and Dasha were a passing thought, a moth fluttering by his nose on its way to the firelight.

"I think that'd be a noble thing, Radiance," Razo said.

"Precisely!"

22

The Grape Harvest Festival

The early-autumn air was in constant motion, gusts of cold, bursts of warmth. The entire world felt ready to happen. With less than a week remaining, Megina thought they had little to lose and declared it was time for the Bayern to celebrate a Tiran festival.

"It's Tira's most important feast day. Look sharp, act humble, don't be quick to draw your weapons. Perhaps the sight of Bayern celebrating among them will hearten the citizens."

At dusk, Razo wandered to the Bayern stable, watching tree shadows, peering through barracks and palace windows, thrumming to the beat of *five days left, five days left*. Enna and Finn were waiting at the stable, and she seized upon Razo at once for his version of what had happened the day before. He gave it gladly, emphasizing his clever deductions—how the fellow's haircut had reminded him of other Manifest Tira assassins and his astounding observance of the telltale copper ring.

"Wish I'd been in Megina's room. I mean, I wouldn't've burned him," Enna said, though no one accused, "but I could've burned the sword out of his hand, and then he'd still be alive for questioning."

Razo thought this was a good moment to describe the curious scene that had occurred after the swordplay.

"No," said Enna, pleased.

"Yes," said Razo, also pleased.

"I can't believe it."

"Believe it. Talone and Megina were *looking* at each other in *that way.*"

Enna leaned back against the stable wall, laughing, and sighed at the sky. "Who'd ever've guessed? That's lovely, that is."

Finn smiled but took himself a bit apart, his body half-turned away from Enna. Something felt wrong to Razo, distance and tension buzzing between those two. He did not know what it meant.

Megina and Talone arrived, striding quickly from the palace. Razo, Enna, and Finn spied on them from behind the stable, waiting for their captain to do something ridiculous like throw her over his shoulder. But he was all business, counting men and assigning duties. Megina did not meet his eyes.

"Are you sure, Razo?" Enna whispered.

"Look, he's blushing," Finn said in jest.

"He'll lose her for sure, acting distant and untouchable like that," said Enna. "He's got to speak up now, make sure she knows how he feels."

Finn snorted. Enna turned slowly, giving Finn a glare she usually reserved for everyone else. He shook his head, meaning, *Never mind.*

"What, you think I'm being hypocritical?" she asked.

"I've told you my mind, asked you dozens of times—"

"So stop asking or I'm never going to say yes."

"Why not?" Finn's voice was strong as a rope, pulling for an answer.

"You can't just assume, Finn. Look at you, the strong man, the warrior, all muscles and sword, always knowing exactly what I'm going to want, standing ready whenever I need water or an arm or a kiss."

"What's wrong with that?" said Razo, his stare blank.

"Stay out of this, Razo."

"Enna, why're you doing this?" asked Finn.

"What, you don't like the way I am anymore? Is that it? You want me to be as perfect as you all the time?" Enna slapped his chest. "Why *do* you have to be so perfect, huh? I'm waiting for you to lose your cool, Finn, just once. So go on! Why don't you make a fool of yourself for me?"

Enna stared up, Finn stared down. Razo scratched his neck and started to back away. "I . . . uh, I'll just . . ."

"Don't bother," said Finn. He punched a tree trunk as he left.

Razo gave Enna a thump on the shoulder. "That was

Finn you were berating, not some nasty Tiran body burner. What's the matter with you?"

"I don't know." She swatted his hand away, her voice still angry. "Maybe I'm scared, or . . . I'm just . . . I don't know."

"You better know. You'd better know something before you start talking to Finn like—"

"Look," said Enna, "saying I'll love someone forever isn't as easy as . . . as pulling yarn from a ball. It's all knotted and kinked inside me. And if I let someone tug on me again . . ." She winced to keep herself from crying. "Ugh! Do you know what I'm saying? I let someone before, and I was wrong and he was bad, and then Finn came and he was perfect, and I thought I was easy with it, and I am easy with him. He makes me feel like Enna. He makes me feel . . ." Enna sat on the ground, Razo dropping down beside her.

"I don't understand you, Enna. If you love him . . ."

"I do, but it's not that easy. I hate how he just assumes everything's fine. Why can't he ever do something . . . something big, something dramatic, something frightening, woo me, show me that he loves me that much?"

"Finn's just not that way. He's the quiet kind."

"Is he? Or does he just not care as much as he used to?" She halted. Her voice frowned. "And I can't keep the disquiet away, the whispers that say he could betray me, too."

Razo blew out his lips. "Aw, Enna-girl. Not Finn, never Finn."

"You're right." She said it lightly, as though she did not have the energy to argue. "So, you over Bettin?"

The question was so unexpected, it made him choke on his own spit. "No, and I won't ever be, so save your voice telling me it's done. I know it's done, but I decided to love her always, and that's not something a boy can just undo because she's gone and everyone says to get over it already."

From the direction of the gardens, Razo could just make out Finn shuffling toward them, one long, yellow flower clutched in his hand.

"He's bringing me a flower," Enna whispered, her tone flat, edged with disappointment.

Finn seemed to hesitate, then tossed the flower to one side and turned back around.

"Finn, wait!" Enna jumped up and ran after him.

Great crows, Razo thought, *we're every one of us a tangle too thick to pick.*

As the Bayern moved out, Razo glimpsed Enna and Finn talking as they walked. Finn's head was lowered so she could hear his quiet voice. She took his arm, they moved closer, but neither smiled, and Razo widened his eyes with the realization that Enna and Finn might not always be Enna and Finn. Suddenly the stones beneath his sandals did not feel so solid.

The group took no horses or carriages—the celebration of the grape harvest began everywhere at midnight and paraded down the avenues, converging in the heart. With Enna on her left, Talone on her right, and Bayern's Own encircling her, Megina held aloft an oil lamp and offered a hearty greeting to anyone she passed.

All along the streets, artists gave of their talents freely—theater groups strutted their rehearsed stories on the plazas, painters scratched at the pavement with charcoal, and poets wrapped their words around passersby. In Bayern, drums drove festival music like a heartbeat, but the Tiran lap harps and flutes lacked that pulse, sliding down the streets and into Razo's ears, ghostly.

The Bayern crossed paths with others they knew from the palace. Even Ledel was there, though Razo recalled Victar saying that Ledel often disappeared on feast days. Razo checked that his sling was at hand.

Victar and his friends were holding their oil lamps aloft and singing a grape walker's song: "Let it gush through your toes till it pleases the nose. What I crush with my feet will be bitter and sweet." Dasha pranced from the head of the group back to Megina, then out to skip beside Victar and his friends, full of song, her hands sticky with grape juice. Razo realized he was aware of her even when she disappeared from view. It was a pleasant, subtle sensation, like being in a noisy tavern but through the clatter and roar still being able to recognize the intonations of a familiar song.

The festivities massed along the banks of Ingridan's three central rivers—the Autumn, the Heart's Finger, and the Tumult—and the romp of the crowds pulled the company to the shores of the latter. The tiled banks were full-moon white under the eerie light of the oil lamps. Hundreds of tiny candles floated in hollowed apples, darting through the water's ripples.

Razo stood well back from the edge, remembering his last encounter with a river, the blinding impact that had seemed to yank his body from his soul, and the peculiar noise of deep water—

"Hello, tree rat!"

Razo leaped back, terrified of plummeting into another river. His legs slammed into something solid, his balance surrendered, and he found himself sitting in a fountain with a soaking bum.

Dasha applauded. "You seem to do that a lot, falling backward."

"Just around you, apparently." He squeezed some water out of his leggings and sat on the fountain rim, Dasha beside him. She wore the front part of her hair knotted on top of her head and stuck with a silver pin. He was tempted to pull the pin and let her hair fall. "Did you make me stumble into the fountain?"

She laughed. "I might be able to coax some water over the side, but I can't force a person to throw himself in. Besides, with you I wouldn't need to."

Her tone was so happy, he wondered why he had been avoiding her, then recalled that she was a royal bride-to-be. Not that it changed anything for him.

"I see the whole lot is out tonight," she said. "I am surprised you came, actually. Aren't you worried about Lady Megina?"

"She's as safe as a bunny in a box." Razo squeezed water from his tunic and nodded in Megina's direction. Finn stood to her side, his gaze wary. Enna loafed on her other side, laughing at a three-woman theater troupe's farcical reenactment of childbirth.

"Finn may be the best swordsman in the Own," said Razo, "and that Enna-girl . . . well, if I were a tick, I wouldn't bite her ankle."

"Are you jealous of Finn?"

The question was quick and flat, and it made Razo blink.

"Because he's a swordsman? No, he works hard—"

"Not that, because of Enna."

Razo barked a laugh. "Enna? Hardly."

"But you seem so fond of her. You give her a nickname, and nicknames are always a sign of affection."

"What, Enna-girl? That's just because of my sister. I'm the youngest of six boys, and when Rin was born, the family and neighbors were so elated not to have another boy, everyone took to calling her Rinna-girl. When I first met Enna in Bayern's capital, she reminded me of my sister—a bothersome, nasty little thing you can't help liking."

"So why don't you call me Dasha-girl?" she asked.

"Because you don't remind me of my sister."

For some reason, that made Dasha blush. She flicked water in his face, though she had not dipped her hand into the fountain. "You're gaping at me again, tree rat."

"Wait, wait," he said, wiping his face. "You just said that nicknames are a sign of affection. Well, you call me tree rat. . . ."

Dasha stood, pulling off Razo's green lummas and wrapping it around her own neck. "Aren't you hungry? I think you should buy me some toasted cheese."

Razo dashed over to Finn and Enna first to see if they wanted anything, as they could not leave Megina's side. Enna looked to where Dasha was hopping on her toes by a group of musicians.

"I don't trust her, Razo," she said.

"So you told me." That Enna did not like Dasha, that Dasha might not be what she seemed, made him feel black and crumbly inside. He'd already decided to trust her, and that was that. "Do you want toasted cheese? Or anything else?"

"No, thanks, I'm not—"

Razo felt heat. It surged past him like a livid wind, singeing the sleeve of his tunic. He gasped at its bite and stumbled back. The barrel beside him exploded into flame.

The music yelped and ceased as though stopped by a hand around the throat. Hundreds of Tiran turned to the fire and stared.

"Enna, that must've been a fire-speaker."

"I know," she whispered back.

Razo dropped on his belly as another scorching gust *swoosh*ed overhead. Had he been the target? Behind him was a wooden stand spilling fruit. For a frozen moment, he saw the round woman who kept watch at the stand, a little boy reaching for a bunch of blue grapes, and he shut his eyes, afraid to see them seared.

Then, wind. From beside him. He opened his eyes. The fruit stand did not burn.

More heat followed, more wind chased it away. Nothing was visible to the eye, but Razo knew what Enna could do. She was anticipating each barrage of heat; she was winnowing it from the air, scattering it before it reached its target and became fire. He watched her, the way her gaze sought the sky as though counting stars, her fists clenched and unclenched, her breath held each time she sensed new fire on the air.

Razo wondered what it must feel like, to know the voice of fire and wind, to sit inside them, feel them coming, heave them into motion, stamp them out again. It was a power that he knew he would never share. No voices of wind or fire or water reached for him. Watching Enna, he thought it must be a marvelous thing to be able to do so much, to feel so powerful.

The flows of heat stopped. Enna wiped her brow, blinked long, holding still as if listening with all her skin. Finn was beside her, holding her arm in case she was weak, but Razo thought she glowed with contentment.

"Good work, Enna-girl," he whispered. No one was burned, and no one knew who she was. Slyly done.

"I think he's out," she whispered. "The fire-speaker. He's probably new at this. You can burn for only so long before you can't hold any more heat and need a rest. I think he's done for the night."

The fruit merchant dumped a bucket of water over the barrel fire, but no one else moved. Razo felt the eyes of the crowd on them, a new and unpleasant touch of heat. A horde of Bayern standing in front of a mysteriously charred barrel had to look bad.

"I am so sorry!" Dasha addressed the food vendor, gesturing grandly as though to draw attention. "I am so sorry. I tripped and my lamp dropped. The wine had saturated that barrel, and it just took to flame. Did you see that?" She looked at Razo, tilting her head, her expression innocent.

Razo jumped to his feet. "Oh yes, that was a thing. That wood must've been soaked clean through. You're a clumsy bit, aren't you, dropping your lamp like that?"

The corner of her mouth twitched. "I tripped."

"Yes, a rather ham-fisted thing to do," he said, staring right back, daring himself not to smile.

The merchant glanced between them. "Well, my barrel is ashes now, and I—"

Dasha handed the lady a coin. The crowd lost interest, conversation renewed, music breathed merriment back into the night.

"Well done," he said.

"Did Enna . . . ?"

He nodded. "Stopped it cold. Now at least we know this isn't some lunatic sticking people in his kitchen hearth. We've got a genuine fire-speaker on the loose."

He examined the crowd. Most of Ledel's men were interspersed with the Bayern, including Victar. Tumas stood on the fringes, glowering, his horde of hulking friends on hand. Ledel himself was no longer in sight. Searching for Ledel, Razo caught sight of a man watching a troupe of actors. He was thirty or so years old, his hand was drumming the cloth at his waist, and his hair was cropped short. On one finger, Razo thought there was a band of green skin, like the stain a copper ring would leave behind.

"Enna, see that fellow over . . ." He started to point when the man began to walk forward, all the while keeping his eyes on the actors. "Shh, pretend not to see him."

The man shouldered his way through Ledel's men. He was steadily approaching Megina.

"It's one of them, I'm sure," Razo whispered. "If we stop him before he attacks, it'll look like we're just attacking random Tiran, but if we don't, he could hurt Megina."

Enna nodded. "I can do this. Finn, be ready, so I don't have to go all the way. Please."

The man edged in, his eyes averted, his expression casual, but Razo noted that his whole body was tense. Then, like a snake, he sprang.

"Manifest Tira!" The man pulled a very long dagger from his belt.

Razo felt a *whoosh* of heat at his side. The man yelped and dropped the dagger. Finn kicked him in the chest, sending him to the ground, his sword at the man's throat. The Bayern made a tight circle around Megina, Talone shouting instructions.

Razo was watching Enna. Despite the attempted assassin at her feet and the crowd simmering around them, she leaned back her head and smiled right up at the stars.

Megina sighed. "And I guess that's the bell for bed." She waved at the crowd and shouted, "We're all fine! Thank you. Enjoy your festival!"

Patrol guards removed the dagger-happy fellow from beneath Finn's boot, tied and took him off, and the crowd jeered and threw grapes and melon rinds. Razo wondered if they despised him for attempting to kill the ambassador or for failing.

Dasha returned to Thousand Years with the Bayern, yawning behind Razo's nicked lummas. "I could be banished from Ingridan for getting sleepy at a midnight festival."

"Really?" he asked.

She rolled her eyes as though imitating his own oft-used expression.

"Well, you never know, my lady, different cultures and such, and what with the baby eating . . ."

They did not talk again as they walked home, the surging crowds of the streets conversing for them. He did not feel tired. A fire-speaker among them. Burning barrels in a crowd. Willing to kill Tiran citizens in order to make the Bayern look guilty. And another assassin.

Were Manifest Tira and the body burner connected? He considered how Manifest Tira always went right for the ambassador, whereas the fire-speaker had targeted items near the Bayern. Manifest Tira fanatics were bold, throwing their own lives in peril just to get a swipe at Megina; but the fire-speaker struck from the shadows. It seemed Talone's guess had been right—the two groups must be separate. So who was the fire-speaker?

Razo listened to the muttering roar of the crowd and heard no answers.

23

From the Spying Tree

azo could not sleep. Festivity rattled and clanked in the city, vibrations of merriment running under his cot, up into his bones. He stuck his head under his pillow but could not stifle the jangle of music as it staggered on with punchy energy.

His cot began to feel like an enemy holding him captive but refusing him sleep. *Four days left*, he kept thinking. So he left the sputtering snores behind and climbed his spying perch in the tree outside Ledel's barracks. He leaned his spine against a branch, holding himself steady with his feet against the trunk, and stared at the shredded blackness the leaves made of the night sky. The bells tolled the time: two hours before dawn.

Razo was in the blissful inebriation of half-sleep when a grating whoop shocked him awake. Three of Ledel's men slurred and shouted their whispers, lurching into their barracks. Razo's skin was clammy with dew, and he thought he had best get down in a hurry.

He did not want to risk waking in the tree after sunrise, Tumas at sword practice under the branches.

He was rubbing his arms and warming himself enough to move when a creak made his skin feel alert. Someone was emerging from the back of the barracks, pushing a small cart like the ones the gardeners used. The wheels groaned, speaking of too much weight, then stopped cold with a screech of metal. The cart apparently would not budge. The someone lifted the cargo out of the cart and threw it over his shoulder.

Razo struggled to see in the gray rind of moonlight. Hanging from under the canvas was a shadow the shape of a limp hand. He could not see color in that muted light, but the raised hairs on his arms told him it was most likely burned black.

This is it, this is it, he chanted to himself. He had caught the murderer in the midst of the dirty deed.

The someone steadied the weight on his shoulder and started toward the Bayern barracks. Razo sat up, straining for more detail to identify the man. He held another branch to catch his balance and leaned forward. And heard the branch whine.

The someone stopped. He threw the body back in the cart and came toward the tree.

"Something up there," he said in the singsong way a father talks to little children. It made Razo's stomach try to

flee up his throat. There was a rasp to his voice Razo knew.
There was the outline of those bulky shoulders against the
thin moon peering. That hair that Razo remembered was a
dirty yellow was loose and hanging over his shoulders,
looking strangely feminine on the warrior.

Ledel moved closer to the tree, his steps making no sound.

"I can see you up there. You don't look like a branch, and
you make too big a bird. If you are one of mine, I promise
not to bite." He snapped his jaw twice.

There was no room up the tree to swing a sling, and
Razo guessed the captain could burn him out of it at any
moment. His only option was to run.

Razo scampered through the branches and dove onto the
barracks roof. He bounded across the apex until his foot
slammed down and his leg disappeared into splinters up to
his knee. He pulled it out, leaped off the far side of the
roof, and, ignoring a twisting pain in his ankle, ran like a
squirrel from an errant sling stone.

He did not dare stop at the Bayern barracks and instead
tried to lose Ledel by weaving between buildings, behind
trees, never giving the pursuing murderer a chance to get a
good look. He hoped.

His frantic heart pounded vigor into his body; his terror gave him an eerie thrill. He could not escape into the
palace without the sentries stopping him for questions.
The palace gate with its many guards was uncomfortably

near now, so he zigzagged and crisscrossed and finally ducked into the stables. Bee Sting would whine if she saw him, but he knew Enna's horse, Merry, was peculiarly calm, considering her rider, and slept like a buried stone. He dove into her stall, covering himself with straw.

His breath would not slow and made him wish he were still running. *Stupid choice, Razo,* he thought. Hiding meant staying in one place where big brothers or burning men could eventually come.

And then, a heavy breath and footsteps. A pause. The steps resumed and paused again, as though examining every stall. And kept coming nearer. Razo tried to hold his breath, but his lungs heaved as his heart raged. His panting rustled the straw, sounding like the crackling of a fire. He stuffed his mouth into his elbow and tried to time his breathing with the horse's gusty inhales.

The footfalls stopped for a longer moment, and a horse grumbled for a treat. That would be his own Bee Sting. He heard a pat as if Ledel stroked her neck, and then the steps passed by. After several moments of silence, Razo allowed himself to scratch his nose.

Slowly, he started to ease upright. A crunching sound set his heart pounding even harder, and he hesitated. Silence. He had to get out and hide that body before others found it. Again, he began to rise from the straw. A twitter, a growl, a hush. Silence. Razo pressed a fingernail into the skin of his forehead to keep himself sane. He had to go, now. *Go!* He heard a squeak and eased himself back under the straw.

I'm in a cursed stable, he thought. *It's never going to be totally quiet. Just go.*

Silent as a cat (or so he hoped), Razo ascended from the straw, crept from the stall, and slammed right into someone. And squealed. A shrill cry of surprise answered his squeal. It was not Ledel.

"What're you doing?" asked Razo. "You likely stopped my heart, sneaking around like that."

"I work the stables," said the Tiran boy, his eyes still wide. "I should call a sentry, you know. What were *you* doing in that stall?"

"I was . . . I . . ." He sneezed, and a flake of straw flew out of his nose. "Uh, the festival. Didn't quite make it back to my cot, I guess."

The boy squinted. "You're Bayern. You the one who goes around with the prince? I heard someone tried to kill you right in front of him."

"Nothing happens in Ingridan but everyone knows," said Razo. He stared out the door, wondering if the body would still be there. "Sorry about the startle. I'll go now, if that's all right."

"Go ahead. I'm not going to rat on the prince's friend. Um, did you know you have hay in your hair?"

"Of course I do. It's fashion."

Razo plucked the straw from his hair when he was well out of sight, removing an impressive handful.

Sneaking back to the barracks took a painfully long time, hiding from workers and sentries and from the sun as it shuffled over the horizon. There was no need for stealth by the time he reached the Bayern barracks. The soldiers were up and outside, milling around, tension humming in the air. A few of Ledel's men stood off, whispering to each other, as if trying to figure out what was going on. Razo found Talone under his spying tree.

"A body," Talone whispered. "A sentry found it beside a gardener's cart, covered it up, and sent for Lord Belvan. Ledel showed up soon after, helped Belvan's men get it out of sight. You look surprised."

"Just about Ledel helping to hide it."

"You think he's involved?"

"He's our man, Captain. I've nothing to prove it but the eyewitness of a Bayern, and I doubt any court in Tira will accept that evidence."

"Hm. I trust Belvan to keep this quiet, but Ledel's bound to let rumors of this body trickle out. Lady Megina should take Belvan's advice and we should leave before—"

"We've still got four days, Captain. Release me from other duties. Let me keep trying."

"The risk is too great," said Talone. "If we're here when they vote for war—"

"And if we leave now, there'll be no chance at all. We've got to keep trying. I can do it, Captain, please..."

Talone nodded. "Good luck, soldier."

Razo watched Talone leave, and only two things stopped him from racing after him and taking it all back—Talone had responded as though he trusted Razo, and Razo was beginning to have a plan.

He took to his heels again, first collecting Dasha from her chamber, where she was already dressed and up, and then off for Enna, who left Megina with Finn and other guards. Razo explained what he needed from them as they jogged across the grounds, Enna always slightly in the lead.

"Proof that Ledel's the fire-speaker. And in a hurry, before he burns someone else." Razo did not mention what he'd seen from his tree perch, or he would also have to tell the part where he ran and hid. "He's rotten with motive, and Victar mentioned he disappears sometimes for whole days. You've both been around him before, and you didn't notice anything?"

"I can never be sure," said Enna. "It's the wind that tells me that sort of stuff, and I'm not as good as..." She glanced sideways at Dasha. "I'm not so good at wind. I'd have to consciously beckon the wind that's touched a person and listen to hear if it talks of heat and strange fire on the skin... but even then it's not always clear."

"That is fascinating," said Dasha, putting on a respectful smile. "The water is touching me constantly, but I have to be really close to someone, touch them even, to tell if there isn't as much water hanging in the air around a person, as though more heat than normal is burning the water away. I never noticed anything unusual about Ledel, but I guess I was only looking for a Bayern fire-witch." She flinched after speaking the phrase and looked aside at Enna.

"So, Dasha, do you ever feel *compelled* to use water?" Enna asked.

Dasha opened her mouth, but for a moment she did not speak. "Sometimes I feel . . . pressure all around me. When I do something small, like fill my hand with water, the pressure lifts for a time. A day, a few hours. But that's all I do, just small things."

Dasha looked at Enna, eyes wide, hoping for approval. "Hmm," was all Enna said.

When they drew near, Enna stopped. "You don't think you're coming with us, do you, Forest-born?" she asked with a laugh.

Razo glanced at Dasha, wondering if she knew what it meant to be Forest-born. "Why can't I?"

"Because, sheep boy, your face is—"

"Is a signpost for all to read, I know. I'll wait here."

Enna grabbed Dasha's wrist and muttered to her as they hurried away.

Razo sat in the petite shade of a flowering bush, flaking the bark off a twig until it was smooth as water wood. He watched Dasha and Enna amble around the barracks, look at

Dasha's sling, pretend to practice on Ledel's training circle. Several soldiers came and went. Tumas passed by with painful slowness, and Razo kept his hand on his own sling until the man left Enna and Dasha alone. Then Ledel emerged. Razo slapped his neck, a sudden crawling sensation making him think he was besieged by spiders.

Dasha, her gait a happy skip, went to Ledel, apparently asking him some innocent question. Enna sidled up. They waited a bit after Ledel left to return to Razo.

"And, and?" he asked as the girls approached. "Ledel's the fire-speaker?"

Both shook their heads.

Razo felt his mouth gape. "Are you . . . are you sure?"

"Ask her," said Enna.

Dasha smiled meekly. "We . . . it was Enna's idea . . . we combined talents. Enna moved the wind around Ledel and straight to me so I didn't have to touch him. His heat seemed normal to both of us. We tested everyone who passed by, and that other soldier—"

"Ah-ha! I knew it was Tumas, that nose-breaking, mossy-breathed, rotting hunk of—"

"No, not him," said Enna, "but his friend, the young one."

"Yes, he had something," Dasha agreed.

"Yes, something." Enna nodded, thoughtful. "Not like . . ."

"Not like you, Enna," said Dasha.

"No," Enna agreed. "Maybe he's just new to it, but I

wouldn't even've sensed a scrap of fire-speaking in him if it hadn't been for Dasha. Razo, I don't think he could be the burner from the grape harvest festival."

"Come on, you two, if he's got the fire-speaking, then that's it. Tumas's friend is our man, and Ledel's helping him."

"Maybe . . . ," said Dasha. Enna nodded as if anticipating what she was going to say next. "Maybe there's more than one."

"Hello!" Victar stalked up, trailing his group of friends. "What a stale air in the city. We need a brisk sea wind, this autumn heat is beginning to ferment."

"Hello, Victar," Razo said, trying to sound casual. "Yes, it's pretty stale."

Razo was not in the mood to keep up with Victar's chatting. The mystery still bound his hands; his mind was limping and no closer to a conclusion. After a few moments of inept silence, Dasha stepped in. Razo watched them chat and dug the tip of a sandal between two paving stones.

"Come here a moment," Enna said in her carefully even tone. Razo tensed, anticipating some rebuke. Instead of scolding, Enna drew inward a bit, as though some buried sadness wrapped a string around her attention and tugged.

"Razo," she whispered, "I've got a thought, and I'm hoping I'm wrong. Tell me what the bodies looked like."

Razo sniffed with one nostril. "Couldn't you ask me something pleasanter? Like, say, what I'd like for lunch? . . . No? Well, they're black. Stiff, charred, unrecognizable."

She closed her eyes. "I don't think they were actually murdered, Razo. Not *set* on fire, as such."

"Believe me, they were burned, sometimes still smoking."

"But it sounds like . . . like Leifer." Her eyes flashed to his briefly. She meant her brother, who had used his talent with fire-speaking in the first battle of the war and grew so hot with it that he had burned to death. "When the skin's how you described it . . . it's not like someone set on fire, more like someone who burned from the *inside*."

"They burned themselves up?" Razo tugged on his hair. "I'm stumped. I'd been so sure it was Ledel, but now . . . Great crows, Enna-girl, what a hornets' nest. Anyone could be involved."

"Including her," Enna whispered, nodding toward the sound of Dasha laughing with Victar. "She knows I've got fire-speaking. I don't mind telling you, I'm feeling as vulnerable as a goose in the cook's fist, and I don't like being scared."

He inhaled deeply. "I promised during the war I'd watch your back. I'm still keeping that promise, Enna-girl. I swear."

Enna rubbed his head and left to return to the ambassador. Razo took another decent look at Dasha. She had said she did not know the pale-haired soldier, yet she and Victar seemed friendly enough now. But why would she lie? And if they were friends, perhaps Victar had told Dasha that Razo was just a Forest boy and how that meant that he was poor and lowly and should not be dangling himself around a no-ble girl's shoulders.

A clack of wood drew Razo's attention to the training ring. Ledel was practicing sword with his secondman, and his eyes looked hollow and bruised with sleeplessness. Razo rubbed a self-conscious hand through his hair to check for forgotten bits of hay and thought, *Four days left.*

24

A Parchment Map

The next day, Razo wore his plain white clothes and skulked around Thousand Years. Once, Ledel left the palace grounds alone, and with a dry mouth and antsy heartbeat, Razo followed the captain from a respectable distance. He lost sight of him just west of the heart and skittered around side streets for hours, anxious at the sound of his own footsteps and wishing he'd asked Enna and Finn to help spy.

But I can't get her any closer to the danger, he reminded himself, *or she might burn again.*

After lugging himself back to Thousand Years, he skipped dinner to collapse on his cot for a quick snooze.

When he woke, feeling tumbled and giddy and half-dead, he found he'd slept through both evening and night. In the distance, the bell tolled dawn with a mockingly happy *ping.* Razo lurched out of bed, still in clothes and sandals, and rubbed his eyes fiercely, in the way his mother used to say would wake up his brain. The assembly would vote for war in two days.

Half-asleep, he jumped back into his routine of walking a broad circle around Ledel's barracks. It had rained in the night, and the fat worms lay gasping on the paving stones. Razo was hopping around, trying not to squash them, when he saw Tumas prowling the early morning.

Razo slid between two bushes, earning a mouthful of cedar greens. Far ahead, Tumas entered the abandoned barracks where Razo had taught Dasha slinging. He stayed inside just a few moments before leaving again. He was coming awfully near Razo's hiding spot. Nearer still. Razo held his breath and tried to look like a tree.

Tumas veered, heading in the direction of the Thousand Years west gate. Razo spat green and waited until the pork-chop-eared soldier had gone a good distance before bustling out to follow.

And then he jumped right back between the trees.

There was another of Ledel's men entering those same empty barracks. He stayed a bit longer than Tumas, then left again, also empty-handed, and took Tumas's path toward the west gate.

Razo made sure no one else paraded down the path, then slid from tree to tree, behind buildings, moving in the flow of early-morning errand runners, and came at the building from the back side.

He stole a look through a window. Nobody home.

The stale odor accosted him, cots rotting where they stood, all silent in mourning the dead. The floor was dusty, and he could see footprints muddling around a cot near the opposite door. So as not to leave his own marks, Razo leaped from cot to cot until he came to that spot. He sat down, heard a crinkle, and leaned over the edge. Between the thin straw mattress and the slats, someone had stuck a parchment. Razo pulled it out.

There was a crude drawing but also a lot of script. He cursed, wishing not for the first time that he knew his letters. He'd have to get some help.

Then voices. Razo skipped across a few more bunks and slid beneath one. Dust stirred around his face, and a fat brown spider ambled out of his way. He pinched his nose, stifling a sneeze, then heard people enter.

A rustle at the lifting of a straw mattress, a sigh of old wood.

"It's supposed to be here. The captain said Tumas would leave it under the third cot."

"Captain hinted the new place would be downriver from the old. Maybe we can just sniff around and find it."

"On all that riverbank? Not a chance. I'm certain he said the third cot, but we had better check them all."

Razo swallowed.

"No, don't bother. That dunce Malroy probably took it with him. Maybe he'll show it to Lord Belvan and ask for directions."

The men laughed.

"Well, the captain will be busy enough without us today. He's invited half the company. Why so many? I asked him. He wouldn't say, but Tumas whispered to me that the captain's getting impatient with just a body here, a body there. Plans an all-out attack, wants as many warriors as he can trust. Tumas hinted it had something to do with the assembly, but I don't . . ."

The voices moved away. Razo whined with another strangled sneeze.

He waited, hurting his brain with the effort of trying to hear new voices or footsteps, and glared at the fleas dropping from the filthy mattress onto his arms. His thoughts drifted, tangled in the skittish movements of a spider.

Ledel did not have fire-speaking.

One of his men did, but he was not the fire-speaker from the festival.

That soldier had said, *The captain invited half the company* . . .

Weeks ago after a feast day, Belvan's men had found an empty warehouse littered with burned wood.

Two men were missing from Ledel's company, supposedly to join Manifest Tira, but Razo recalled that Ledel was the one who had claimed that. So where were they, really?

And that first day, when Ledel's and Talone's companies sparred on the training ground, Ledel had said, *. . . we'll see how well they perform as soldiers without the fire fighting for them.*

Initially, Razo had taken the comment as an insult, an insinuation that the Bayern were just the lackeys of a fire-witch. But as he heard it now in memory, he realized there had been jealousy, a twinge of sadness on the word *soldiers*, of longing with *fire*.

So, two of Ledel's men were gone, and Enna said the corpses had most likely burned themselves to death. Razo shuddered. That captain was up to something very, very bad.

Razo poked his head out, slithered from under the cot, and stepped from bunk to bunk to the door. When the area seemed clear, he ran to the palace. The parchment crackled under his tunic.

Enna was gone. Conrad was guarding the ambassador's chambers, and he reminded Razo that today was yet another feast day, the day of apple cakes.

"For women only. From what I gathered, Enna and Lady Megina joined the assemblywomen and others at the heart, making apple cakes and griping about men, no doubt. Finn and Talone will be hovering nearby and wishing they could have some cake. Maybe they'll toss 'em a core. As it was, they had to get special permission from Lord Belvan to let the men go at all. There was some rather intriguing talk of dressing Finn and Talone in skirts. . . ."

Conrad laughed. Razo disappointed himself by not being able to get his own laugh past the rock in his throat. Another feast day. A thought shocked him like touching static metal. *The bodies have been appearing after feast days. Ledel*

must go someplace that's emptied because of the day off and teach his men
to burn.

"Any idea when they'll be back?" asked Razo.

"Evening or night. Enna's sour expression told me that
it promised to be a long day."

"Conrad, do you know your letters?"

Conrad snorted. "Not likely."

Razo thought of going to the prince for help—surely
the man knew how to read—but no, he would not allow
suspicion of Dasha to squash and squeeze him.

She had not joined the feast day celebrants yet and was
still in her rooms, breakfasting on bread dipped in a greenish oil, olives, and cold ham. Razo gave her the parchment,
sat on the floor, and took over the meal. He could not help
whimpering a bit as he ate. It was a cruel, cruel mission that
denied him his five meals a day.

"It's a map," she said.

Razo had figured that. He winced as he bit into an in-
tensely sour olive. There was something satisfying about
food too bitter or spicy to eat without a grimace, making
him feel as though he'd accomplished some difficult physi-
cal feat.

"You really never learned to read? Well, the scribbles
are directions to the Rosewater River, west side, lower docks
near the river mouth. It's all shipping warehouses that far
down the Rosewater. One of my father's warehouses is in
that area. So, when do we go?"

She smiled, her eyebrows up.

He swallowed his bite of ham. "We?"

"Come on. I shared my breakfast with you."

"Dasha, I don't think . . . I'm just going to scout it out, and scouting's better with one. . . . I'm not even going to ask Conrad to come because . . . I mean, we could be seen, and there're fire-speakers on the loose . . . um, no."

"Hm." She pursed her mouth, looked at her fingernails. "You know the assembly court requires two witnesses to support an accusation. I suppose you have some other Tiran to go with you?"

"Oh."

By the time Razo had finished the breakfast platter, she was ready. He had insisted she wear something drab and unassuming, so she replaced her Bayern-dyed blue lummas for a quiet peach one and took the silver butterfly pins out of her hair. She combed it and plaited it on each side, and he watched, as mesmerized as though his gaze were caught in the melting gold of a campfire.

"Something wrong?"

Razo blinked. "Huh? Uh, no, let's go."

He thought of trying to get to Enna, Finn, and Talone, but he knew how the heart was during other feast days. During one festival, he'd not been able to actually walk through and had moved by leaning into the crowd, traveling slug slow as the people adjusted around him. That would waste hours—Ledel might move locations by then. No, he had to go now, before someone else died. He would not try anything foolish, just peep a bit, like his old scouting missions during the war.

In and out, nobody hurt.

25

A Slinger and a Spy

D asha was chatty at first, and Razo tried to follow her conversation, but his thoughts were looping, his muscles twitching for action. By the time they had skirted the chaotic stirrings in the heart, he realized she had been silent for some time.

"Why didn't you go with the other women this morning?" he asked as they hurried down a side street.

"I was in no rush to arrive." She shrugged. "I've had apple cakes before."

A doubt tickled him, a flea bite in his mind. He ignored it.

The morning was dirty gray, the sky musty with clouds. All the women were in the heart, the men and children home, and business on hold for the sake of the feast day, leaving the streets sad and empty. The mood was lashing around Razo, and he felt tethered by anticipation.

They crossed the last bridge over the Rosewater and continued south, civilization beginning to thin out.

For long stretches, the west bank of the Rosewater was weedy and desolate, dotted with isolated shacks. The mouth of the river widened toward the peculiar flatness of the gray sea, and the banks became messy with docks in different phases of newness and decay. Warehouses crammed together, elbowing for a bit of river side.

In case of an unexpected plunging into the river or other mishap that could damage parchment, Razo had left the map with Conrad, so Dasha was looking for landmarks from memory.

"That one . . . No, wait, that's it. That's the one."

They hunkered behind some crates at an adjacent building and watched for guards before moving in closer. The wooden docks scraped the banks as the water heaved up and down in a tired rhythm, the wet breath of river sloshed against the shore, an open door clacked in the wind. No human sounds. Then the wind blowing off the ocean shifted, swooping between them and the warehouse. Razo smelled smoke.

They dashed from their hiding place and crouched beneath the warehouse window. Razo inched up to peer through the slats and felt Dasha move beside him.

There was Ledel, sitting at a table in the nearly empty building, looking over a book. Two soldiers stood behind him, one his secondman, the other the young soldier Dasha and Enna had identified as a fire-speaker. Crates in various

stages of ash were stacked and flung in every corner. Ledel
pointed at an empty crate in the center of the room. The
young soldier's squinty-eyed expression became even more
crooked in his concentration, and a hiss of smoke puttered
from the crate's corner. Ledel shook his head and gave some
command to his secondman. Now the crate ruptured with
flames.

Razo turned his back to the wall and slid down to sit.
Dasha was beside him.

"Did you see?" he whispered.

She nodded.

"My bet is Ledel tried to learn fire-speaking himself and
failed, and so enlisted others," said Razo, thoughts pulling
through him like a tug-of-war he was winning. "He must've
read about fire-speaking in one of those books and is training
some of his men, but not doing such a great job of it. They
burn themselves up while trying to learn fire-speaking, and
then he makes use of their deaths by planting the bodies near
the Bayern to increase public suspicion. Ingridan will believe
there's a Bayern fire-witch running rampant, increasing the
desire for war, and after the assembly votes for war, Ledel
will have half his crew to offer up as flame-tossing warriors."

Razo's grin at his own cleverness shifted into a grimace,
and his voice croaked. "He's making an army of fire-
witches, Dasha. He'll set Bayern blazing."

Dasha's eyes were gray-blue today. "We need to tell Lord
Belvan and the chief of assembly."

"Right." Tell Lord Belvan, let someone else take care of it. Razo wished he were armed with fire-speaking or wind-speaking, could swing a sword like Finn, could rush in right now and end it. What was he doing here, anyway? A Forest lad, the weakest member of the Own?

You're a slinger and a spy, he reminded himself. *Your job is to find, war scout, not to fight.* He looked at Dasha, her ear cupped to the wall, and felt glad, at least, not to be alone.

With a warehouse full of danger pressed to their backs, Razo's thoughts jumped to a tiny shack, rain seething outside, his arm around her shoulders. He thought it would feel awfully nice to hold her again like that but reminded himself that she was the prince's intended bride. He tugged playfully on her lummas.

"You were right about coming along. They might not believe a Bayern boy, but a noble Tiran witness . . ."

"And a pretty one at that," she said.

"I didn't say that. I mean, but I will, if you want."

She considered. "Let's get out of here first."

They crept away, testing the quietness of their own toes against stone, and huddled outside the next warehouse.

"I heard something," whispered Dasha.

"I did, too, coming from the way we want to go."

"Let's go back and skirt around. . . ."

"But if we get caught, there's no way out except the river."

"Oh. Well, if we need to, I could make the river a way out for us." She clenched her hands. "If we have to."

Razo nodded. "Only if we have to."

They listened to the uneasy silence, edged out, and sneaked toward the river.

Then came the unmistakable congested grumble of Tumas. "Where in the blazes is it? Captain, you around here?"

In the narrow alley between two warehouses, there was no place to hide. Tumas rounded the corner, his gaze grabbing them.

Dasha cried out and sprinted toward the dock, Razo right behind. The sound of running feet followed. Razo pushed himself harder, loosing the sling at his side.

Before he could get a stone in his palm, a fist came down on his head. He thudded to the ground as he saw Tumas grab Dasha by her hair.

Razo fumbled for his sword, but another set of arms encircled him, lifting his feet from the ground.

"Almotht got away," came the voice of Tumas's friend.

Thick, hairy arms held Razo from behind, pinning his arms to his body. Razo bit into a hand and heard a yelp, but the soldier adjusted to the hangman's hold—arms under his, hands locked behind his head.

Dasha was screaming and kicking in Tumas's arms, and he yanked her head back until she whimpered and stilled. Her neck was exposed, and as Tumas reached for his dagger, Razo understood, with a shock that burned as it burst through him, that Tumas would kill them both.

Tumas looked at his captain, who was standing in the

doorway of the warehouse. Ledel's frown was frightening.

"Bring them inside," he said, and disappeared.

The soldiers threw Razo and Dasha on the floor of the warehouse, tied their hands behind their backs, and bound their ankles. Tumas ripped off Razo's sword, sling, and pouch of stones, but just like the assembly guards, he mistook the distance sling cinched around Razo's waist for a common belt.

"Here." Ledel tossed the short sling to his secondman. The tanned, lean soldier held it between two fingers. The ends began to smoke, and he shook it away as it fizzled and trickled into ash.

"Shame," Razo breathed. He had made that sling himself, braided it from the black and white hairs of the sheep he used to watch for the king. He looked at Dasha. Her face was down.

Tumas prodded Razo's gut with his foot. "It's that Bayern boy, the one that put himself on Hemar's knife. Captain, I told you he was no good, always sneaking, looking around more than he ought." He pressed a finger to one nostril and blew out the other. A lump plopped beside Razo's sandal. "How did he find us here?"

"He followed you, no doubt," said Ledel. "How long have you been lumbering around, lost?"

"Not long." Tumas sniffed, embarrassed.

"Look at his girl." The squinty-eyed soldier was squinting now with purpose, his eyes on Dasha. "Isn't she—"

"Lady Dasha." The scar down Ledel's jaw was as white as teeth.

Dasha tossed her head, flicking her braids behind her shoulders. "Captain Ledel, your men tied me up."

"Yes, I did not realize—"

"So now that you realize, why don't you untie me?"

Razo's stomach felt like a chunk of ice.

Ledel crouched beside Dasha, lifted her chin with his finger, a gentle, mentorlike gesture. The hollows beneath his eyes were purple, as though he had not slept in days. "What are you doing with this Bayern boy?"

"He was looking for you, and I wanted to see what he intended to do."

Ledel rubbed his scar. "But you ran from my men. You kicked Tumas in the face."

Dasha's eyelids lowered and twitched back up, a half blink. Relief burst in Razo's middle. He could read that expression—she was lying to Ledel, which meant she was not working with the burners. But apparently Ledel caught the lie as well.

"I see. You're on this boy's side." Ledel rubbed his eyes and mumbled to himself behind his hand. "I never wanted it to come to this. I would never harm a daughter of Tira. This is all for Tira . . . for Tira." When he looked back at Dasha, the whites of his eyes were veined with red. "If only you understood. Lady, all of Tira aches for what I can provide—a justification for war. The incomplete conflict rankles this nation like a wound left unstitched and seeping."

"It was a hard loss," said Dasha. "But—"

"No, you listen to me." He was on his knees before her, holding her shoulders. "You nobles make the decisions, but you need to listen to those of us who understand war, who do the work. War is the best tool of civilization. Rules must be followed, or the tool of civilization becomes the catalyst of chaos. Do you understand? The Bayern were the ones who twisted battle out of the ancient pattern of man to man and sword to sword, instead exploiting one fire-witch to burn hundreds. The thought even now brings bile to my mouth."

"Lovely thought," Razo mumbled.

"But what you do here," said Dasha, "you're taking up the tool you say disgusts you."

"I know! And I cannot abide my own face for the thought of it. But I love my country more than myself. I will sacrifice my own honor to redeem Tira." His hands on her shoulders were shaking. "Will you, Lady Dasha?"

The two locked eyes. Razo stared back and forth, his breath too large to come out of his lungs. *Say what he wants so you can get out of here!* he thought.

Dasha blinked. "I will do—"

"Stop. You are going to lie to me again." Ledel stood, turning his back to her.

"Captain." Ledel's secondman stood by his shoulder. "What do we do with her? If we—"

"When all of Tira demands the Bayern be punished for burning Lord Kilcad's daughter alive," said Ledel, deadly calm, "he will rush home and demand we resume our war."

"You hypocritical monster!" Dasha's voice lifted as though she addressed hundreds. "The assembly will find you out. My father will stab you through the neck in the assembly itself, and all of Ingridan will applaud."

"Tomorrow night, the assembly will be a smoldering clump of ash."

"Are we going to burn them, Captain?" asked the young soldier.

Ledel stared at Dasha, his eyes vacant, but his forehead tense as though he were in pain. "Yes, you are going to burn them."

"But tied up like that, Captain? You have always told us—"

"Soldier!" Ledel pressed his lips together and closed his eyes. His voice softened, pleading. "Yes, you are right. But Bayern's foul play forces us to make exceptions to the rules. We are running short on time to accomplish our goal. That idiotic Manifest Tira is in very real danger of turning the entire city *against* its cause with its clumsy assassination attempts. Besides, rumors abound that the prince will announce an engagement soon, and the timing suggests he means to take sides. At just the moment when our mission becomes even more urgent, we are offered a means to accomplish it with Lady Dasha's death.

"If you're not ready to be a man, I'll give this task to someone else." Ledel stared at the soldier until the young man took a step back and shut his mouth. "I'm done waiting for the others. You four are my core warriors, and I need your skills perfected. Perhaps having live targets today will motivate you to—"

"Having more trouble making fire-witches than you'd thought, Captain Ledel?" Razo's voice scraped out of his throat, as dry as week-old bread.

Ledel did not even look at him, just pointed his gloved hand. "You do not speak, prisoner."

"Had hopes of a whole army, did you, but they just keep burning themselves up? Just like the rest of you will. What, did he use poor folk at first, but they kept dying?" Ledel was crossing the room to Razo now, picking him up by his neck. "So he decided to use his own men. I count two of you gone already; how long do the rest of you have?"

Ledel punched Razo in the gut and dropped him on the ground face-first.

"What ith he talking about, Captain?" asked the large soldier.

"When Bayern talk, they vomit lies," said Ledel. "Ignore it. Burn them."

Tumas grinned, and the secondman cracked his knuckles and stepped forward. The young soldier kept staring at Dasha.

"But . . . but, Captain . . . she's a lady, and a Tiran—"

"Tumas? Tumas, I'm here!" A girl entered the warehouse, smiling sheepishly, sashaying her way to Tumas's side. It was Pela.

"Pela, I told you not to come," Tumas said through gritted teeth.

Ledel growled. "Tumas, why is this girl here? What have you told her?"

Pela sidled up to Tumas, putting a hand on his chest. "I want to learn the fire witchery, Captain Ledel, for Tira—" She recognized Razo and squealed. "Look! I told you that Bayern boy was trouble. He was always asking questions about Captain Ledel and the rest of you. I tried to take care of him for you, I promise I did. I don't know how he survived the bloodbane berries I put in his tart, those Bayern aren't all human. And when I tried to get him caught by Belvan's men in Lady Dasha's chamber—"

"Shut up, will you?" said Tumas. "I told you all this was a secret—"

"But I'm tired of waiting."

Pela and Tumas began talking over each other, and Ledel just stood there and stared at Pela, eyes dark with some thought Razo did not want to guess.

Razo seized the moment to focus around him. No

weapon lay within reach. The warehouse doors opened to a gray glimpse of river, too far away to attain at the speed of crawl. He saw that Dasha was staring at the Rosewater, her hands trembling behind her back. In her eyes, Razo saw a little girl running after her grandfather, laughing behind her hand at the marvelous game, then watching as he slouched into the river, facedown.

"Dasha," Razo whispered, "they're going to be shooting heat at us. Enna, she'd use the wind to blow that heat away, cool it off before it could become fire. Could water do something like that?"

"It might, but what you're talking about would take buckets of water." She looked up, her expression somber. "The clouds are heavy today, and I might be able to nudge them to release the rain, but I'd have to be standing out in it to use it right. Maybe the river . . ."

She closed her eyes. Through the open doors, Razo saw the river agitate, the waves flowing side to side, building momentum, getting higher, splashing up on the dock. A small pool formed on the sagging wood platform. Then it started to slide its way toward them, a tiny rivulet running just behind Tumas's back as he argued with Pela. The sweat on Razo's forehead pricked like needles. *Don't look, don't look,* he prayed. The stream found Dasha's feet and wrapped around her ankles like a cat, curling up and settling into a pool. It fattened, and its edges crawled out, gushing over Razo's toes, up to his ankles.

Razo wanted to ask, *Couldn't you call the river to throw tidal waves at them or something?* But he considered that water was not a weapon like fire, and Dasha had never used her gift for more than idle play.

"That's enough!" said Ledel.

Razo jumped, but the captain was talking to Tumas and Pela. Dasha's eyes opened, the river calmed, the water stopped coming.

Ledel turned his troubled gaze to Dasha, and he pulled a fat dagger from his belt. "Tumas, your friend compromises our safety by coming here. I will show you all that I am not afraid to kill a lady for Tira's sake."

Tumas took one step away from Pela. The pastry girl went very white. Ledel advanced, and she turned to run, but he caught her by her neck and brought the knife down hard. Razo looked away, his eyes burning. He heard Ledel command Tumas to get rid of her body. A few moments later, there was a splash.

"Do you see?" Ledel's eyes were wild, his voice scraping as it rose higher. "That is all it takes. We have killed one daughter of Tira, let's not fight over one more. We are so close, men, so close! Show me you have it in you to take Tira back. Use this opportunity to practice for what's to come. Burn them."

At that precise moment, thunder crashed against the horizon. To Razo, it seemed but the echo of bad news.

ight rain soon." Tumas squinted out the door and up at the sky, apparently unconcerned about Pela's death. "It's already soggy in here. Look at that puddle—"

"Are you ready to be a man?" Ledel asked the young soldier. "Or do I release you and ask someone else to burn the boy?"

"No, please, Captain, I apologize. I am ready."

Razo dropped onto his side and rolled around in the dirty pond. When he looked up again, the soldiers stood shoulder to shoulder ten paces off, as if lined up for target practice. Without warning, the air between Razo and the young soldier rippled and heaved as a column of heat shot forward. Razo buried his face in his arm.

He heard a hiss and peered over his sleeve. The air around him steamed, then trickled into nothing.

Dasha smiled quickly. The sight made Razo's heart whack his ribs.

Again, the air was a whirlpool of heat that flashed into vapor before Razo's face, stinging his eyes. He had only a moment to breathe cool air before barreling heat left the secondman as well, tearing toward Razo like a charging bull. Once more the attack exploded into hot spray that nipped Razo's skin.

"I don't know what's happening." The secondman's eyes shifted to Dasha. "Let me try the girl."

"Avoid the face," said Ledel. "We want her body recognizable."

"Don't—" Razo started, but a barrage of shapeless fire was already storming at Dasha. Her hands dug deeper in the water, and the heat exploded into steam. The air was still misty when it trembled anew with heat, and then again and again. Her eyes were closed, her face tensed.

Ledel glared at Razo. "Do the Bayern know something that can counter fire? All three of you at once, target the Bayern boy. Burn him until he breaks apart."

Razo could not quite rally the nerve to stick out his tongue. The attack was a hurricane of heat, rolling toward him, cresting, then cracking into hot vapor. His wet clothes dried, his face burned as though he'd spent a noon hour staring at the sun. Some strings of heat escaped Dasha's screen of water and set tiny fires on his clothes. As best he could with bound wrists and ankles, he rolled on the ground, suffocating the fires. Dasha's pool was drying to thin mud.

In desperation, Razo turned his back to the soldiers. He felt a thread of heat set fire to the rope around his wrists.

"What in the seven rivers is going on?" The attack stopped at Ledel's shout.

Razo held very still while Ledel yelled at his men, letting the rope burn behind his back, biting his lips to blood to keep from yelping. When the pain became unbearable, he sat back, smothering the fire against the dirt. He pulled the rope between his wrists, groaning as it rubbed his blistered skin, and felt the rope fray and then fall away.

"Let me kill him, Captain," said Tumas. "He might be the only Bayern that can stop their fire."

Ledel cursed and heaved over the table, scattering his papers and books to the ground. "Fine, we'll burn the girl's body later. Just kill them both."

"Uh," said Razo.

"Wait," said Dasha.

Tumas charged, clouted Razo twice on the head, seized his tunic, and shoved, sending him flying. Razo slammed into a stack of crates with an explosion of wood. The blows had set his vision crooked in his head, and the whole room leaned and rolled as though he were underwater.

He was wincing in anticipation of Tumas's next strike when he heard a slosh and a thud like a large body falling in mud. Tumas grunted. Dasha emitted a little note of delight, no doubt pleased her sudden mud had worked to trip him, but then the others were yelling, grabbing her. When Tumas gained his feet, he went for Dasha.

Razo leaped up, and the broken crates crumbled around him, spilled jars of spices. He ripped the long sling from his waist, fastened it around his hand, and seized a small glass jar for shot. His head felt far away, as though still being pummeled by Tumas's fists, and his eyes refused to clear, but he was fairly certain the orange smudge was Dasha, the bulky figure was Tumas, and that he was strangling her perfect neck.

If you ever made one shot in your life, Forest boy . . .

Razo wobbled on his bound legs, spun the sling, and let the shot fly. It cracked as it struck Tumas's skull. Razo heard glass shards tinkle to the ground before the thump of the big man's body. A dusty sweet odor invaded the air— cinnamon.

Ledel had crossed the room before Razo's unsteady vision could detect his movement. "The boy burned his hands free."

There was a blurry swipe of Ledel's sword, and Razo thought he was skewered for sure, but instead the blade nicked the sling from Razo's hand and cut it in two. Razo felt a stitch in his gut. He'd made those slings with his own two hands. He dropped to the ground and started to roll away, but Ledel grabbed a fistful of his hair and hauled him to his feet, holding him forward for the soldiers to see, like a roasted duck on display in the meat market.

"Who checked the boy for weapons? He had a sling, you imbeciles!"

"Tumath ith alive." The large soldier crouched over Tumas. "No, wait, he'th dead."

Ledel's scar turned a livid red, and he shoved Razo into the center of the room. The throbbing in his head, the danger, the ridiculousness of being almost killed again and again, was making Razo feel giddy.

"You are pathetic!" Ledel shouted. "You fail to burn two trussed prisoners while this rodent breaks his bonds on your own fire and kills Tumas."

"You know, you're right, they *are* pathetic," said Razo.

Ledel backhanded Razo's face. He stared at the floor and shut his eyes against the dizzying splurges of light.

"Captain, he *was* doing something sneaky, or maybe it was her." The secondman nudged Dasha with his foot.

"You can't let them. There will always be someone doing something to stop you." Ledel's voice climbed to a pleading range. "The point is, you must be quicker and deadlier. I know you want to see Bayern burn, but wanting isn't enough. You know, I'll just do it myself."

Ledel reached for his sword.

Razo's body seemed to be drowning in the river again, his ears full of its song, and the whole world slowed. His last breath lasted a lifetime, allowing him a moment to say farewell.

"I like roasted pork," he said quickly. "And vinegar cucumbers, and those barbaric red olives." If he was going to die, he'd better say something worthwhile first. "And Dasha. I like you."

"I like you, too, Razo." Her voice crunched on the words.

Ledel hefted his sword, angled to slice through Razo's neck, but before he could thrust, smoke began to drape from the hilt. Ledel bawled and dropped the weapon, examining his red palm.

"What are you fools—"

"Not them," someone said.

And Razo laughed. He laughed because two figures had just entered through the warehouse's riverside doors, and even though his vision was still a little slurred, the shape and move of them was as familiar to him as the taste of cheese.

"We're bunnies in a box, my lady," Razo whispered.

Enna was walking toward Ledel, scrunching the parchment with the map into a ball, and Finn was beside her, his sword drawn. She tossed the paper ball into the air, where it burst into flame, raining soft ash. Ledel cursed himself.

"Not them," Enna said again. "Me."

And then, wind.

27

Rainstorm

The wind pushed between Razo and Ledel, forcing the warrior back and giving Razo an inch to roll away, grab Dasha, and crawl from under their feet. He saw Ledel dive for his cooling sword and fling himself at Enna, but Finn caught the attack against his own sword, and metal clanged.

"This is your moment!" Ledel hollered at his men as he attacked Finn. "Prove yourselves. Burn the fire-witch!"

Razo freed Dasha's wrists and then attacked the rope at his ankles, his eyes on the fracas. While Finn kept Ledel busy in combat, Enna was facing the three burners. Razo thought grimly that Ledel must be proud of his men now, who seemed to need no greater motivation than a Bayern fire-witch facing them down.

All Razo could see of the fight was a trembling in the air, but he knew Enna was using wind to battle the volleys of heat before they could become fire. Wind zipped and zoomed around them, breaking heat like bread, shoving the warriors into one another. Her eyes were hot, but her face was rigid with fear.

The secondman shouted in frustration and drew his sword, then screamed as the red-hot hilt burned his hand. The large soldier advanced on Enna with his fists, but before he could swing, he stumbled back, his sandals flaming.

"Enna can't . . ." Razo fumbled for his sling and remembered it was gone. "Dasha, if she can't stop them with wind, if she has to burn, if she kills again . . ."

"We'll help her," said Dasha, tugging the rope off her legs. "I need more water, for this I can't use just what's in the air." She stood and ran toward the landside door.

Razo was going to go after her when he saw that a crate near Enna had started to crackle and the hem of her tunic was smoking. Enna was not able to hold back the fire on her own. Razo scrounged the ground for anything to throw. He hurled a wooden slat, and it slapped the lisping soldier in the face. His eyes turned to Razo.

Razo dove for the ground as a stack of crates behind him erupted with fire. Slapping flames out of his clothes, he found himself surrounded by burning rubble. He dropped lower, trying to get under the smoke.

Thunder sounded again, clashing with the ache in his head. The sky dimmed as though someone had blown out a candle; the day became gray wool, and then, rain. Through the landside doors, he could see Dasha standing in the rain, her face up, her palms open.

She's done it, she's called the rain down, Razo thought.

He glimpsed water oozing down the faces of the soldiers who battled Enna, into their eyes, soaking their clothes. They swiped at it madly.

"What the . . . We've been discovered!" Someone cried from the landside doors.

Razo shouted warning to Dasha as another of Ledel's men arrived. He tried to kick his way clear of the blazing debris, smoke choking the air, and watched helpless as the soldier ran at Dasha, swinging his sword.

Suddenly, the rain clotted before Dasha's body, slowing the sword, pushing it away. The soldier stumbled but spun around and attacked again. Once more the raindrops thickened, twisted, and slowed the blow. Dasha cried out as the sword's flat side struck her shoulder. The soldier tossed his sword aside and reached through the rain for Dasha's neck. Water rolled from her hair and face, over his hands, up his arms, and into his mouth and nose. Razo could see him gurgling, spitting water, drowning where he stood.

Razo finally cleared his burning barrier and bolted for Dasha. Another errant wave of heat rushed over his head. He dove for the ground and felt the heat singe his hair. Without Dasha's help, Enna was struggling against the three burners.

When Razo looked back toward Dasha, he saw the soldier spring forward, knocking Dasha under the roof of the warehouse. Razo gained his feet and sprinted, aiming to ram the man into the wall.

Dasha held out her palms. The soldier twisted back to punch Dasha but paused, his face contorting. Razo faltered.

"What're you . . . ?" Razo saw now that sweat was beading on the man's face, on his hands, dripping, huge globs of water streaming from his skin. A gurgling noise bubbled out of his throat. She was pulling water right out of the man's body.

"Dasha . . ." Razo put a hand on her arm, trying to still her. "Careful, Dasha. Easy."

The look on her face was too close to how Enna had looked there at the end of the war—eyes pained, but face void of expression. He took her hand.

"He's subdued, Dasha. You can stop."

Dasha's hands lowered. The soldier slumped over his feet, coughing, face white, lips blue. Razo found rope and tied him. Dasha's limbs trembled, her steps wobbling as she walked back into the rain.

"Sit down. Rest," he said.

She shook her head. "We're not done." She crumpled, and Razo caught her under her arms and stood behind her, his arms around her waist to hold her up.

Dasha was right—it was not over yet. Through the rain, he could see the terror tight in Enna's face and how her hands trembled, and he knew she was not as strong with wind as she was with fire. It would be so much easier for her to just burn those men. A cord of heat escaped the wind and scorched Finn's pantleg as he battled Ledel.

"Hold on, Enna-girl," Razo called out.

Water massed again on the brows of the three burners, poured down their faces, over their hands, soaking up the heat, taking the bitterness from their attacks. Still they fought. Enna's wind speech seemed spent, and she was using her fire-speaking to stop them now. Instead of brushing away their attacks of heat, Razo guessed that she was pulling the heat into herself and setting the fire loose elsewhere. Soon spurts of flames were rupturing the air around her and breaking the hard dirt floor. Broken crates crackled until water doused them into gusts of black smoke.

At last, the young soldier was slackening and looking eager to be defeated. Ledel's secondman knelt on the ground, still fighting but groaning in pain. The lisping soldier collapsed onto the now muddy floor, gasping for breath.

Razo felt a shudder ripple through Dasha like lightning through the sky.

"That's probably good now," he whispered. "I think Enna can handle the rest."

The rain faltered, then drizzled away. Dasha turned to put her head on Razo's shoulder, tucked her hands on his chest, her body trembling like a candle flame. He pulled her close and rubbed her arms. Her skin was ice.

He brought her back under the roof just as the young soldier fell to the ground, his head in his hands. The secondman was lying face-first, his back shaking as though he either wept or laughed. The lisping soldier slumped down, and

Enna put her foot on his back and called to Razo to bring rope.

But Finn and Ledel's sword fight still thundered on. Neither lagged or swayed with fatigue. They seemed to be trapped in a contest of perfect balance.

"Finn, let me," said Enna, her fingers dancing with impatience on her skirt.

Finn's expression supplied no response, his eyes never leaving his opponent.

He can win, Razo thought. *He's the best sword I ever saw.* And he wanted Finn to win, on his own, to show Ledel, to show Enna, too. But he knew all it would take was one delayed block, one slip in the mud, and Ledel's blade could find its mark. It seemed not such a bad thing to let Enna do what she did best.

"Let her, Finn," said Razo. "Please."

The two warriors locked swords up to the hilts, their faces close together. Finn shoved Ledel and stumbled backward. They paused, looking at each other from across the room, their swords ready. Neither charged.

Ledel's eyes left Finn for the first time. He took in the sight of the big soldier, cussing and spitting, trussed like a hog. Dasha was binding the young man's wrists with half of Razo's distance sling. The secondman had stopped trembling, but he did not bother to lift his face from the mud. The last soldier, still pale and blue lipped, lay tied by the door.

In a movement quick as a wasp, Ledel flung his sword at

Enna, but a wind shoved the sword off course and into the pile of broken crates. Then everything about Ledel's face that Razo thought of as his captainness pulled down. His scar changed from impressive to ugly, his jaw did not seem so fine and square, his shoulders narrowed, his chest caved. He howled and fell to his knees, covered his face in his hands, and sobbed.

The former captain did not fight back when Finn secured him with his own lummas. Once he was immobile, Ledel's crying subdued into shaking breath, and that eerie silence tickled Razo from his scalp to his bum. He scratched.

The four of them stood together, turning around, looking at the bound soldiers lying all over the room. The strange after-rain sunlight, sharp as needles, shot through the doors, glaring brilliant on the Tiran white clothing.

"I think I figured out who the murderer is," said Razo.

Enna was wide-eyeing the situation, her fingers on her lips. She whispered something.

"What was that?" asked Razo.

"I didn't kill any." She turned around again, memorizing the scene, her face solemn. "I had to keep them fighting, you know. Until their fire was used up. So that they couldn't burn, not until we got them back to the palace and safe. In a stone dungeon. And I think it worked. My skin got numb to the wind after a while. I had to burn to keep them from striking me, but just . . . just a little. Not kill. We didn't have to kill anybody. Except that one—is that lump there

Tumas?—but he was dead when we got here." She walked over to Finn, her face just a handsbreadth from his. She put her hands on his chest and exhaled. "I did it. I kept my promise."

"I love you so much," said Finn, his eyes full of Enna.

She squealed in joy, and he hugged her and spun her around as she declared that she did it, she'd done it. And when they stopped spinning, they started kissing. Razo realized he had never seen them kiss before. He tried not to watch, but the sight of people kissing drew his eyes like a fistfight in a marketplace or a gurgling baby smiling right at him. When he tore his gaze away, he felt even more awkward when it fell on Dasha.

She was smiling at Enna and Finn, her nose crinkled.

"Let's leave them to, uh, *guard,*" said Razo, "and we can fetch Lord Belvan."

Lord Belvan, Razo had said, but he was mostly thinking about Talone. *I did it,* he would say to Talone. *We did. It's done.* He might even hop up and down as Enna had, but without the kissing Finn part.

Razo and Dasha left the warehouse and walked along the riverbank, all panic drained from their feet. The rain had stopped. Sun and bright dashes of blue sky melted through the clouds, and the warmth dried their clothes. Purple bruises encircled Dasha's neck, one bulged on her cheek, and her sleeve was torn at the shoulder. Razo knew he looked no better. Funny that he felt like crowing.

Dasha took his hand, careful not to touch the burns on his wrists, and swung their arms back and forth. The motion made Razo realize how alive he still was. He felt like saying something obvious.

"I'm glad we didn't die."

She adjusted her fingers around his hand to get a firmer grip. Though she held only his hand, somehow he felt her touch in his chest, in his gut, in his head.

"We almost did, though, didn't we?" she said. "That would not have been fun."

"No, not really. Would you prefer to be killed or maimed?"

"Killed . . . no, wait. Maimed how?"

"Lose an arm but still live."

"Maimed. Would you prefer to lose an arm or your face?"

"If I lost my face, could I still eat?"

This discussion lasted them their journey home. They crossed two rivers before finding a penny wagon still running on a feast day. The heart was subdued, empty of both business and celebrants, the festivities cut short by rain. The uncannily sweet fragrance of apples stained the air, a lingering scent that emanated from everywhere, as though the white stones themselves were the fruit's opened flesh. It seemed a small miracle that the rain had not washed the smell away, the kind of wonder that filled Razo's chest with *ahh*. Like the curiosity of rain laced with sunshine. Like the marvel of picking ripe fruit right from a tree. He liked being with Dasha and having these thoughts at the same time. It felt natural, in the way that dancing goes with music.

His mouth was full of other questions for her. *Would you really marry the prince? Do you think a person can decide to love only one girl his whole life, then lose her, then find someone else he loves more and change his mind? Do you think that's possible?*

Instead he asked, "Would you prefer being baked to death under the sun or eaten alive by ants?"

Dasha did not have a chance to answer. They were passing through the gates of Thousand Years, Lord Belvan found them, and the bedlam of a crisis solved sucked them into meetings and testimonials until they were spat out again just in time to sup and sleep.

When night pulled down over his ears, Razo burrowed in his cot, his arms around his face. His bandaged wrists smelled of greasy burn ointment, his sleeves still whiffed of smoke, and on his skin lay the thin, cold smell of apples.

28

A New Ship in Port

azo woke to the sound of rain pouncing on the barracks roof. Thunder hissed and lightning scratched the sky, then the rain calmed and curled up, intending to stay. The purr of storm drowned out the hourly bells, and Razo found he could roll over and dream some more. He slept until noon. When his stomach and curiosity finally sent him running to the pastry kitchen, a few minutes of floor sweeping earned him a plate of painfully spicy fish patties and a bucketful of news. The girls talked over one another, practically skipping about with the happy tidings of a fresh scandal.

"Never mind the weather, Razo, business in the heart will be brisk all day. No one could rest comfortably at home when scandals are afoot."

"It's simply too juicy—Captain Ledel and many of his men arrested, one killed, several trained as fire-witches . . ."

"A conspiracy to frame the Bayern, Lord Kilcad's daughter herself an eyewitness and nearly a victim . . ."

"This will be a trial that ruins nobles and military men and catapults attorneys into assembly seats."

Razo wiped a tear sparked by the awe-inspiring spice in his food. "From all I've heard, Tiran attorneys are slipperier than sausages. Any chance Ledel could get off?"

The pastry chef shook her head. "I doubt it. The city already hates the man for his duplicity, and public opinion is half of any trial."

He was not eager to share the news of Pela but finally told all, including the poisoned pastry and her murder. The kitchen went so quiet, all he could hear was the hearth fire nipping at the wood. A quick scan of the faces—surprised, sickened, solemn—made him believe that Pela had been acting alone.

That afternoon, Razo shared the pastry girls' assessment with Talone in Megina's receiving room, where they drank purple grape juice as thick as food and watched the rain smear the world away.

Megina nodded, her eyes on the blurry world outside the shutters. "I've made some mistakes. . . ."

"Megina," said Talone.

She shook her head. "There were times when I was too cautious, particularly after Veran was murdered. Razo was an ambassador for the people I couldn't reach. I'm trying to say thank you." Megina smiled. "And I have more good news. This morning, three separate citizens offered up the names and locations of the remnants of Manifest Tira. The chief of assembly told me the informers had known of Manifest Tira and their plans for some time. When asked why they came forward now, all three mentioned the disgrace of a military leader trying to trick the public into war. Two also cited the rumors that the prince's choice of bride would cement relations with Bayern."

"Razo, you're friendly with the prince," said Talone. "Do you know whom he intends to marry?"

"No, I don't." Frustration seeped through his words. Talone apparently mistook it as anger for not having better information.

"No matter, Razo. If you never discover another secret, your duty to Bayern has been paid in full. And I'm grateful to you, son."

Razo could not help but grin foolishly. Talone's compliment put him in hasty danger of crowing like a rooster and strutting along the back of the sofa, so he changed the subject.

"What about Enna, Captain? Ledel and his burners, down in their dungeon, know that she's—"

"Last night, Megina told Lord Belvan about Enna. He's taken it upon himself to be the only person to interrogate the prisoners, and he has assured us that he will keep Enna's secret until she leaves for Bayern with the next traveling party. She will be safe."

The next day, the assembly voted for peace.

The celebration banquet was subdued, more an exhale of

relief than a shout of joy. Only the prince was all sparkling eyes and graciousness.

"Razo's-Own! Of course you single-handedly used those villains' faces to clean your sandals. Pardon me, I meant to say, perhaps *handedly* but certainly not *single*, or so I have heard. Well done, Lady Dasha."

"Thank you, Radiance."

Dasha smiled at the prince, and Razo watched her nose very carefully for any signs of crinkling. She was polite, but she did not oversmile or ask the prince if he would prefer to be horsewhipped or pecked to death by tiny fish. Razo took this as a good sign, until an exuberant Victar swept Dasha into his entourage and got her laughing at a face puppet he had carved from an apple. Now there was definitive nose creasing.

The very next day, Razo was leaving the barracks for the palace when he spotted Dasha's orange hair across the courtyard. He jogged toward her, intent on pinning her down about the prince and marriage once and for all, but she cut off his greeting.

"Can't talk now, Razo. I have something I have to do."

"What is it?" he asked. "Maybe I could help."

"Uh, sorry, it's nothing really, but someone is waiting for me, and I can't . . . I'll see you later, all right?"

Razo watched her twitter away and felt as though someone had whipped a tree branch into his gut.

"Razo!" Enna hurried toward him. "Have you seen Finn?"

"Finn's gone, too?"

"What do you mean, 'gone, too'?"

"Nothing, it was a stupid thought, never mind."

"I can't imagine where he's . . . he used to be so . . . it's like he's pushing me away on purpose, like he really wasn't . . ." Enna's interest in scanning the horizon faltered. Her eyes fell to her ragged fingernail. "Never mind, you don't want to hear this." She cleared her throat. "I wanted to tell you something else. Your friend Dasha, she did well, you know? She distracted the burners with the water, keeping them from slipping fire past me to hurt you or Finn. And soaking the scoundrels like she did probably saved them from burning themselves out."

"I think it was hard for her." Razo chose his words carefully, aware that if he played it wrong, Enna's current agreeable state could vanish in a huff. "She got really spooked when her grandfather drowned himself. She pretends not to worry, but I know she's fully anxious that what she did back there will plunge her headfirst into his fate."

Enna nodded. Razo suspected she understood more than he did.

"I looked over the book Ledel had found on fire-speaking," said Enna. "It's ridiculous, just fragments of ideas and none of it clear about exactly how to push all the heat back out of you again. No wonder they burned themselves up. If there's bad information out there, someone desperate, like Dasha, say, could stumble on it and try to learn fire speech and get herself burned. What I'm saying is, I'll teach her."

Razo leaned back against a tree and breathed out. "That's about the best . . . Will you really, Enna-girl? Really?"

"Yes, of course." Enna smiled her good smile. "When the weather chased us away from the apple cakes festival, Conrad was all anxious about you, said you tried to act composed but your worry was pretty easy to read, and he showed me and Finn your map, said he was supposed to keep it safe for evidence or something but thought you might need our help now instead. Right when he said that, it was like something struck me. There aren't many people in the world I trust, but you're one of them, and if you say that Dasha's trustworthy, even though she's Tiran, and if you say she'll do good with it, then I believe you."

"Thanks, Enna." He smiled, showing off the space between his teeth. "So, what is happening with you and Finn? Are you still . . . ?"

"I don't know, Razo." Her voice dried up, and she shook her head as she left.

Razo hurried the opposite way, following the direction Dasha had gone. He had to know. He skulked outside her chamber, listening. No voices, no sound but the clatter and ting of a harp played dreadfully. Was Dasha plucking it with her toes? The noise jarred Razo like his teeth scraping metal, and he waited by the door, arms folded. A serving boy with a tray sneered at him as he approached, nudging him out of the way to knock.

"Lady, I have the food and drinks you called for."

Dasha opened the door, her cheeks turning red when she saw Razo. Behind her in the room, he could see Finn, seated with his back to the door. Without a word, Razo left.

He wandered the palace grounds, kicking loose rocks hard enough to bruise his toes. He stooped to pick up an egg-shaped stone to add to his pouch, remembered Ledel had destroyed his slings, and hurled it into a whitewashed tree planter.

"There you are!" Conrad jogged toward him. "Talone sent me to find all the Bayern stragglers. We're meeting at the stables in half an hour. You'll never guess—Isi and Geric are in port!"

"Something good today, anyway . . ."

"What do you mean? What's—"

"Never mind. Conrad, could you go tell Lady Dasha? She's in her chamber. I'm going to go fetch His Radiance."

"Excellent!" said the prince when Razo extended the invitation. "I was very much in the mood for an outing. A man needs to stretch his legs, see the world! Now, who is it again we are going to see?"

The prince did not ride horses, so a carriage was assembled. Finn and Dasha showed up late, Finn going to Enna's side as though all were normal. When he rested his hand on his sword hilt, Razo noticed Finn's fingers were red in the very same places where Dasha sported harping calluses.

The docks were lively and jammed, heavily salted from the briny air and the sweat of sailors. One ship in the harbor bore a banner carrying Bayern's sun and crown. A rowboat worked the waters toward shore, Isi and Geric on the bow, their cheeks tanned from the sun. Shouts of greeting erupted from both sides.

"Hello!" Geric waved, full of energy. "Well, that was very pleasant. No reason for the travel to take two months—we spent six days on horseback, two days on a river, four days on the ocean, and here we are!"

"It's not always so fast, Your Majesty," said a bearded man whose face was as weathered as oak bark. His accent was crisp, his words lilting up, marking him as a man from Kel, Bayern's northeastern neighbor. "That was an abominably good wind we followed."

"Just happened to have a good wind, did you?" said Enna. She and Isi exchanged devious looks.

As soon as Geric's foot touched soil, Conrad leaped at him, pulling him into a grappling hold. Enna was the first to grab Isi coming down the plank.

"Where's Tusken? He must be huge!"

"Poor lamb, we had to leave him home! I know, I know, but I couldn't inflict that journey on a one-year-old. Finn, I cajoled your mother out of her Forest house and into the palace for once. I couldn't trust my boy to anyone but Gilsa."

"I can't believe you actually left him!" said Enna. "You must feel wretched."

"Wretched and lonely and torn in half, but if you think *I'm* suffering . . ." Isi glanced back at Geric, who now had Conrad in a choke hold, and lowered her voice. "You should've seen Geric. The first two nights away, he actually—"

"What are you telling them?" Geric looked at her suspiciously.

"Nothing!" said Isi with an impish smile. "Nothing. I'm not saying a peep."

Geric released Conrad and shook his hands out in front of him with a gesture of defeat. "All right, all right, I might've been upset—"

"Upset? He sobbed!"

"—but I'm no more upset than any father would be. It's not that I don't trust Gilsa, but . . ." Geric had to pause for emotion. "But he's my boy."

Enna stared openmouthed, as though she saw some strange new creature in a menagerie. "He's more heartbroken than you are, Isi."

"I know! Who knew Bayern men were so demonstrative?" She pulled Geric in to kiss him.

Enna's glance slid ever so briefly to Finn, and Razo thought again of her saying, *Why don't you make a fool of yourself for me?*

Then someone stepped off the boat whom Razo had never met before. Someone as yellow-haired as Isi.

"What a sight!" she said, holding her hands to her chest and taking in Ingridan as though she drank honeyed milk. "It's positively delicious. Look, I can see three rivers from here. How many are there again?"

"Seven, my dear. Seven rivers." The prince stepped from the shade of his carriage. He looked striking, his green- and blue-dyed clothing brilliant against the backdrop of white city and red-tiled roofs.

"Isi, Geric," said Razo, "may I introduce His Radiance, the prince of Tira."

"Oh!" said Isi. "This is wonderful."

"A pleasure, sir," said Geric.

"Please, Radiance," said Isi, "allow me to name to you my sister, Napralina-Victery Talianna Isilee, second daughter of the queen of Kildenree. She was visiting us in Bayern when Lord Kilcad suggested we travel to Tira to address the assembly before their vote. We passed a trader ship en route who gave us the news—we missed the vote but are here in time for the celebration!"

"I could not be more delighted." The prince crossed his hands on his chest and bowed his head in a pleased and solemn manner that Razo had never before seen on his face.

Napralina curtsied prettily. She had the light eyes and happy smile of someone who has never known hardship and thinks the whole world a bunch of grapes. Razo was thinking her eyes were not as interesting as Dasha's when Isi gave him a significant look.

"Oh!" said Razo, understanding.

"Oh, what? What is it?" asked the prince, looking around eagerly as though afraid to miss whatever spectacular thing Razo had discovered.

"Oh, nothing, oh, it's getting hot out here under the sun. Oh . . ." Razo fidgeted. "Oh, I mean, Radiance, why don't we walk back to the palace? You could show Princess Napralina the docks and such."

"Splendid idea, Razo's-Own! I was weary of the carriage. Come, my dear," he said, extending an arm to Napralina. "Those ships there with seven sails are from the Wasking Islands. You'll adore the Wasking. They have the most musical accents. Nom, do say something so she can admire!"

They walked away, accompanied by the prince's Wasking entourage. Geric was speaking with Talone, Megina, and Dasha, so Isi, Razo, Enna, and Finn took a moment to huddle together. Isi locked arms with Enna and Razo beside her. Razo noticed that though Enna and Finn stood side by side, they did not touch.

"Napralina was telling me how bored she was with Kildenree," Isi said, barely moving her lips. "How she wished Geric had a brother, how much she would like to become a princess of a foreign land."

All their eyes followed the pair.

"And then you got Enna's letter, huh?" asked Razo. "About finding a bride for the prince?"

"It was Razo's idea," said Enna.

"Seems like it was a good one," said Finn.

Razo thought so, too.

"Do you think it'll work, Razo?" asked Isi.

Razo considered. The prince's choices resonated with the citizens of Ingridan. Even so, marrying a Bayern woman when feelings were still tender could cause havoc among some groups. But an attachment to the queen of Bayern's Kildenrean sister—unmistakable side taking without the risk of going too far. He wondered what name Napralina would give the prince.

"I think it could be rotten great."

29

A Few More Secrets

azo had not worn his old brown uniform since first adopting the Tiran clothing. He vaguely recalled rolling it up in a ball and stuffing it into Enna's wardrobe some months back, so he stopped there a couple of nights after Isi and Geric's arrival to prepare for their welcoming banquet. Finn was who-knows-where again, but Enna was in her room, sticking little silvery things in her hair the way the Tiran ladies did. Apparently, her distaste of all things Tiran had begun to wane.

He grabbed his ball of wrinkled uniform and ducked behind Enna's dressing screen to get presentable. He thought he would like to look good tonight, all laid out in his Bayern army splendor. Just to honor Isi and Geric. No other reason.

He pulled on his leggings. That is, he pulled them halfway on. He could yank them up his thighs, but the bottoms left his ankles bare like little-boy knickers.

"What mischief's this?"

He wrenched his long-sleeved tunic over his head and tugged down. The hem used to hit the tops of his thighs, but it barely covered his waist, and the chest and shoulders were so tight that he had to pull himself tall just to breathe. And then, of course, his boots proved too short for his toes. He glared at the back of Enna's head, then had to laugh. It was a pretty solid prank.

"Ha-ha!" he said, emerging. "Do you like my new attire?"

Enna's eyes widened as Razo strutted a little circle. She choked, then leaned forward to laugh as though her delight were so heavy that it weighted her chest. He pranced on his toes as he imagined girls must do when showing one another new dresses.

"Tight tunic and short leggings, the newest Bayern fashion," he said in a high voice. "It's an Enna specialty."

"I can't take credit, though I wish I could," said Enna, still laughing.

Razo ceased flouncing and set his features to look dead serious. "Don't play, Enna-girl. You can't make me believe Finn did this."

"Finn? What're you . . . ? Razo, it's you."

Razo re-firmed his expression to be even more deadly.

Enna barked a surprised laugh. "Don't you realize, you Forest yokel? You hit a growth spurt this year."

"Please, I'm not as gullible as I used to be. This's another of your tricks, like the short stirrups on my saddle."

Enna put out her hands as if to say, *What can I do if you don't believe me?*

Razo snorted. "I'm eighteen years now, and my brothers stopped growing when they were . . ." How old had they been? Sixteen, seventeen? His clothing had seemed tighter these past months. Was it possible that all of a sudden his body took to the idea of getting taller?

"Am I really?"

Enna flicked her hands in the direction of his bare ankles as if saying, *There's your evidence.*

Razo nudged Enna out of the way and placed himself before her mirror. He had not seen his reflection in months or more. The top of his hair had been singed in the firefight and was not long enough to stand up impressively. His face sported several rather impressive bruises, and his skin was speckled red from the scalding water of Dasha's fight with the burners. But something else was different—a firmer jaw? A longer chin? He squeezed his arm muscles and nodded, impressed at their girth, then glanced at Enna to see if she had noticed. She was smirking.

"Stand up." He pressed his back to Enna's and patted the tops of their heads. "I'm taller than you."

"Barely. Don't let it go to your head."

"No, wait, let me say that again—I'm taller than you!"

"Barely," Enna said again.

Razo did not care about *barely*. He strutted and frolicked, swaggered and sashayed, chanting his ha-ha's and feeling the magnificence of his new size.

"You're still a head shorter than Finn, *at least*," she said.

"You can't burst my pig bladder balloon, Lady Hair Ornaments. I know that I'm quite imposing."

He changed back into his Tiran garments, and they sauntered down to the celebration, exchanging jabs, verbal and of the elbow kind, and were laughing to the point of the occasional snort when they crossed into the banquet hall's heady fragrance of a thousand oil lamps. Finn was sitting on a pillow at their table, his back very straight, his thumb flicking a spoon as though to relieve nervous tension.

"What's funny?" he asked.

"Razo's taller," said Enna.

"That *is* funny," said Finn.

Enna did not sit beside him.

The feast was more fancy than hearty—orange fish with heavy mustard sauce sweetened with dates, minced clam meat stuffed with peppercorns and pine kernels on bread soaked in wine. It was not until the chief of assembly's speech during the pickled melon course that Razo realized what this was—a farewell gala.

"The honor of this royal visit . . ." *blah blah blah* ". . . excellent tidings from Lord Kilcad on the peace he greeted in Bayern . . . hope of ongoing relations . . . and bid a fond farewell to those Bayern who will now be returning home."

Returning home. Razo had not thought . . . Of course, the

assignment was meant to carry through only until after the assembly's vote. Megina would stay, but he imagined many of Bayern's Own would leave and others come to take their place. Razo would be sent back to Bayern's capital, life as normal returned, no war, no worries. That would be all right. He supposed.

Home. It would slay him if he never saw his ma or Rin again, he loved being Uncle Razo, and there were some happy moments with his brothers, when he was not spitting dirt and pine needles out of his mouth; even so, the memory of the homestead pinched him like the clothes he'd outgrown.

He leaned on his elbow against a floor pillow, thinking how well he liked the lounge and lunch customs of Ingridan. And he was pretty attached to his lummas now and to the kind of weather that permitted sandals. Wind on the toes was a good thing. He even liked the summer with its breathless heat. The smell of tangerine blossoms so sweet and unreal, it felt wicked. The way the ocean gulped the city to a stop, the ships that made his toes itch to climb aboard. Eggy fig cakes and sour, sour olives, dark bread seeped in greenish oil, fish and wine sauce unbearably sweet. Dasha. He would miss these things. A pressure in his chest told him that he already did.

Just as he was feeling his most sentimental, the music began. Four ladies with harps and fiddles settled into the center of the hall and played a melancholy tune, one he'd heard sung on every feast day. The sound of it went down his throat and twiddled with his stomach, and the words hummed themselves into his mouth.

> Ingridan, pour yourself inside my skin
> A city of seven rivers
> My blood runs in all your rivers

Dasha was one of the harpists. He watched her very closely and wondered if he'd already lost the opportunity to tell her that he liked her ankles, and that lock of hair that slipped loose from her braid, and when she was too happy to keep from bouncing.

When the song ended, everyone moaned as they applauded in the Tiran custom for giving homage to a song of their homeland. Razo was expecting another tune to follow, hopefully one a bit more robust to tap away the flavor of homesickness, but all the musicians rose and left, except Dasha. She held out her harp, and wonder of wonders, Finn stood, crossed the room, and took it from her.

Razo looked at Enna. Her face was so obvious and gaping, he decided she could never tease him about that again.

Dasha gave Finn her seat, made sure his fingers were on certain strings, then stepped back.

The room was shivering in stillness, everyone watching the Bayern soldier with a Tiran harp, his sword hilt clanking against its bow. His entire face was red-turning-purple, but his lips were straight and serious.

"I want to play a song for my love, Enna," he said.

Razo heard Enna emit a tiny sound, much like a squeak.

Either Finn's fingers missed half the right notes or the tune was as near to the sound of a wounded cat as Razo had ever heard. After what he could only guess was an introduction, Finn sang. Enna squeaked again.

> Tell her that she is my rose
> Tell her that I love her
> Whisper that I've gone away
> And I'll love no other

Finn was fairly large, decently broad, certainly strong, but as he sang, his voice sounded ten years old. It squealed over high notes and trembled and sometimes rasped and disappeared completely when the song sank too low. To Razo's mind, the song did not suffer much by losing a few of those absurd lyrics, but Finn sang them with bone-deep earnestness.

Razo's throat tickled as he tried not to laugh.

Finn's voice faded out, his thick fingers plucked the final notes, up the harp to the thinnest, shortest string and its piercing adieu. He placed the harp on the ground, his hands trembling as they never did when holding a sword. The silence of the room begged, *Should we applaud?*

Razo looked at Enna, ready to share a smile, and gulped when he saw her face. She was sobbing.

"Great crows," he whispered. There were more mysteries in this world than he could ever solve.

She teetered to her feet and ran sloppily across the room, around tables, leaping over outstretched legs. Finn had his arms out, and they embraced right there in the middle of the hall.

"Of course I'll marry you," Enna said. "Yes, Finn, yes, of course."

The silence shattered into walloping applause.

Razo clapped so violently that his hands hurt, and he still felt like laughing, so he did, though he was not laughing at Finn—the laugh was just stuck in his throat like a hard bite of apple, and he needed to get it out. Strangely, it made his eyes water.

Dasha was clapping hard, too, and the Bayern were whooping. Isi and Geric both cupped their hands around their mouths and shouted huzzahs. The prince gestured toward Finn and Enna in case Napralina had missed it, and she nodded happily. Talone, who'd been standing by the door, crossed the room and sat on a pillow beside Megina. She smiled without turning her head.

The thought occurred to Razo that if he had not been applauding close friends in a raucous room, he would have felt very lonely just then. He clapped harder.

When the banquet dwindled and the guests had drifted away, Razo still sat on his cushions, stacking bread crumbs into a miniature fortress. A hand touched the back of his neck.

"You're still here," she said.

He could smell a faint cloud of tangerine perfume and, underneath it, the heartier fragrance of ocean brine. The scent played him, and he felt full of the hum of her tune.

"Want to go for a walk?" His voice sounded just the right kind of casual, even if he could not quite school his face into a nonchalant expression.

The Ingridan autumn air was pleasant and cool and carried with it a round feeling like something complete—a full moon, a full plate, the end of a good day. The wind from the west smelled brown and parted the ocean from the air, filling it with harvest wheat.

They followed the Pallo, the slim river of Thousand Years, out the gates and across the avenue to where city architects had joined it with the tiled ways of the Tumult. The river was high, just one pace down from the edge of the bank. Razo watched their reflections drizzle across its surface as he told her of Enna's offer to teach her fire. Dasha stared straight ahead, her mouth agape.

"That is ... that's just ..." She ended in a whisper. "Thank you."

Razo thought about taking her hand and then did not. Dangling just above the horizon, the moon looked so perfect and round, he longed to pluck it from the sky and pop it in his mouth.

"I have not seen you much lately." She was wearing tiny silver bells in her hair. They tinkled when she turned her head, as though laughing at the water sounds rushing beside their feet.

"I haven't seen *you*," he said.

His tone straightened her spine. "Well, where have you been? With the girls from the pastry kitchen?"

"With . . . what? What would you mind if I were?"

"I think it's disgusting the way some boys cavort with poor girls."

"You do?" Razo had not thought she could be so haughty.

"Yes. I've seen it a thousand times, noble boys like you playing with their hearts with no intention of making true on promises, just because they're beneath your rank and—"

Razo laughed. "Oh, you're worried about *them*. . . . Wait, ho there now, would it make a difference if you knew that I'm no noble?"

"You're not?" She kept walking.

"No. Razo of the Forest, as poor as a tree rat in the winter." He tried to read her reaction to the news from the corner of his eyes while whistling a jangled tune, then stopped when his dry mouth turned the whistle into a scratch. "So, does that make it all right if I cavort with pastry girls?"

"I suppose." She sounded reluctant.

Razo's own spine straightened. "What's with pointing fingers at me anyhow, noble girl? What about you and Finn?"

"Finn? He wanted my help to learn the harp so he could play it for Enna and he asked me to keep the secret."

"Oh, right. And the prince?"

"If you are referring to his intentions toward me, my father wrote me to ask my opinion, and I said I declined. By the way, did you see how smitten he seemed by the queen's sister?"

"Yes, actually. Well . . . well, what of Victar? You said you didn't know him and then—"

"I made a point to know all the men in Captain Ledel's company after you told me your suspicions. We have become friends, of a sort, but he is just that type I was referring to, a cavorter and a heartbreaker. He makes me laugh, but I don't like him much."

"No, no, no, you do too like him. I saw you with Victar, you with your smile and your nose all crinkly."

She stopped short. "My nose what?"

"All crinkly. Your nose crinkles when you smile especially big, when you're really pleased." He accused her with his glare. Then, of all inexplicable things, her eyes began to tear. "Uh, did I say something . . . ?" He rubbed his neck. "I'm always saying something . . . I'm sorry, I didn't mean to—"

"You noticed my nose," she said with a little squeak.

Razo had nothing to say to that.

"No one has ever observed that about me before, or never told me. It means you're noticing me. It means you care."

"Well, of course I care, any dolt could see—"

"Do you really?" She placed both hands on his chest and looked up.

It was about the best invitation he'd ever had to kiss a girl, and he was not about to let the moment escape. But this was no teasing girl who patted his bum just to see him squirm. This was someone who made his heart clatter against his ribs. He did not feel quite as cavalier as he would have liked. His mouth was dry, his lips were dry, his head felt light, and he suddenly had the crazy notion that Dasha's hands were holding him down from the sky. He thought he had better say something quick, and the first words that touched his tongue were, "My heart's really pounding."

"I know," she said. "I can feel it."

"Oh," he said.

Quit stalling, he told himself.

So he bowed his head and closed his eyes, and somehow his lips found hers. He kissed her once, then let her lips go, but it was about the sweetest thing he had ever tasted, better than fig-and-egg cake, so he went back. A longer kiss. He peeked. Her eyes were still closed. He kissed her again and felt her mouth smile under his.

"You were stalling," she whispered.

"I was not."

"You were, too. You were scared."

"I'm not the least bit scared, my lady, see?" He swept an

arm under her knees and picked her up, kissing her again as he did. "Not scared a whit."

Razo took one step off the pier and plunged them both into the autumn water. He bobbed back up like a duck after a feeding, lay on his back, and let her float him, the water under his body as strong as a net, massaging his back with thin, rippling currents.

His shoulder rubbed against a small boat, and he grabbed the side and clambered in, pulling Dasha in after him. He reasoned that as it was not being used, no one could mind if he borrowed it for a little row. The exercise warmed his muscles. Dasha looked extremely pleasing just then, as wet as an otter, but then the water rolled off her unnaturally fast, down her legs and onto the boat's floor, leaving her clothes wrinkled and dry.

She drew something out of the linen pouch she carried at her side.

"A sling!" he said.

"Two slings, even." She held the oars while he examined each, admired the weaving, the coarse green material.

"These are more durable in this humid climate, and I've heard that hemp slings might even be more accurate than wool ones. Though I don't know how it would be possible to improve your aim."

He bound the slings around his waist and took up the oars again, eager to be doing something besides staring at

Dasha with an undoubtedly gushy expression. She let her fingers drag in the water, and he wondered what the river's dreamy voice was telling her.

"Will you be going home now?" she asked.

"If that's where my captain orders me." He could not say those words and look at her at the same time.

"Do you miss it?"

"Bayern? Sure I do. And the Forest, and my ma and sister, too, though . . . I don't know, whenever I go to my ma's house, I feel like a stinky little boy again caught stealing a lick of honey." He laughed, wishing he had not used the word *stinky*. "I mean, nothing changes there."

She was quiet for a time, her fingers tracing ripples on the river. "My father's tenure as ambassador to Bayern will be short. He desires to return to Ingridan and the assembly."

"Hmm, I wonder who'll replace him."

They met eyes, smiling, both daring the other one to speak the idea. Razo gave in first.

"You've thought of bidding for the position yourself?"

Dasha batted her eyelashes in mock diffidence. "I would need a personal guard, of course."

"It'd be best if your guard was a fellow who knows Bayern pretty well."

"We could spend summer and autumn in Bayern, winter and spring in Tira."

"Home in time for the tangerine blossoms," said Razo.

"Home?"

He had meant Tira. He smiled again. She sat facing him, her hand on his knee, her eyes holding his gaze. He felt no need to look away.

"Razo, don't worry that you are not of a noble family."

"I wasn't. Unless you were."

"It might be a concern for my father, but he may assume, as I did, that you were chosen for the ambassador's party because of your status in Bayern." She paused. "Will it be a problem in your country? Would a marr . . . uh, you know, a close relationship between such persons as, say, you and me, would it be forbidden?"

Razo had to smile at Dasha, suddenly turned shy.

"I don't think so. At least, our king, Geric, he married my friend Isi, who was just an animal worker like me."

Dasha grinned in delight. "Your king married a commoner?"

"Well, I guess Isi was in fact a princess of Kildenree, but when I knew her she wasn't a princess at all, not until after . . . Well, it's a good, long story."

"Keep rowing, Lord Razo," said Dasha. "I'm eager to hear about the princess who wasn't a princess and how she met Razo of the Forest."

So he began the tale, how he'd left the Forest to work as a sheep keeper in the city, and in his second year there, he met the new goose girl, a quiet girl who always hid her hair.

Razo dug the oars deeper and drew them back. The pull

felt good, and he thought he could keep rowing forever, perhaps even to the ocean. The water was smooth under them, Dasha was listening with that forgotten smile her lips always kept at the ready. She edged closer so she could place both her hands on his knees, her face open to him. Razo's heart stirred. He wanted to touch her again, but she wanted him to keep talking.

And that was all right for now. Telling his story felt like the next closest thing to giving her a kiss.

Acknowledgments

Thanks to the community at slinging.org for looking over the slinging passages and steering me clear of mistakes; all the sheroes at sheroescentral.com for helping me think through the title; Holly Black and Tiffany Trent for inspired input; Victoria Wells Arms, of course, who is a radiant example of editorial greatness and makes me look better than I actually do (though my husband argues here that I look pretty good); speaking of my husband, Dean, who takes such good care of his crazy writer wife, while being the greatest papa this world over; speaking of again, my own marvelous papa, Wally Bryner, who taught me how to cast a lure and shoot a bow and feel confident; the tremendous Jeff Bryner, who inspired some of the best bits of Razo; Amy Lu Jameson, for suggesting that a Razo book would be welcome; and the coolest kid in the world, Max, who took great naps.

A note about *River Secrets*
from
SHANNON HALE

Ah, Razo. Never have I had such a character as Razo. Some characters give you a landslide of trouble trying to figure out, some sprout from the ground fully clothed and ready to play. Razo was the latter. He appeared out of nowhere in *The Goose Girl*. From the beginning his voice was so distinct to me, I could almost hear him speaking. There was a scene in *Goose Girl* where Razo had some dialogue, but in a later rewrite I had to take him out of the scene, so I attributed the dialogue to someone else. Ever since, that scene has bothered me because Razo's voice is so unique to my ears—clearly that's Razo speaking those lines, but he's not in the room!

Razo isn't even mentioned in my original outline for *Enna Burning*. About halfway through the first draft he showed up unexpectedly, insisting himself into the story until he became a central character. *Enna* was a really difficult book for me to write, but the Razo bits were fun. I knew what Razo would say and do, I understood his relationship with Enna and Finn from the beginning, so his parts just flowed. He was like an old, comfortable friend who helped me get through the telling of that story.

After *Enna*, I didn't think I'd write another Bayern book at all, and yet here it is. And who is the main character? Razo, of course, that wily, sneaky kid. He got his own book out of me, the rascal. By far the greatest joy in writing *River Secrets* was spending that time with Razo, seeing the world from his point of view, hearing the things he'd say, laughing at him and with him.

And he's done it again. At this writing I'm working on a fourth Bayern book. The main character is Rin, Razo's little sister, and in an early draft I mourned that Razo just didn't fit into the plot. He'd make a brief appearance near the beginning but would be left behind. And guess what? You got it—he's weaseled his way into a bigger role yet again. Bless him.

I love all the characters in Bayern, good and bad, but if I had to pick just one to hang out with one day, it would have to be Razo. And maybe he'd teach me how to sling. And then I could take him to an all-you-can-eat buffet. And we'd chat. And laugh. Maybe I should give him a ring. I sure love that boy.

From

SHANNON HALE

During the process of writing *River Secrets*, I wanted to be closer to Dasha, to make sure I understood her. I chose a scene—the end of Chapter 18 and beginning of 19—and wrote it from Dasha's point of view. This was a writing exercise only, never meant to be part of the finished book. It's a rough scene, never edited, but I thought you might enjoy it anyway.

Dasha's Chapter

Dasha was fingering a peculiar silver brooch when she spotted that sneak, Tumas. Just the sight of him made her hands feel dirty. She left the shop, vaguely aware of the merchant shouting lower prices at her back, and ran after him.

The streets outside the market hushed; the day stilled. In the solitude, she was aware of the thickness of the air. She parted her lips and breathed in, tasting water on her tongue. Everything was so heavy. The clouds were crowded, their presence pushed down on her. The hairs on her arms tingled, suggesting that the sky was full of lightning unspent.

She glared up. "I am not playing this game."

Clouds jostled each other, eager to unload their weight. She felt that familiar pull on her skin. All she would have to do is feel it, close her eyes and feel the clouds release, the rain break apart, the world sigh in relief, and she knew it would happen. The desire tugged on the corner of her mouth like a hopeful smile, but her belly felt black and heavy. Again, the image of her grandfather pulsed behind her eyes—the defeat on his face, his skin wet, his body leaning into the river. It was a sight so familiar in memory, it was like the smell of home. A home where she did not want to stay.

"I won't do it," she whispered.

She ripped her attention away from air and sky and realized that Tumas was no longer in sight. She kept wandering, hoping to find him. Ever since the day she saw him climbing a tree to peer in Enna's window, she had kept watch on him. Why had he been spying on Enna? Did he guess that she was the fire-witch?

Dasha harbored a mad, hopeful fancy that once she knew what Tumas was up to, she could go to Enna and tell her, that Enna would be grateful to Dasha for looking out for her, that they would become friends, and Enna would understand about the water and the desire and offer a cure. . . . Dasha smiled sheepishly. It was a lovely fantasy, but it crackled and fell away under scrutiny. Enna would, naturally, be suspicious. No friendship was likely to spring up between them. Relations between Bayern and Tira felt like holding a glass pane above her head, balanced on her fingertips, her arms tiring. But perhaps she could talk to that boy Razo. . . .

Then, suddenly, there he was, standing over something dark. The day dimmed as though taking a long blink. He was gaping down at a body. A burned body. He pushed it to the bank and sent it into the river, mumbling something to himself. Curious to hear, Dasha stepped closer.

Razo looked up, and the expression on his face pierced her—shock, pain, fear. Didn't he recognize her?

"Razo," she said, so that he might hear her voice and remember that she was a friend. But his eyes were crazed.

"It was you," he said, stepping away.

He was backing up, toward the river. She should have reached out to stop him, but for an instant his movement made sense to her; she herself felt drawn toward water—it seemed only natural. It was not until his body tumbled over the edge that she realized it had been a mistake.

The wall beneath her was sheer, no hand- or footholds, and the current was pulling him hard toward the sea. She ran alongside.

"Swim that way!" She pointed to the other bank, where tiled steps led out of the water. "You can climb up there! Swim away from me!"

Razo was thrashing madly, churning water, his neck bent back, his head up and pleading for air. A wave struck his face, and he disappeared, leaving a trail of bubbles.

"No, no, no," Dasha breathed, running, watching for him to come back.

He can't swim. The thought slapped the hesitation out of her, and her fear of the threat water promised her lifted as the very real threat of his immediate death weighed down.

From so far away, her link to the river was weak, connected only by the invisible water that hung in the air. She needed direct contact to communicate this need to the river, so she ran off the edge, a final thrust from her feet pitching her into a dive.

The impact shoved away her sense of her bodily self. She floated underwater, dazzled by the touch of so much water. Its song filled her ears and its sense spoke of tiled banks and garbage wood, the skeleton of a dog in its depths, spots where warmth gathered and other plunges of raw cold, down where darkness sparked with drops of sunlight and up where the surface undulated under strokes of air—the river's touch exhaling a thousand images. Dasha pled with it to speak to her of a boy inside the river, air leaving his lips, body falling down.

Then she found him. Her eyes closed, and she could see the image of him in her mind, carried to her by the water. She was too far to touch him, but the water touched all.

Moving water was like dreaming. When she was only half asleep and pierced with slivers of dreams, she could change the story they told, move herself into a different story, a nicer one, a dream story where she wanted to stay. Water was like a dream—not something she could hold, not easily changed like clay in her hands. She had to will it, want it, see it before it would obey her. And even then, it was a slippery thing to hold.

Dasha kicked and rose upward, all the while keeping with her the picture of Razo as he sank down, his eyes open. She held that thought fiercely and imagined him now head up, body rising. Her face broke through to cold air.

He was near the surface now, too. She forced herself to feel the water roiling beneath him, lifting him, snaking beneath his body, carrying him across the current. Moments after she felt it, she was relieved to see it happen, the water complying with her vision. Dasha swam behind him, watching the ripples of water spray around his body. She did not ask the water to carry her. Just the thought of how much she had already done filled her with a dark panic that threatened to weigh her like a stone. She had to work with the water to save Razo, but she would make as little contact with it as possible. Already she was feeling a strange, lovely tingling in her fingertips and toes, almost as though the tips of her were in danger of being lost, the river taking her into itself, forgetting where Dasha ended and water began. It was a gorgeous sensation, and one that frightened her, shooting an unearthly cold through the insides of her bones.

Ahead of her, Razo reached the bank and pulled himself out. Dasha was a few laps behind.

She fluttered her legs one last time underwater, feeling as light as a butterfly, as sleek as a snake. She kicked herself out of the water and onto the bank, and the sense of her body returned, as heavy as the world.

Razo said something to her, but she did not hear it. Though in the hard air now, her head still felt underwater, sound softened through a river. Her feet to ankles hung in the water, and against her skin she heard the river muttering in its swift, cold voice, passing on images of all that touched its banks, all that passed over its surface or lay in its depths, ruffled by the pull of the current like leaves are in a wind. How easy it would be just to fall back in, how lovely not to have to struggle anymore on dry land.

Her awareness of the clouds pulled at her skin, dragging her gaze up from the water. The dampness in the air tickled her face and arms with the knowledge that the gravid sky was groaning with the weight of rain. She knew lightning would flicker in the west the moment before it flashed. Her soul felt pierced, and she remembered that she was fighting something. She remembered Grandfather. She had promised the flowers blooming around his grave that she would never succumb to what had taken him, to the lies of solidarity the water gibbered. She'd had to save Razo, but she would not toy with that curse anymore. She would live.

Razo was pulling her to her feet, and she followed, tearing herself from the river. Thunder laughed at her, and she glared up.

I won't play. I am done.

READ ON FOR A SNEAK PEEK OF THE NEXT

Book of Bayern

Forest Born

✦

Spring gusted into summer, and every day Rin ran. She ran over pine needles that snapped and moss that hushed. She zigzagged and changed paths, bolted through sunny clearings and back into cool shade. She sweated to exhale the tightness in her chest, to hide from a world that felt crowded, hostile, and too dense to breathe.

The exertion helped some, but today guilt cut her run short—Ma had need of her, and her brothers and their wives too. She took one look toward the deep Forest, longing to test its promise that she might lose herself entirely in its echoing silence. Someday perhaps. But now she veered toward home.

When she reached the clearing of the homestead, she rested her hands on her knees, waiting for her breathing to slow. There stood her ma's house, one room built of wood, shutters wide open in the summer afternoon, fir boughs on the roof turning brown. Dotting the small clearing were five other houses, built by her big brothers for their own families. Everywhere children wrestled and shrieked and chased. The whole place bustled, motion constant, the family like a huge beast with a thousand parts.

Rin spotted Ma, a sobbing grandchild on her hip and a long wooden spoon in her hand. Rin's mother was nearly as wide as she was tall and looked sturdy enough to face down a root-ripping storm.

"Brun, your Lila there is making a ruckus that'll scare the squirrels into winter," she shouted as she crossed the clearing, sounding loving even as she scolded. "See to her or I will. Gren, don't you knock over that pot I just filled if you want to live to supper! Jef, you sack of bones, get back to work. I didn't raise you to nap like an overfed piglet. Look at you children—what pretty needle-chains you made! Now don't go scratching each other's eyeballs. Tabi, let go of your brother! He's not a branch to swing from."

Rin followed Ma through the clearing and to the fire pit on the far side of the little house. When Ma began to stir the pot hanging over the fire, Rin took the spoon from her hand.

"Rin, there's my girl, only sensible person for leagues. Keep the stew from burning while I patch up Yuli's knee, will you? I can't think what those children meant by . . . now wait just a minute." Ma peered at Rin's face. "What's wrong?"

Rin tried to smile. "Nothing, Ma."

Ma sat Yuli on a bench, his sobbing more habitual than urgent, and put a hand under Rin's jaw. "You sure? You've been quiet lately . . . but it's not so much the quiet as something inside the quiet."

Rin shrugged, though her insides were turning to ice. Had Ma noticed these last months how often Rin ran off? Could Ma see that she was shaking inside? Would she speak the words, would she pronounce the problem and then make it right?

Ma felt her forehead, her cheeks, made her stick out her tongue, prodded her belly, listened to her elbows for creaks, pulled down her earflaps to look for rash. "Seem fine. You not feeling fine?"

Rin shrugged again. She'd never bothered anyone about the spiny things in her heart. It did not seem right to complain, especially not to Ma, who worked from the moment her eyes opened until she groaned as she lay down at night. Maybe everyone felt knotted like that but it just was not something spoken aloud. Or maybe only Rin was all wrong. If so, she'd never speak it, especially not to Ma.

"Could you . . ." Rin stopped.

"Ask me, Rinna." Her mother rarely told her what to do. Rin was the child who never needed scolding, who heard what her mother wanted before she'd even finished speaking. But Ma commanded her now, with fists on hips and eyes almost angry, daring her daughter to stay quiet. "Ask me."

And so Rin was surprised into saying exactly what she was thinking. "Could you hug me?"

Without hesitation, Ma pulled her in close, hugged her as if she were a tiny baby scared to be in the open world. Rin's head pressed into her mother's warm shoulder, and she breathed in wood smoke and juniper.

"My girl," Ma mumbled against her daughter's head. "My treasure. My perfect girl. How I love you and love you."

Rin wished she were six and could fit on her mother's lap, and every bad feeling or big scary terror could be drowned out by that ferocious love. There inside her arms, Rin's ache soothed a bit, but the snarled unease did not untangle. Rin had not believed one embrace could fix what was wrong, but she'd hoped enough to try.

"Thanks," she whispered.

Ma hugged her firmer still and smattered her head with kisses before letting go and returning to Yuli, whose cry had become offended.

"Anytime you want a hug, my treasure, you just blink," Ma said over her shoulder as she wiped Yuli's knee with a wet cloth and gave him a heel of bread to chew. "Can't think what's the matter with me if my little girl has to ask for love."

"I'm all right," Rin said, eager to hide it again. "Maybe I'm just feeling lonely for Razo."

"Yes, I bet that's it. That'll be it."

Rin scraped the bottom of the pot to keep the stew from

burning and tried to lose her worries by concentrating on the sounds around her—Yuli's shaky breaths, Ma's comforting mumbles, someone chopping wood, hollers from the children's game of owl and mouse. And the constant murmuring of the trees—wind in the high branches, pine needles clicking together, the soft knocks of cones, the creak of wood. But she could not shy away from the same thoughts grinding in her head: *hide yourself, try not to be who you are, you don't belong in this good family, even the trees think you're all wrong, you've got to go away, away.*

But where would she go?

In the yard everything quieted, then silence burst with hollers and calls of greeting. Could it be Wilem? He had not returned to the homestead since that night four months ago. Many times when she'd been running, Rin had almost turned toward his home. For what purpose? She did not understand why she'd felt so desperate for him to kiss her or why the trees now kept their peace to themselves. But surely nothing she could say could fix it.

Rin tiptoed around the side of the house. In her nervousness, her hands rose to cover her mouth.

A couple dozen members of her family gathered, her Ma squealing and administering hugs. In that sea of dark heads, Rin caught sight of orange. Her heart beat harder. There was only one person in all of Bayern with hair that color—Dasha, the ambassador from the country of Tira, and her brother Razo's girl. That meant Razo was here too.

Rin could hear Dasha saying, "It is a pleasure to return to the homestead again, Mistress Agget."

The Tiran girl had taken to referring to Ma as Mistress Agget, a formality that actually made Ma blush. All the folk known as Agget-kin called her Ma, including her grandchildren, who referred to their own mothers as "my ma" to avoid confusion. Even the nearest neighbors called her Ma. Only Dasha would stiffen things up like that. Apparently she was wealthy, her home in Tira a palace. "Isn't it wonderful how she's so comfortable here too?" Rin's family often said. But early last spring when Dasha had first arrived at the homestead, Rin had detected shock in Dasha's expression, even a little disdain. So why had Dasha stayed with Razo? That was what Rin wanted to know.

At last she glimpsed her brother, just exiting his mother's embrace. Razo looked the same—he was the youngest and shortest of the brothers, his cropped dark hair sticking straight up. Just the sight of him made her want to giggle. He was her best friend. And she had been his best friend—until Dasha.

Rin smiled, straightened, and waited for Razo to look for her, because he always did. She was usually standing a ways back, and he would call her Rinna-girl and push everyone aside to hug her or wrestle her or challenge her to a race or just knock his forehead against hers and smile.

His glance was roving. Her stomach tingled in anticipation. Then their eyes met, and in that moment before he could speak, a shock split her as she realized, *I can't tell him either.*

All these months she'd been planning what she would say on his return. "Razo, how can you stand to be away from the trees in the city? Or don't you feel anything from them? I used to think with them, through them, and feel calm. But not anymore." If she said that much, she'd also have to explain. "But then I kissed Wilem, and the trees changed toward me. I must be really bad if even the trees want me gone, and maybe if Ma knew me inside instead of out, she wouldn't love her girl anymore." If she could explain, perhaps he could help her make sense of it and fix it.

Only now did she understand that she could not admit it, even to him. He would not know how to mend her or the trees, and she could not reveal her secret ugliness, not without the risk of losing his love. That comprehension knocked her as if she'd fallen back-first out of a tree.

Razo waved. "Rinna-girl!"

Katie Jeske

SHANNON HALE

is the Newbery Honor–winning author of *Princess Academy*, *Book of a Thousand Days*, and the highly acclaimed and award-winning Books of Bayern: *The Goose Girl*, *Enna Burning*, and *River Secrets*. She has also written a novel for adults, *Austenland*, and a graphic novel with her husband, *Rapunzel's Revenge*. She lives with her husband and two young children near Salt Lake City, Utah.

Visit Shannon on the Web for more information about all of her books, including deleted scenes and other fun extras!

www.shannonhale.com